The Girl From Poor House Lane

The Girl From Poor House Lane

FREDA LIGHTFOOT

CANELO

First published in the United Kingdom in 2004 by Hodder & Stoughton
Ltd.

This edition published in the United Kingdom in 2019 by

Canelo Digital Publishing Limited
57 Shepherds Lane
Beaconsfield, Bucks HP9 2DU
United Kingdom

A CIP catalogue record for this book is available from the British Library.

Print ISBN 978 1 78863 390 1
Ebook ISBN 978 1 78863 257 7

Look for more great books at www.canelo.co

Printed and bound in Great Britain by Clays Ltd, Elcograf S.p.A.

Chapter One

1905

'Make no mistake Kate O'Connor, this is the best chance you're going to get so don't mess it up. There's many a lass who'd give their eye-teeth to work for Mr Tyson, hard taskmaster though he might be, and who can blame him when you see some of the ne'er-do-wells he has to rely on for labour? Just watch that lip of yours and you'll happen be all right. And think on, Kirkland Poor House is closing before the week is out, so you'll have to cope on yer own from now on.'

With red hair which loudly proclaimed her Irish background, and apple cheeks made rosy by the sweet country air of the Westmorland fells, eighteen-year-old Kate O'Connor could easily have been taken for any simple, fresh young country girl. But looking closer, an interested stranger might note a bone-thin body, one that had not seen a good solid meal in a long while; a pair of scrawny ankles in too-large boots jutting out from beneath the loose-fitting gown made for some other, more voluptuous and better class of woman altogether. They might note that what little was visible of her skin was encrusted with ingrained dirt, the hair which fell about her slender shoulders matted and uncombed for all a portion of it was carefully knotted on top of her neatly shaped head.

'Oh, I can cope all right,' Kate tartly responded. 'I'm not afraid of hard work. Don't you fret none about that. Ye wouldn't find me accepting any of yer po-faced charity, not if I didn't have me babby to think of.'

Though she had only visited her homeland a couple of times as a child, there was a lilt to her voice, a musical intonation of sound that she'd perhaps inherited from her father, or had been born in her. And if she appeared alarmingly fragile, the fire within gave off a radiance to warm the soul. The grey eyes were alive with pride and passion and an anger as fierce, and as stormy, as the Lakeland skies. And something else: a softer inner core she was doing her utmost to hide, a sadness which still held the bleakness of grief. Whoever had made her hate the world with such a vehemence, would not be let off lightly. That much was all too plain in the obstinate set of the small square chin, the way the eyebrows winged defiantly upwards and the nostrils flared with courage, revealing a rare beauty made all the more poignant by the outward image of a wayward young girl.

That steady gaze, the proud, proprietorial manner with which she held her child, the very truculence of her stance proved that however low she had fallen, however downtrodden, the fight had only just begun.

The woman wagged an admonishing finger then jabbed it against Kate's thin shoulder, nearly knocking her over. 'Mark my words, girl, pride comes before a fall. You were glad enough of our so-called charity once over, not least when your poor husband was called to his maker. Think yerself lucky you were fed and sheltered here, in Poor House Lane. Next time it'll be the Union Workhouse on Kendal Green, then you'll be sorry. They'll not treat you so kindly, and you'll have to work even harder making Harden cloth from flax and hemp, laundrywork happen, or emptying chamber pots. See if you like that any better.' And with this parting threat, the woman nodded her head with gleeful satisfaction and slammed shut the door.

Kate stood for a second in silent contemplation of that battered, filthy door she knew so well, scratched and pounded upon by a million hungry hands over the years, all of them paupers, like herself, who had come pleading to be let in, to be fed and watered by the unfeeling guardians within. They would queue for hours in the soft Westmorland rain for a bowl of watery soup or luke-warm porridge, then hurry back to the hovel they'd been assigned in Poor House Lane to feed their children, while others would stand where they were in the rotting filth of a stinking yard, eating it quickly before anyone stole it from them. They might be given free coal in severe weather, a warm shawl, or a pair of boots that some poor soul no longer needed since scarlet fever or 'the visitation of God' had perhaps carried them off. And they were daily encouraged by the overseer to adopt the habits of 'prudence and virtue', no doubt on the grounds that it was their own fault that they were starving.

Perhaps, if Kate had been more fortunate in her family, she might not have needed to come knocking on that door at all. Things could have been so different. Her father had first come to Westmorland as a young man in 1870 as one of the navvies working on the new sewerage system, installing it over a period of five years so that for a time he'd enjoyed relative stability and prosperity, sufficient to take a wife and start a family, producing a son first who they named Dermot, after his own father. But Kate's mother died giving birth to her just a few years later and the two youngsters had to be cared for by various well-meaning neighbours while her father moved on to other building work: the new Market Hall, Sandes Avenue and Victoria Bridge. He'd passed quietly away in the flu' epidemic back in '92 when Kate had been barely five or six and Dermot had just started an apprenticeship with a shoemaker.

Losing her beloved father had been terrible, all such a blur she couldn't quite remember the details but while Dermot managed to board with his master, for Kate it was one short step to Poor House Lane and the Guardians.

The only bright spot in a grim youth was when she'd met and fallen in love with Callum, married at just sixteen and gone to live with him behind his tiny cobbler's shop. Then the River Kent had flooded, as it frequently did, not quite so bad as when at age eleven, in 1898, the worst floods in living memory nearly washed away the new bridge Daddy had helped build. But bad enough to deprive her of a beloved husband, just as if the gods resented this little bit of happiness she'd found.

In Kate's eyes he'd died a hero's death trying to save her from the floods which had swamped their humble dwelling. Having got her safely clinging to a tree, her lovely Callum had lost his hold and been swept away by the swirling waters.

But what was the use in complaining? This was where she lived now, in one room of a cottage right opposite where the pigs were kept.

Poor House Lane was typical of many of Kendal's yards, which were a distinctive feature of the town. These might be known by a number or a name, but all led off from the

4

single main street that ran from north to south, parallel with the river, in this case close by the church in Kirkland through a narrow entrance that led to a row of ten or eleven cottages which might house thirty or more families at any one time. The walls were built of limestone, blackened by age and grime, and high enough to block out most of the sunlight that might creep over the slated roofs. And within the narrow confines of the yard with its shared privies and central open sewer running over the rough cobbles, was found a degree of security by the seething mass of folk, all victims of poverty like herself, who needed to draw strength from each other.

A short flight of stone steps led to the upper floor of each of the cottages, and it was up one of these that Kate now went, holding her child close to her breast and ducking her head beneath the low lintel. Here, in number five, she'd been allotted a plank bed with a pillow and blanket, a straw pallet she scoured every day for bugs, and the facility to warm milk for her baby. As she entered, she saw that Millie, with whom she shared this room and had become a dear friend, was still asleep; no doubt having been kept awake half the night by her own brood which she'd produced at yearly intervals, regular as clockwork, since she was fifteen. All of whom were constantly ailing from something or other.

Kate poured a small quantity of the milk she'd been given into a pan and set it on the hob to warm by the meagre fire, then sat on the corner of her bed, cuddling her child and humming softly as she lay him on his back on her lap to change his wet napkin. Freed from the encumbrance of the damp flannel, young Callum kicked his legs with exuberance, big grey-blue eyes fixed on hers, his beaming smile lighting up the gloomy room.

'You didn't get much then, only the milk.'

Kate glanced up. Millie's old mother-in-law, Ma Parkin, sat rocking herself in a corner, cradling the youngest infant in her arms, while doing her best to keep the others out of mischief by having them unpick a moth-eaten old woollen jumper they'd no doubt picked up off the rubbish tip. The rest of the Parkin tribe were either at Kirkland school, if they'd felt inclined to go that morning and managed to avoid the truant officer, or out with their father, Clem. Clem had only one arm, having lost his other to gangrene, following an accident at work, and could do little more than clean middens, or search for scraps to sell or use in their hand-to-mouth existence. Generally speaking he was a patient, kindly man who adored his wife, though if he did get any money in his pocket, he was fond of stopping off at the Cock and Dolphin and spending a good part of it on booze on the way back.

'That's right Ma, just the milk. And it's all for you me grand boy, is it not?' Kate crooned, tweaking her baby's dimpled cheek and kissing him. 'How many teeth can I see? One, two, three, four, ah 'tis too many to count now. Aren't ye the clever one?'

The old woman heaved a sigh, cursing softly under her breath. 'What are we supposed to eat to keep body and soul together then, bloody muck off t'cobbles?'

Kate said nothing, but the small crust of bread she had carefully secreted in her pocket seemed to press heavily against her thigh. She was fond of Ma Parkin yet she couldn't give it to the old woman without depriving her own child. She meant to soak the crust in the last of the milk for his supper, so that at least he didn't go to bed hungry. She washed and dried his little bottom with great care because whatever pains she took it was always a little red and sore, there being nowhere to properly dry his napkins.

She neatly pinned on a clean one, then poured the warmed milk into the curved bottle, fixed on the rubber teat which he at once grabbed and began to suckle greedily. At fifteen months he was really getting too big for this to satisfy him, and Kate would've liked to give him something more solid, but the bit of bread was all she had. She'd given no thought to her own supper yet, relying on providence, Millie or Clem to provide it. She had a couple of pennies tucked into the pocket of her shift, but that would have to last until she'd got paid, which could be a few days, even a week or more before she produced anything worthwhile.

'It'll all be better soon,' she told her child, rubbing her nose against his and making the baby chortle with glee. 'Mammy's going to make us a fortune, so she is, sewing shoes like yer clever uncle. Except that unlike yer Uncle Dermot, and most round here, I'll save every penny, so I will, then we can get out of this God-forsaken place and start to go up in the world. Won't that be grand?'

Ma Parkin gave a snort of disbelief.

'I will so,' Kate insisted, just as if she had spoken.

A loud sniff this time. 'I wish I'd a penny for every time I've heard that.'

'Ah, but I'm the lucky one, Ma. It might not look like it to some, but this is a red letter day for me.'

The old woman gazed back at her, blank and uncomprehending.

Kate simply smiled and returned to talking to her child, who was much more responsive. 'I will so,' she repeated in a whisper against the baby's soft cheek. 'I'm not having my fine little man being brought up in this hell hole, so help me.'

At her brother Dermot's suggestion, she'd gone knocking on Tyson's door just a few days ago, spoken to the foreman and got herself some outwork, stitching the soles on to women's shoes. She couldn't believe her good fortune. Kate saw this as the first step on her road to freedom; an escape from the Poor Law Guardians who'd largely brought her up after her father died. As a child she'd worked in the mornings on the carding and knitting, learning the basics of the three R's in the afternoon, if she could stay awake long enough to take anything in, that is. After she left school at twelve she'd been found a bit of domestic work here and there but most people didn't care to have a pauper child about the place, so it was never easy to make ends meet.

Only months after Callum had been drowned she'd been forced to move back to Poor House Lane, worse off than ever. Heavily pregnant, she'd been grateful for their care, rough and ready though it might be, if only for the sake of her son who she'd given birth to within these damp, rat infested walls. At least the guardians had provided her with a midwife, seen that her child was born alive and well, and put food in her belly at a time in her short life when she hadn't cared whether she lived or died, heartbroken as she was over losing her lovely husband.

Each morning and evening since that day, she'd joined the queue for food at the door of the Poor House which gave the lane its name; do her allotted chores, then spend the rest of the day helping Millie to clean the overcrowded room, do the washing and care for her numerous children.

Desperate as Kate was, and grateful for a roof over her head, she'd somehow never become inured to the squalor of their living quarters: running with damp and vermin and stinking of stale urine, vomit and the sweet sour odour of rotting decay, with Millie making no effort to keep it clean. The state of it still turned her stomach. You could pick the bugs one by one off the crumbling walls, though they as quickly returned; see the cockroaches scurry across the floor; hear the mice and the rats squabbling and squealing.

'We can't put up with this! The pigs live better,' she'd cried, when she'd first clapped eyes on her new quarters. But no one cared about Poor House Lane now that the big new workhouse up on the hill was in operation.

Millie had simply shrugged her shoulders in helpless defeat, all the fight in her having long since seeped away, destroyed by lack of sustenance and too many demands upon her which she'd no hope of fulfilling. Kate had briskly complained to the overseer, whose response had been the loan of a brush and a bucket of whitewash with the curt instruction to clean it up herself if she wasn't satisfied. This was accompanied by a lengthy lecture on how she should consider herself fortunate that the Misses Tyson were generous enough to provide such implements for the betterment of the poor.

'The Misses Tyson, whoever they might be, should be ashamed of theirselves for having such shameful places in their fancy town,' Kate had tartly replied.

When he heard what she'd done Millie's husband Clem had ranted and raved at her. Filled with fear for his family, for once, he'd thoroughly lost his temper. 'Were you trying to get us evicted, was that the way of it?' he'd roared, his face so scarlet with rage she'd feared he might burst a blood vessel. 'Where the hell would we go then? Will thee tell me that? In t'gutter? Or have you the ferry fare home to Ireland?'

That was the moment when Kate had finally realised how very serious her situation was, how she too was trapped with no hope of escape, her future in ruins. She'd no one to rely upon but herself. Worse than that, she had a small baby entirely dependent upon her for survival.

She'd long ago learned that she couldn't expect any help from her brother, who never had a penny to his name, wasting it all on beer and the turn of a card, far too much the rabble-rouser to be anything like dependable. It was a wonder he hadn't ended up on Correction Hill, the fights he got himself into. Being deprived of a father seemed to have affected him badly. Dermot was filled with bitterness, carrying a grudge against society as big as a rock on his skinny young shoulders.

But for Kate, a lesson had been learned, and from then on she struggled to be as accepting and uncomplaining as everyone else in the yard, although she found it far from easy. She strove to keep herself clean, going frequently to draw water from the Anchorite well on Kirkbarrow, the hill that backed onto Poor House Lane.

The walk gave her a chance to smell the sweet green grass and breathe fresh, clean air into her lungs. She'd take her time walking back through Vicar's Fields and think herself in the country. Then, with her face and hands scrubbed till they were red-raw with the effort, she'd spend hours trailing around the streets of Kendal in the vain hope of persuading someone to offer her work. Mostly, they took one look at her tell-tale, institutional clothes and her scrawny appearance, and shut the door in her face.

Some days though, especially when the rain sheeted down and even the comforting sight of Kendal castle was blotted out by cloud and mist, she'd lose even the will to do that much, and would simply get through the day using as little energy as possible so as not to worsen the constant and gnawing pangs of hunger.

Oh, but today was different. She at last had a proper job so wasn't she the lucky one? And even if it was ill paid and Mr Tyson didn't enjoy a reputation of being the most amenable or caring of employers, it represented a whole new beginning for her, a chance to give her son a better future.

Her first morning was to be a training session with the foreman. A small, rotund man with a bristly moustache and a manner to match, he had hard, self-seeking eyes, one of them with a slight cast in it, which left Kate unsure as to whether he was looking at her or addressing someone else entirely.

The sight of this strange little man filled her with trepidation and for some reason she felt reluctant to enter the shabby little workroom with the big counter where he handed out leather, sometimes ready cut into soles, sometimes still in the bend, which was an oddly shaped piece looking as if it came straight from the cow. She hovered uncertainly at the door.

'Well, are you coming in or not? Don't waste my time if you're not up to the job. You lasses are too flighty to my mind. Reckoning you want work, and then not turning up for it.'

The thought of anyone having the energy to be flighty in Poor House Lane struck Kate as so funny that she almost laughed out loud. But managing to keep her gaze downcast, she meekly responded, 'Sure, I'm a fine worker, so I am.'

'Women never are any use. On the work front, that is.' And he smirked, giving a dirty little laugh as if he'd said something amusing.

'Well I'm different. So long as I know what's expected of me.'

He rubbed the snot from his nose with the back of his hand. 'Don't stand about then. Get in here and I'll show thee what's what.'

He made her sit on a stool, pressing himself hard against her back, entrapping her within the circle of his arms as he began to demonstrate the job to her, in a sketchy, hasty sort of way. He smelled strongly of leather, which was not unpleasant, and something else she couldn't put a name to, that was. As he adjusted her hands, showing her how to hold the shoe he let his own hand slide over her breast, giving it a quick squeeze before circling her waist and finally dipping into her crotch, fondling her with a boldness that shocked her to the core.

Kate leapt to her feet, knocking away his hand and dropping the shoe and leather sole in her haste to escape his probing fingers.

'What the hell's wrong with yer, girl? Can't a chap be friendly? You'll have to learn better if yer to work fer me, lass. Show proper gratitude.'

'And why the hell should I?' She was breathing hard, her cheeks rosy with outraged fury. But the foreman simply smiled at her, revealing yellowed, tobacco stained teeth.

'Because you don't want that bairn of yours to starve. I'd say that was as good a reason as any. But it's no skin off my nose. If you want the job, pick up them uppers and soles and go and get on with it. But you'd do well to mind yer manners next time, cause I don't take kindly to uppity girls. There are rules, and if you want work, you have to keep 'em. Understood?' His greedy little eyes were narrowed, challenging her to object.

For a moment, she very nearly did. Kate almost told him to stick his job but beggars couldn't be choosers. Kirkland Poor House had shut its doors for the last time, and, as had been clearly explained to her, if she wasn't to end up in a worse situation, sleeping in regimented dormitories in the big Union Workhouse on Kendal Green year after year till she was old and grey, she had no choice but to make a go of this precious opportunity she'd been given. She'd just have to learn how to handle this toad, that was all.

Her son needed feeding, and there was no one else going to see to him, but her. This was her big chance. Now it was up to her.

Chapter Two

The work started well enough. Each week, Kate collected the shoe uppers and leather soles, then set about the task according to the instructions she'd been given. The leather was of the finest quality, soft and supple, and Kate loved the feel of it. Vegetable tanned, with oil and grease and wax rubbed in to give it strength and flexibility, and make it water-resistant, this process was known as currying and could take months as Tyson's prided themselves on tailoring the finest leathers, calf and kid, to a customer's specific requirements. They produced a comprehensive range of men's and women's shoes and boots as well as bridles, harness and military accoutrements. The uppers were stitched together in a room at the factory but outworkers were used to attach the soles by riveting or stitching. This was to be Kate's job.

Dermot too did outwork, usually men's boots: Hessian, Shooting, Peel Riding boots or Napoleon, and fine work-manship was required. He collected the basic materials from the workshop in exactly the same way, and returned days later with the completed boots ready for polishing and finishing. So as Kate started on her new job, for once in his life her brother came up trumps and carefully demonstrated what she must do. She was grateful for his help since Ned Swainson, the despicable little foreman with the self-satisfied leer and wandering eye, offered no further assistance.

Even before Kate had experienced Swainson's too-familiar attentions at first hand, she'd been warned of his low opinion of women, of most people, in fact, other than himself. He evidently believed that Tyson's could not operate without him. It was said that he was so determined to buy himself a life of comfort, that he was filled with a bitter envy for all those more fortunately placed. He was equally contemptuous of those below him, no doubt because they reminded him from whence he'd come, using them for his own ends, greedily making a profit from any little side line he could devise.

'Don't enquire too closely into them,' Kate was warned by the other women in the yard. Women such as Sally Sibson, Joan Enderby and Nell Benson. 'Do as yer told and don't argue. You get off lightly that way,' was their advice.

Her first attempt was a mess but she soon began to improve. Had it not been for what she'd learned by watching her late husband work the leather, and from Dermot, she would have been in a complete fog. When Kate took in the batch of finished shoes, she could see at once that Swainson was surprised.

'Harrumph,' he muttered, turning the shoes over and over with hands deeply ingrained with the dyes used for the leather, evidently seeking some way to find fault with her work. 'Quite the little clever-clogs, eh?' He sounded disappointed that she'd done so well, thus disproving his theory that women weren't up to the job.

Aware of Dermot standing quietly beside her with his own load, and, anxious not to upset the foreman since she needed regular work from him, Kate hastened to set the record straight with what she believed to be a proper show of modesty. 'Not really, me brother here showed me how to do it, as it was me first time.'

'You could have asked me, girl, if there were summat yer didn't understand. We wouldn't want a nice li'le lass like you fretting, now would we?' He accompanied this offer with a smirk that chilled her, so that when he slipped a hand consolingly about her slender waist, letting his fingers creep up and squeeze the fullness of her breast beneath her arm, Kate managed to 'accidentally' step on his toes with the heel of her boot. It gave her immense satisfaction to see him struggle to disguise the flicker of pain that came into his eye, but the flare of anger was all too evident.

He stepped back, scowling at her, smoothed down his moustache with two brown stained fingers and then glowered at Dermot. 'Happen I should pay him then, and not you, if he made 'em.'

'Oh no, he only demonstrated. *I* stitched them.' It had been harder on her hands than Kate had expected: waxing the thread, holding the two parts of the shoe together with a special tool called a clam, and pushing the hog hair bristle which served as a needle through the tiny holes she'd pricked with the awl in the stiff leather, and she certainly wanted to make sure that she got her just rewards for her labours. 'It's all my own work, isn't it, Dermot?'

Before her brother had the chance to reply, the foreman brusquely interrupted. 'Happen he's got too much time on his hands if he can afford to give demonstrations, and he's not doing his own work right.'

'Ye'll find no fault with them,' Dermot said, setting three pairs of boots on the bench before him. 'My work is as fine as ye'll get in London Town, so it is.'

Swainson harrumphed again as he snatched up the boots and turned them over to examine the soles, picking at the stitches, pressing here and there with the heel of his thumb, then resolutely shook his head. 'This in't the leather you were given to use.'

'Indeed it is.'

'Nay, I don't reckon so. This is inferior stuff. See how thin it is. No doubt you've sold the decent leather I gave you for extra beer money.'

'That's a lie, and I'll ask you to take it back afore I knock yer block off.'

Swainson flinched slightly, as if he half expected fists to fly there and then, while Kate frantically tried to calm her brother down. Wasn't she familiar with his quick Irish temper, forgetting that it was her own that had landed them in this pretty pickle. 'If you've been up to more mischief, Dermot, I'll skin you alive, so I will.'

'Indeed I haven't.'

'I think otherwise.' Seeing he was in no real danger from either one of them, the foreman quickly recovered from his show of nerves, determined to reassert his authority as he pounded the counter top with his fist. 'Seems to me you've got too big for yer boots, Dermot O'Connor. You've been stitching yer sister's shoes and then rushing to finish yer own batch in an inferior fashion. I don't believe this li'le lass is capable of doing this class of work herself, not first time, and you happen fancied some extra money to feed yer drinking habit. If you think you can cheat Mr Tyson and get away with it, you're mistaken.

17

Neither of you will get a penny out of me today.' And he tossed both the boots and the shoes Kate had stitched under the bench, as if the very sight of them offended him and he'd no wish to clap eyes on them again.

Dermot looked as if he might leap over the big wooden counter and throttle the foreman with his own bare hands. Kate, equally incensed, got in first by yelling at the top of her voice, 'Ye can't do that!'

The moustache twitched and the eyebrows shot up into a thatch of dark, greasy hair. 'I can do owt I want to. I'm the foreman, in case you haven't noticed? What I say goes.'

'But it's not fair. Dermot only showed me how to get started. I put every stitch in meself. By hand. Look!' And holding out her hands Kate showed him the welts and segs and coarse patches scarring the rough skin. He was unimpressed.

'Show me a woman round here with soft hands and I'll show you a whore. It proves nothing. The pair of you is nowt but offcomers. We don't want no Irish rubbish here. More trouble than you're worth. Be off with you.'

Dermot took a step closer, his voice dangerously low. 'Why don't you stop hiding behind that high counter and come round this side and say that to me face. Go on, show me what a fine, strong man ye are. I dare you.'

Uncertainty flared in the mean little eyes as the right focused furiously upon Dermot and the other roamed wildly, as if seeking escape. But aware of his power, Ned Swainson soon recovered his composure. 'I could give you the push for that alone, you knows. However, you've caught me in a mellow mood today, so get on with your next batch and we'll say no more about it. Just see that you do better next time. But you'll get not a penny out of me for this lot.'

A wave of sickness came over Kate. 'No money? Next batch? But how will we eat till then? I've a babby to feed. Dermot has rent to pay. He's only just finished off his apprenticeship, with nothing behind him and he has to find a place to live. You can't stop the pay for both of us. We'll starve, so we will. Besides, we didn't try to cheat anyone. We've done a grand job and deserve to be properly paid for it.'

'Are you questioning my judgement, young woman?'

A stain of red spread over her cheekbones and the fighting spirit returned to her stormy eyes. Fists firmly planted into her slender waist, she faced him head on. 'I certainly am. I'm questioning your right not to pay what's due to us.'

It was Dermot now who was urging Kate to be quiet. 'Will ye shut yer face or ye'll get us both the sack.'

Swainson gave a harsh bark of laughter. 'You never spoke a truer word, lad. Take it or leave it, it's all the same to me. Do the next batch, or you can sling yer hook and never show yer faces in t'shop again. Suit yourself.' And giving a shrug, he removed the bend of leather he'd just placed on the counter top and put it away again.

Seeing her brother's shoulders slump and her own dreams slip away did nothing to calm Kate, rather the opposite as fresh anger kindled deep inside her, hot and fierce. The soft Irish lilt had never seemed more pronounced and more at odds with her temper, than it was at this moment. 'Indeed it looks to me like you're the one doing the cheating round here, not us at all.'

'For God's sake, Kate, shut yer noise. He'll hang, draw and quarter us, so he will.'

'Not before we get our money, he won't. We'll have that off the bastard first, to be sure. You can string me up when I've fed me babby and not a minute sooner, Ned Swainson. So, what's it to be?'

'*Mr* Swainson to you, girl, and you'd do well to hearken to your brother's advice, if'n you wish to keep your job.'

'Indeed? And where's *Mr* Tyson? What would he have to say about all of this, I'm wondering? Now wouldn't I like a word with the grand man himself, and hear his opinion on the way we're being treated.'

'Hear what the grand man himself has got to say about what, may I ask?' And Kate turned to find herself face to face with her employer. Behind her Dermot began to quietly mutter, 'Oh, Hail to Mary, Mother of God...'

Eliot Tyson viewed the scene before him with the jaundiced eyes of one who has seen it all enacted too many times before. The underfed waif, the rapscallion brother, both no doubt ready to swindle and cheat while being anxious to save their own skins, obstinately maintaining they had right on their side. Eliot was all too aware that his reputation among the outworkers was not good, yet despite common opinion, he believed himself to be a fair and just employer, if somewhat neglectful. He provided much needed employment in the town in a business which was expanding rapidly; paid above the going rate and contributed generously towards a recreation room for his workers, and an annual outing for them every July.

He didn't greatly care for Swainson, who was admittedly a bit of a bully, but the task of keeping outworkers in line couldn't be an easy one. Many of them were only too eager to get one over on him, at the least opportunity. The most favoured method was substituting cheaper quality leather for the soles, while selling off the better stuff to dealers. Another way was farming out work to women at a cheaper rate while pretending to do it himself, so that a man could take on more than he could personally cope with, which easily boosted his own income.

Eliot glanced at the girl and saw, to his surprise, that she was a beauty, from what he could see of her beneath the grime. She'd obviously made some effort to clean it off, for which he gave due credit, even if the attempt didn't meet the standards he was personally accustomed to. Her eyes were the softest grey he'd ever seen, admittedly with not much evidence of compassion in them at this precise moment; and the lashes long and curling. But her hair was filthy and matted, more like a rook's nest, save for its fiery colour. He considered it with a detached fascination, trying to put a name to the particular shade: auburn; ginger; titian; no, none of those. But how could he even begin to guess? It would take several buckets of hot water and a large cake of soap to discover the answer. Startled out of his reverie, he realised that she was speaking to him directly and Swainson was jumping about like a cat with his tail on fire as a consequence.

'You'll address your questions to me miss, not bother Mr Tyson with your prattling.'

'I'll speak to whosoever I wish, and since you've just given both me and my brother the push for doing an honest week's work, we owe you nothing, I'm thinking.'

Eliot hid a smile, for the girl's forthright manner was refreshing, and having a decidedly unsettling effect upon his surly foreman, which was most amusing. 'If he sacked you, I'm sure he must have good reason. Perhaps you'd best listen to him, and go quietly.'

The young man beside her, he noticed, was growing agitated, plucking at her sleeve and begging her to hush. His own thatch was not quite so red and cut exceptionally short but the pair were undoubtedly related.

Eliot resigned himself for a long, convoluted tale of self-pity from all parties concerned. Instead, she marched right up to him, hands on hips and sticking her chin in the air, with steam practically rising from her ears, she began to rail at him. 'Not while I've breath left in me body. I never did anything quietly in me life, and I don't intend to start now. Just for the record it's this man you should be watching, not me. He's the one doing the cheating which you'll discover to your cost one day, mark my words. But you can stick yer rotten job. I don't work for them what twist me and steal the bread out of me babby's mouth.'

Startled and perplexed by her daring, Eliot narrowed his eyes in a questioning manner as he swung around to his foreman, demanding clarification. 'Is what she says true?'

'Not a word of it, sir, as you well know.'

'Hmm, as I would expect. Then can you perhaps explain to me, briefly, and in words of one syllable, what this fracas is all about?'

'No, he cannot,' cut in Kate, before Swainson had chance to draw breath. 'Because he hasn't a leg to stand on, isn't that the truth? Me brother here showed me how to do the work since that eejit didn't have the time nor the patience to show me right, and for some reason this is not allowed and so we've both got the push.'

'The work is rushed and inferior,' Swainson blustered, finally finding his voice.

''Tis not. It's just that your foreman here doesn't believe a woman to be capable of such quality work.'

'And the boy hasn't used the right leather.'

'I have so.' This from Dermot, who suddenly took it into his head to speak up and defend himself.

But a tell-tale flush was creeping up his neck and along his jawline, a sure sign of guilt in Eliot's opinion, one he had seen too many times before. He came to a swift decision, more out of admiration for her cheek than anger, and because he was in a hurry. They were expecting the Whinerays for supper this evening and he was anxious to get back home to soothe his wife's jitters. Her nerves always played up when she found herself required to give precise instructions on menu and flowers and goodness knows what else. Of late, her depression had been such that she couldn't even control her own servants, particularly the dreaded Mrs Petty. Amelia had grown far too indulgent of her cook's failings, a woman easily diverted from the task in hand by her facility for fanciful superstition and gossip.

'Give the young man his cards but keep the girl on. He seems to be the one at fault.' And she has a baby to feed, added a small voice at the back of his head. But Eliot didn't say this out loud, in case he failed to disguise the envy in his tone. It always seemed so utterly unfair that those who had least to offer could breed so easily, while he, who had everything – a fine house, a thriving business, a beautiful, adoring wife – couldn't get himself a son for love nor money. A child of either gender would, in fact, have been most welcome. But, apparently, it was not to be.

Having issued his judgement, Eliot Tyson turned on his heel and walked smartly away. The last thing he wanted was for any of his own workers to feel sorry for him.

–

The supper party was not a success. It had begun badly when he'd found his tail coat had not been brushed and his white tie was crumpled and dingy so that he would have to use the black one instead. Really, this household had gone to pot ever since Beckworth had retired. He should somehow find the funds for a new valet despite dear Amelia's insisting she enjoyed laying out a clean shirt and handkerchief for him. She'd had young Dennis polish his shoes and press his trousers, but the boy had put out his velvet smoking jacket by mistake so the tail coat was still hanging, unbrushed, in the wardrobe.

Eliot had always been most fastidious about his appearance and now quietly completed these essential tasks himself rather than upset his wife by pointing out the inadequacies of her preparations. He'd painstakingly shaved the whiskers from his chin with a cut-throat razor, slapped cologne on the long, narrow cheeks and jutting jaw, then brushed his hair, striving to flatten the dark curls into some sort of order. His own brown eyes stared broodingly back at himself from the mirror, already expressing doubt as to the wisdom of hosting this occasion.

Did he really wish to become involved in local politics? Was this a wise move on his part? Almost as if he wished to fill the gap in his life, as if he needed to keep every hour of his day fully occupied. Yet could he afford to take his eye off a business which seemed to be flagging of late?

Tyson's Shoe Manufactory had been his father's pride and joy, and his undoubted obsession. Eliot was all too aware that he would never be able to match up. Hadn't his father told him so a dozen times? George Tyson had started the company from scratch, cycling the length and breadth of the country as a young man in order to win orders, devoting his life to building up the company, but his success had brought little happiness in its wake, resulting in him rarely showing his face in the gracious home he provided for his family. His wife had grown bitter and disillusioned and, not surprisingly, had ultimately refused him her bed, so that he'd turned to other women for consolation and had taken a string of mistresses.

With the business an endless bone of contention between his parents, Eliot had watched in helpless misery as the pair barely spoke a civil word to each other, living entirely separate lives within the claustrophobic four walls of their home.

George Tyson had jealously guarded his creation, declaring that he wished his sons to climb above trade and any necessity of earning a living for themselves. He'd assured them that there would be no need for them ever to work, that there would be sufficient money for them to live a life of ease, as gentlemen.

Charles, the younger son and apple of his father's eye, accepted this unquestioningly, preening himself on his own good fortune. Eliot was different. He wanted to be a part of the company, to be active in its growth. But when he asked if he could learn the business from the shop floor upwards, his father had simply laughed, telling him he knew nothing about shoes, and never would. That he should stick to his books and his gardening.

But then nothing Eliot ever did, or suggested, was considered good enough so far as his father was concerned. He dubbed him a 'mother's boy' in that sarcastic, derogatory way of his, all because Eliot took his mother's side in the inevitable and frequent arguments between them.

Feeling rejected and unwanted, he had buried his disappointment by spending much of his youth studying art and history at university, and in travelling, at least until his father's stroke. That had been so dreadful, so incapacitating, that George had been forced to allow Eliot to take over, albeit with furious resentment, viewing his son as an interloper and resisting him every inch of the way.

This cold and empty childhood was perhaps the reason why a desire for a child so consumed him now. Eliot still longed for the family life he'd been deprived of as a boy, to be the kind of father his own never was. But even that was denied him.

Tonight, dinner had been late, no doubt due to yet some distraction in the kitchen, and yet the lamb was woefully underdone, too bloody for his taste. Young Fanny, the bows of her starched apron sticking out like cow's ears, had spilled soup on Gilbert Whineray's pristine white cuff. The wine hadn't been chilled for nearly long enough and darling Amelia was taut with tension, as highly strung as a young thoroughbred. Which was what she was, in a way. Far too well bred for her own good. Ah, but what she lacked in organisational skills she more than made up for by her beauty.

She had looked utterly delightful in a coffee and cream lace gown, a pink rose tucked into its trim waistband. Her skin was clear and rose-flushed, lips generously curved into a gracious, rather wistful smile, and her eyes as bright as a summer sky. With her blonde hair puffed out entrancingly about the pale oval of her lovely face, his wife sat at the head of his table with all eyes upon her: a perfect vision of loveliness, a picture of serenity. Only he was privy to the true turmoil within. But then Amelia looked wonderful whatever she was wearing, even in the thick woollen stockings and tweed skirts she adopted to 'help him' with the gardening, which never managed to become mud spattered however inclement the day. And when she was asleep, neatly curled up like a child with one hand cupped beneath her cheek, she was never anything but entrancing.

Oh, how he adored her. She was the sweetest, most delightful woman he'd ever met, and despite everything he had never, not for a moment, regretted marrying her. She was his very reason for existence. Without her, he would be nothing.

But yet he longed for a child.

When all their guests were gone, Eliot came out of his dressing room to find Amelia already sitting up in bed, cheeks flushed, blue eyes bright as they always were after such an evening. 'It went well, don't you think?' she asked excitedly. 'I thought Mrs Petty surpassed herself with the pear tart, didn't you? A quite unusual dessert. I'm sure Olive Whineray was thoroughly impressed.'

Dear Olive, he noticed, had left half of it untouched, the pastry being slightly soggy. He leaned over and kissed Amelia's soft, pink cheek. 'It was wonderful darling, as ever. A superb evening, and I'm sure it will bear fruit. Whineray is keen to have me on the Council.'

'And will you agree to it?' She sounded anxious, knowing his doubts.

Eliot suppressed a sigh. 'I dare say I might in the end. It can do no harm to be seen about more, I suppose. But what about you? You must feel quite worn out with all the preparations and organisation you've had to do.'

Her cheeks, if anything, flushed even pinker. 'Not in the least. I feel perfectly marvellous.'

And so he climbed into bed, turned off the light and made love to his wife. But sadly, as he knew only too well, their passion for each other would bear no fruit at all.

Chapter Three

'I'm done for. This is it, the end. If I'd known that helping you get started in the job would lose me mine, I'd never have offered. Years of apprenticeship, a trade at me fingertips, and now I'm all washed up, finished before I hardly get started.' Dermot stood in the midst of the muddle and squalor of the single room Kate called home, Millie and Clem anxiously looking on. Only Ma Parkin was oblivious to his distress as she sat and hummed some ditty, surrounded by a gaggle of children. His hands hung at his sides, shoulders slumped, dejection written all over him. 'What am I supposed to do now? I don't even have a home to go to, not now me apprenticeship is over and I've no money coming in to pay rent.'

'You could stop here, with us,' Millie offered, generous to a fault, as always, even though she had nothing to give.

Dermot gave her a weak smile and said nothing. He'd no wish to give offence but the idea of bunking down with Millie, Clem and their noisesome brood didn't bear thinking of.

'What about yer master?' Clem put in, clearly thinking that a man fortunate enough to have two arms and a trade as well as youth on his side, didn't have too much to complain about.

'Old Gabriel barely has enough work to keep himself going, he's certainly none to give me. I've already asked him. I was depending on Tyson's.'

'Couldn't you get work some place else?'

'And who would that be with, would ye mind telling me? What other employer of size do we have hereabouts? None that won't be influenced by the fact Tyson laid me off. No, I'm done for. There's no other word for it.'

'Aw, don't keep going on about it, Dermot. I know what I've done to you, and I'm right sorry for it, so I am.' Kate could hardly bear to look at the bleak misery in her brother's face, see the tightness of his jaw and the way his mouth trembled very slightly despite his best efforts to prevent it, just as it had done when he was a boy. 'I never meant for this to happen. It was just that it was all so unfair, I couldn't bear for Swainson to cheat us. He wouldn't accept that a woman can do as good a job as a man.'

'You and your blethering pride.'

''Tis not *my* pride at fault, but his. To blame you for helping me wasn't right, not right at all. The miserable scoundrel. I'd wring his scrawny neck with me own two bare hands if ever I got the chance.'

'Ach, don't start again. I'm the one who has to suffer, not you. You're fine and dandy, so you are. It's me what's got the push.' He pounded a fist into his chest, made to storm off but then realising there was nowhere for him to go, stayed where he was, flapping his arms about in frustration. 'What am I going to do, Katy?'

He hadn't called her by this pet name in years, not since they were children together. Kate felt a lump come into her throat and couldn't help but wonder what Daddy would have said, to see how her show of temper had landed their Dermot in this mess. She could almost hear his soft tones just as if he were standing right beside her, the lilt in his voice as he put the long A in her name. 'Holy Mauther, what've ye landed us in now, Katherine child.' Kate couldn't help but smile at the memory, for all she could feel the prick of tears at the backs of her eyes. She came to a sudden decision.

'I'll put it right. I'll go and see himself. Apologise for being so forward, so filled with pride and impudence. I'll speak to the Father too, get him to put in a word for me. I'll tell himself it was all my fault and it's me should be given the old heave-ho, not you.'

Millie said, 'Don't talk daft, Kate. How will you feed the bairn if you've no work, nor money coming in?'

'Aye, she's right. At least I'm still single.' Dermot had been hoping to change that lonely status and ask Dolly to wed him, once he'd got a bit put by. They'd been walking out for years and they'd both been very patient, but the waiting was driving him mad. He was desperate to bed her, but she wouldn't even let him go beyond a chaste kiss and a bit of fondling till she had a ring on her finger. Now he was further away than ever from that hoped-for happy state.

Kate was saying, 'I'll go up to the Union Workhouse then, so I will.'

'You'd rather be a skivvy in the kitchens or scrub laundry up there, would you, than work for Mr Tyson?' Millie asked in disbelief. 'And what about your dreams for Callum? Look at us, is that what you want for him too?' She became distracted as one of her babies started to howl and picking it up, lifted her blouse and watched in pained resignation as it clamped its greedy mouth tight on to a scraggy breast. It sucked for no more than ten seconds before it began to howl again. 'See what I mean? No food left anywhere.'

Kate shivered. 'Well, they'll feed us up there, at least. We'll manage, don't you fret.'

She'd meant to sound jaunty and decisive, but the words emerged as a hollow-sounding squeak because she could barely get them out for the lump of fear and bitter disappointment that was clogging her throat. Why was it that everything turned sour for her? What had she ever done to deserve such ill luck? Kate didn't care on her own account. Hadn't she endured the rough and ready ministrations of the Board of Guardians for years? But what Millie said was true. She did want something better for Callum.

Besides, they'd take him away from her, she knew they would. They'd put him to work along with the other children by the time he was five or six, crushing bones for fertiliser, or breaking stones. That's if they hadn't already given him away to some better-off family in need of a fine healthy son. For as sure as the Virgin Mary is on the side of all sinners, he wouldn't stay healthy for long, not in that great, huge monstrosity of a place where hundreds of men, women and children were slowly reduced to human wrecks.

It was said that the bed frames were already rusty as the mattresses were rarely dried properly, let alone aired. Kate knew well enough that this was the overseer's way of discouraging malingerers, just as if anyone would willingly choose to be incarcerated in such a hell-hole.

'I'll go and see himself. Put this mess right. Mebbe he'll change his mind and keep us both on, if I ask him nicely.'

'You think Tyson will listen to you? Don't make me laugh, Katy. He'll not even see you.'

'He will, so. I'll make him see me. He won't be able to resist.' Kate gave a little smile, for hadn't she seen a flare of interest in his eyes? She might be poor and uneducated but she knew when a man liked the look of her right enough.

Dermot rubbed his hands through the wild thatch of ginger fair hair that topped his round head and gave a grunt of impatience. 'There ye go again, so damned sure of yourself, so filled with yer own self-importance. He's a happily married man, Kate, and even if he weren't, he'd never be interested in the likes of you, a girl from Poor House Lane.'

'He will so. You'll see. I'll put it right, so I will.'

–

Kate had hoped to leave baby Callum with Millie while she put her case to Eliot Tyson, or even with old Ma Parkin, but when it came to it she changed her mind. The youngest Parkin child had woken fractious and burning up with a fever this morning and Kate had left the cottage as soon as she possibly could, anxious to get away, frantic that whatever was ailing Millie's children this time, Callum wouldn't come down with it too.

Fortunately, he never seemed to catch their coughs and colds, or their frequent bouts of diarrhoea and had so far proved himself to be a happy, healthy child. Even so, Kate never stopped fretting about him, not in that place. It was a breeding ground for disease and fever of one sort or another. Rarely a week passed but what some child in the yard didn't have measles or chicken pox, whooping cough or mumps, and too many of them didn't have the strength or the will to survive. Lice and scabies were all too common, and sometimes there were more serious complaints such as diphtheria or scarlet fever that could carry off an entire family of children in the blink of an eye.

So here she was, dashing across Nether Bridge with her baby tucked under her shawl, the rain sleeting down in typical Lakeland fashion, soaking her to the skin and Kate still hadn't decided what, exactly, she would say when she got to the factory.

'I'm a blethering idiot, so I am, Mr Tyson and I'd like you to sack me instead of me brother because he's desperate to wed.' Would that do? No, that wouldn't wash at all. He'd take her for the fool she claimed to be, laugh fit to bust and probably sack the both of them. Oh, this was a pretty kettle of fish and no mistake.

She paused to wait for a waggonette to go by, stepping quickly back as it sprayed yet more mud and water on to her skirts. 'Shall I say that your clever uncle Dermot is the one with the skills, or is that going too far?' She pulled the shawl closer around Callum so he didn't catch cold as she addressed the question to him. The baby beamed up at her, a happy, toothy grin, and kicked his legs against her hips, making her laugh. 'Or shall I simply say that he's the man, and deserves a job more than me?'

Ach, how could she even think to say such a thing? Didn't she have a little man in her arms who deserved the best that life could offer? Besides, it went against the grain to put herself lower than the male of the species. Even for the sake of her own brother. Come to think of it, particularly for her own brother. Had she lost her senses completely to even be thinking of saving Dermot's position?

'Doesn't he lose most of the money he earns on the dogs, the cards, or the booze anyway?'

With her head down against the tearing wind and rain, she made a dash for it across Aynam Road, splashing through puddles and getting further soaked for her troubles.

Yet, she couldn't let him starve, now could she? Not her own brother. What would Daddy have said? Kate let out a bubbling laugh. 'He'd have said, that son of mine is the greatest lump of useless pudding that I ever had the misfortune to...'

She got no further with the thought.

Kate didn't even see the carriage coming full tilt from the direction of Thorny Hills, where the nobs lived. Wasn't aware of its presence as she rehearsed her thoughts aloud, entranced by her sweet memories, the rain drumming on the pavement and the wind howling in her ears. Not until she smelled the horses, heard the jingle of a bit and a warning snort of alarm from wide, flaring nostrils. The next instant she seemed to be tangled in a mesh of harness, desperately trying to fend off two terrified animals and prevent them from ploughing down herself and her precious child under their prancing feet. Then she felt Callum slip from her grasp.

When she came to, the world was spinning slowly round and small explosions of light were going off inside her head. Kate came to reality with a start and tried to sit up. 'Callum! *Callum!*'

'Ah good, we have life.' Hands pressed her gently down again, a round, cheery face swam into view. It bore whiskers and sideburns, steel-framed spectacles and there was the strong smell of burning feathers under her nose. The stink was appalling.

'Where is he? Where's me son?' She seemed to be on some sort of couch, evidently inside a doctor's surgery and there was no sign of Callum anywhere. The doctor had turned away, was walking to the door as if not wishing to answer her question and Kate's heart plummeted, feeling certain that the bile she could taste in her throat would erupt at any moment, all over the doctor's clean floor. 'Mary, mother of God, will ye tell me where he is before I go demented. Is me babby all right?'

The doctor hurried back to her at a brisk pace, quietly hushing her yet his expression remained stern. 'By some miracle the baby is well. Must have bounced like a rubber ball for there's barely a bruise on him. You have a fine healthy son, my dear, so stop fretting, and stay calm while I fetch him for you.'

Kate sank back on to the leather couch with a sigh of relief, letting the tears slide down her cheek. What would she have done if she'd lost him? It really didn't bear thinking about.

By the time she heard the door open again she was sitting up, making some attempt to smooth her muddy skirts. She'd pushed the tangle of hair from her face, arms wrapped about her thin chest for she felt chilled to the bone in spite of the thin blanket the doctor had draped about her shoulders. Still dazed and in shock, Kate looked up eagerly, arms reaching out for her child. It wasn't the doctor bringing Callum but quite another figure altogether. He emerged from the shadows, bearing down upon her like the angel of doom. His voice rang out, resonating with anger. 'What the hell do you think you were you doing, running around the town with a babe in your arms in this weather?'

Kate took a quivering breath. She recognised him instantly. Oh, why did things always go wrong for her? Wouldn't Dermot kill her, to be sure. She cleared her throat, reminding herself to take care to address him correctly. 'I was coming to see you, as a matter of fact, Mr Tyson, sir.' It was amazing that her voice sounded so calm, when inside she was a turmoil of emotion. *Where was Callum? Was the doctor lying?*

'If you mean to beg for that wastrel brother of yours, you can save your breath. Swainson is certain he cheated with the leather and in any case, I'm reliably informed that he generally spends three days working and two drinking. He can be replaced by a dozen better men any day of the week. As for you, young lady, you should be ashamed of yourself, taking a child out in such a rainstorm. Don't you realise he could have caught a chill, got pneumonia even.'

'Oh, so he'd be better off catching scarletina in the stews of Poor House Lane would he?' Kate retorted, cocking her chin up in exactly the sort of truculent manner she'd vowed not to use with him again, and taking enormous satisfaction from the stunned expression that came upon his face.

'Scarletina? Are you saying there's an epidemic about?'

'I'm saying he's no worse off in the rain than staying in the pit we call home.' Had the man lost his wits completely? But then, wasn't she supposed to be trying to butter him up, to wheedle him into a more benevolent

37

mood so that she could indeed put Dermot's case? She softened her stance, attempted an alluring smile. 'Look, the fact is that me brother had done nothing wrong, nought but help me get started with the stitching.'

'That's not what I heard.'

'He showed me what Swainson should have told me himself, if only he'd had the patience. And there was nothing at all wrong with the boots Dermot made neither. Your precious foreman was just determined to be nasty and have his own way, so help me.'

The look he gave her was scathing. 'What are you saying? That he wanted to have his wicked way with you, is that what you're accusing him of now? What else? Murder and mayhem too perhaps.'

Kate flushed with annoyance, hating how he kept side-tracking her from the point she was trying to make. She wondered whether she dare accuse Swainson of having wandering hands, but decided that was too risky, even for her. Besides, she couldn't prove a thing. But recklessly, not wanting to be beaten, she decided to try a different tack. 'If ye think Tyson's is still producing the quality work it allus used to when your father was alive, ask your precious foreman to prove it.'

'I beg your pardon?'

'Go on, why don't you? Me brother says there's no comparison with the old and new.'

'We're not discussing Tyson business here.'

'I am.'

'We are discussing how you risked your own child's life in order to save that useless brother of yours.'

'I did not risk my child's life!'

38

'Running around not looking where you're going. Do you realise that the child could have been killed?' He kept his voice low although it crackled with wrath. And it showed no sign of the harsh overtones of a Westmorland accent or the slightest hint of a flat vowel, as one would expect from one of the gentry.

'That was not the way of it at all. If you hadn't been tearing down the road so fast in that fancy carriage of yours, ye might have seen us. Do you always drive so recklessly?'

'A gentleman doesn't drive his own carriage.'

'Aw, now why didn't I think of that? Doesn't that make all the difference in the world. Well then you should employ someone who isn't half blind or plain daft. A woman with a babby can't be that difficult to spot, surely to God, even in the rain.'

'You were reckless in the extreme, so don't try to turn the blame onto me, or on to my driver. Not for this unfortunate accident, nor for that other little matter.'

'Little matter?' Kate was incensed. ''Tis our livelihood we're talking about here. You robbed us of it, turned me brother off without a penny.'

'Accept what fate and his own folly has brought, Kate O'Connor. I never back down from my decisions. Never! As I understand it, he got what he deserved. You both did.' His anger and obduracy suddenly seemed awesome, leaving Kate stunned into silence for a whole ten seconds before she found her voice again.

'Then you understand wrong.' Despite her defiance, a tiny shiver ran down her spine at his vow that he never backed down from a decision, rather like a premonition, just as if a goose had walked over her grave.

Tyson stepped closer in a manner she took to be threatening, except in that moment she became aware, for the first time, how very handsome he was. He had a chiselled, sensitive mouth, an arched forehead from which sprang dark, wavy hair that just touched the collar of his greatcoat. The nose was perhaps more hawk-like than aquiline but no one could deny the fine bone structure, even if the lines of his face did look as if they'd been dragged down by some disappointment or other. The eyes were a deep chestnut, yet worry and strain seemed to have created a fog of abstraction in them, the sentiment echoed in the slump of his shoulders.

Until that moment Kate had never imagined it possible to be both rich and unhappy. It somehow seemed a contradiction in terms but she knew hurt when she saw it, only too well, and this new insight surprised her. She longed to reach up her hands and stroke away those cold, harsh lines, to ask him what had put them there. But then the doctor came in, carrying Callum in his arms and the moment passed.

Kate leaped from the couch and ran to gather her child to her breast. Callum stretched out his arms to her, giving her his cheeky, toothy grin and her heart melted with love for him. Cradling him close she began to quietly sob, breathing in the dearly familiar, baby smell of him, admittedly much fresher and sweeter than of late as someone had evidently bathed and changed him, dressed him in clean clothes she didn't even recognise. He looked quite the little dandy, but he was still her babby. Her lovely Callum, whole and well.

'Leave us,' Eliot Tyson instructed the doctor with a brusque nod, and the man discreetly withdrew. 'Sit down.

I'm not done yet. There are things which need to be said, matters requiring attention.'

Kate pouted her resentment. 'I thought it all settled. You said you never changed your mind.'

'I'm not talking about that dratted brother of yours, but this child here, and your inadequate care of him.'

'Inadequate? How dare you, I...'

'Don't interrupt, girl, when I'm speaking.' He was ranging about the room in a restless, agitated manner, as taut as a coiled spring and, wisely, Kate sank back on to the couch and held her tongue.

'I assume there's no husband,' he snapped, glancing across at her with open contempt, and Kate bridled.

'There was once, but he was drownded, God rest his soul. Saved me life, as a matter of fact, but lost his own.'

'I'm sorry.'

He didn't sound in the least bit sorry, or even convinced by her tale, but Kate let it pass. He was striding about the room again, rubbing a hand against his chin, apparently deep in contemplation of something or other and she began to feel alarmed and very slightly troubled. Why didn't he just let her take Callum and go? He'd made it perfectly clear that he'd no intention of relenting over his decision not to give Dermot any more work. This whole trip had been a complete waste of time. She'd put herself and her child through all this agony for nothing and nearly got them both run over in the process.

He was speaking again, in slow, measured tones, almost as if the facts of life had only just become clear to him. 'You can't pretend that your situation is ideal. Living in Poor House Lane as you do, trying to get by on an outworker's wages, running around town in rags and with your child in a pitiful condition.'

Kate gasped, cut to the heart by the insult. 'Pitiful condition? Isn't he the finest boy you could ever hope to see? Sturdy and strong and full of good spirits.'

'Indeed he is. Surprisingly healthy in fact.' There was a moment's silence while he paused to consider the baby seated on her lap, which, as the silence dragged on and lengthened, became ever more strained and awkward, making Kate fidget with discomfort. Finally, he seemed to stir himself and recollect what he'd been saying. 'That's exactly my point. He deserves better.'

'Well, isn't that what I'm trying to do for him? Which is why it's so important I get regular work with decent pay.' She made a sound of disgust deep in her throat. 'Only it seems you have to be on the right side of your foreman to get it.'

'You can't blame Swainson. He's only doing his job. He has to guard against scoundrels who are only too anxious to cheat me.'

'You think everyone is dishonest, just because they're poor? Let me tell ye, there's plenty in the same situation as me, and once you're down, there's no way back up that flaming ladder to a decent life, or so it seems, but that doesn't make us all cheats and liars. Honest to a fault, that's me, so help me God, though not a living soul cares.'

She noticed that he very nearly smiled at this, but then thought better of it. 'I dare say there are indeed plenty in as bad a situation, but that doesn't make it right – for you.'

'Why should you care about me?'

'I don't, not in the least. It's the child I'm thinking of.'

42

'Then think about all the other children, and their poor mothers.'

He ignored this. 'Wouldn't you like a decent life for him? Something better than Poor House Lane?'

Kate felt suddenly overwhelmed with frustration at his stupidity. He was so naïve, so blinkered, he couldn't seem to recognise the day to day reality she had to live with. A situation not helped by a nasty foreman with wandering hands. Didn't she do her level best for her child, poor as she was? Kate got to her feet, filled with a sudden impatience to leave this clean sanctuary, this man whose wits had clearly been addled by soft living. Annoyance flared once more into hot temper.

'Of course I'd like something better for him. Haven't I said as much? Dermot would like to start a family too, if he could afford one.' She made for the door, ready to flounce off home in high dudgeon, to put her child to bed and hope and pray she could find something for his breakfast on the morrow. *And* try to think of some way to soften the disappointment for her poor brother. In any case, where was the point in going round and round in bloody circles, repeating the obvious. Her hands were actually reaching for the handle when his next words brought her to a skidding halt.

'I have come to the decision that it would be by far the best thing for me to adopt him.'

She stared at him in stunned silence for a full half minute. '*What?*'

'That is, for my wife and I to adopt the child. We can give him a much better home than you could ever hope for. He would be properly fed and cared for, schooled and educated, turned into a fine gentleman to live a life beyond your wildest dreams. What do you say to that?'

'I'd say you've run stark, staring mad.'

'It's a generous offer. Take it or leave it. You'll not get a better. How else can you be sure he'll even survive?'

Chapter Four

Amelia gazed at her husband in astonishment. Had she not been so properly brought up, she might very well have allowed her mouth to drop open in shock.

'I'm sorry Eliot, but I think you're going to have to explain this all over again. You plan to do what?'

He'd wisely left the girl kicking her heels in the hall while he brought his wife around to the idea. Despite Amelia having suffered a disastrous end to three pregnancies, the last more than two years ago with no sign of another since, he knew that she still hadn't given up hope. Her longing for a child was such that whenever he'd tried to reassure her that it really didn't matter, that he loved her anyway, it always upset her. It seemed too cruel to simply tell his beloved wife that Doc. Mitchell had confidentially informed him that it was highly unlikely she would ever bear another. Aware of his desire for a family, she longed to provide one. In the end, they'd stopped discussing the matter as it was far too painful a subject for them both, and generally reduced Amelia to tears. Even the small remnants of her dreams that she clung to had seemed better than no hope at all. Until now. 'The boy is healthy and strong, and in need of a good home.'

'You speak as if he were a stray dog or cat.'

'Then I am sorry if I have given that impression. He will, I am sure, grow into a fine young men. He does have a mother who loves him but she is penniless, without the facility to care for him properly. My plan is that we adopt him as our own.'

Amelia looked at him askance. 'And she is agreeable to this? Is she asking for money? What kind of mother is she?'

'A desperate one. And no, she has asked for nothing for herself. The suggestion – the idea – was mine. She isn't, as yet, too comfortable with it but is prepared to consider it, for the child's sake, and is willing to meet you.'

'But handing over her own child, that seems so heartless. Can't you simply give her some work?'

'She has work, but neither home nor family beyond a rapscallion of a brother. She lives in Poor House Lane but wants something better for the boy, and who can blame her? I wouldn't let a dog of mine live there. Will you speak to her at least? Will you agree to see the boy? He needs our help. Can you imagine, Amelia, how it must feel to be starving?'

Amelia could not, unfortunately, imagine anything of the sort. Not out of any sense of unkindness or lack of caring on her part. She held a strong sense of *noblesse oblige*, loved to give to those less blessed than herself, indeed felt it her bounden duty to do so. She would take them the preserves made by Mrs Petty in the kitchens; the flowers or fruit which grew in abundance in their garden, thanks to Eliot's green fingers and to Askew's back breaking efforts. But it never crossed her mind to worry over the differences between her own good fortune and station in life, and those of the blighted poor. 'The rich man in his castle, the poor man at his gate,' were to Amelia facts of life over which she had no control. God had ordered their estates, as the words of the old poem clearly stated, and therefore could not be altered.

Amelia certainly believed that she treated her servants with benevolence and generosity. They were well fed, had access to regular hot baths, fresh air, and ample time off. Some mistresses, she knew, were cruelly unkind to their maids, so it was more than likely that she could be accused of pampering hers. Social change, with its connotations of politics, economics and other business matters, was a philosophy best left to men, in her opinion. It was a part of their rhetoric and therefore quite beyond her. In Amelia's world, a woman should concern herself with the moral tone, with social etiquette. She must train her daughters to be ladies and her sons to take over the business, assuming she was fortunate enough to have children. Which Amelia, sadly, was not.

'I – I'm not sure, Eliot. I'm not certain that I can do that. I mean – take on another woman's child. Indeed, it is asking a great deal of me when we may yet have our own.' She turned her lovely, pale face up to his, eager for his assurance that this was true, but instead read bleak disbelief in his eyes. A small sob escaped her throat and she got up from her chair and fled to the window, pressing her lace handkerchief against her mouth to stifle her tears.

Following his wife, Eliot quickly gathered her into his arms, holding her close against his chest, stroking her too slender shoulders till the weeping eased. 'I don't mean to be unkind, my darling. I would never ask this of you if I thought there was some other way, but you know – we both know – in our hearts, that there is little chance of

47

that now. And if you did have a child of your own, all well and good, then we would have two children. What is so wrong with that? And you will love him on sight, as I did. I know you will. Shall I bring him to you?'

'He is called Callum. Say hello, Callum, to the nice lady. He's only just starting to talk but he's bright as a button, ma'am.'

Kate was aware that she was talking too much but the woman in the dark grey dress, a dull muddy shade that did nothing for her complexion and made Kate think of old ladies and funerals, was sitting bolt upright, saying nothing at all. Kate had placed Callum on the rug before Mrs Tyson then stepped quickly back, mindful of her boots, but the woman had scarcely given him more than a passing glance.

Kate sent a silent appeal up to Eliot Tyson, standing behind her chair. He seemed anxious and uncomfortable and rested a gentle hand on his wife's shoulder. 'Speak to the child, Amelia. Perhaps he would like one of your sweets.'

Obedient to his direction, Amelia took a peppermint drop from the bag on the small round table beside her and held it out to the child with a trembling hand, rather as if he were a rabid dog and she half expected him to snap her fingers off. Callum had never in his life tasted such a thing but curiosity and the sweet, peppermint scent of it, intrigued him. He reached up and grasped it with one small fist and, as is the way with babies, put it straight to his mouth. His eyes suddenly opened wide in delight and he began to suck upon it noisily. In seconds it was gone and he was reaching out a sticky hand for more. 'Again,' he said. Amelia burst out laughing and gave him one.

'What a greedy boy you are,' she said, reaching for another, her blue eyes suddenly shining. 'Say please.'

'Peas.'

Amelia clapped her hands with delight, half turned to look up at Eliot. 'Did you hear that?'

'I did.'

Kate moved a step closer. 'Not too many, ma'am. He'll get belly ache.'

'Oh, of course. I wasn't thinking.'

Satisfied that some progress at least had been made, Eliot muttered something about having one or two matters to attend to. 'I'll leave you two to get acquainted.' And when Amelia put out a hand to him in alarm, he grasped it, kissed her fingers and assured her that he wouldn't be more than ten or fifteen minutes at most.

When he was gone, closing the door softly behind him, Kate felt quite at a loss to know what to do, or to say next. Standing there in her rags and tatty boots on this expensive Persian rug, made her feel like something the cat had dragged in. She glanced anxiously down at her footwear, at the shameful trail of dried mud behind her, and thought that perhaps she should have taken them off, after all.

The house had astounded her. Built of limestone, as was usual in these square, Lakeland mansions, with tall, wide windows looking out over the river, its roof a complicated arrangement of gables, even sporting a tower with a battlemented top in one corner. The coachman, Dennis, had driven them into a big paved yard surrounded by a bewildering number of outbuildings and what she took to be stables, larders and dairies. Kate couldn't imagine how two people could need so much space, and why they didn't frequently lose each other within it. She guessed there must be a number of servants living here too. She'd already met Fanny, the maid who had opened the front door to them, and peered at Kate with frowning curiosity as she'd sat waiting on the carved wooden bench in the hall, with Callum on her knee. Clearly Fanny wasn't accustomed to seeing ragamuffins in their dirty boots spoiling her mistress's polished floor, and had stared pointedly at them.

'Are you here for a job, because by rights you should come in t'back way and see Mrs Petty, the housekeeper,' she'd asked Kate, in her blunt way, implying that she was getting above herself by sitting there, even though the master himself had instructed her to do so.

Kate had shaken her head. 'No, I've not come for a job.'

'I didn't think you could have, because there isn't one going. Not that I know of.' A short silence and then, 'So why have you come, if I might ask.'

Kate had smiled. 'I'm not too sure. Perhaps he's not the only one to have gone funny in the head.'

And since this made no sense at all, Fanny had redirected her attention to the offending footwear. 'Were you planning on going into t'parlour in them things?'

'I wouldn't know.'

'Are your socks any cleaner?'

Kate had managed a little giggle at this. 'What socks? And before you ask, me feet are filthy too, so they are.' Fanny had put her nose in the air and stalked off.

Now it was too late to take the boots off, the damage was done, and she would really have to risk stepping on the rug again before Callum sicked up all the peppermints

Mrs Tyson was stuffing into him. 'I think mebbe he's had enough, ma'am.' And very daringly, Kate did indeed step further on to the beautiful cream rug to reach for her child.

'May I hold him? Just for a moment. He's such a cherub, isn't he? Just look at those enchanting blue-grey eyes.'

Warming to her kind words, Kate picked Callum up and placed her son on the other woman's lap. She was used to others holding him, to Ma Parkin minding him, and Millie once or twice putting him to her own breast when she'd been overflowing with milk and Kate had dried up. Yet this felt different. Seated on this woman's clean, sweet scented lap, he seemed slightly removed from her, distanced by the strangeness of the situation.

Kate saw how poor and grubby her baby really was, even in the borrowed clothes. His eyes were indeed bright, and his hair undoubtedly marked him as her own, but his skin had that dingy quality of all underfed babies, and he was much too thin. Dribbles of peppermint juice ran from the corners of his laughing mouth and when he suddenly reached up and playfully tweaked Amelia's nose between his finger and thumb, making her giggle with delight, Kate saw the woman's earlier resistance instantly melt away. She saw love spring into her eyes, and felt, in that moment, a deep sinking of her own heart.

'Oh, he's wonderful. What a little dear!'

Uncaring now of the rug, Kate marched across the huge expanse of it and made to reclaim him. Callum wriggled his legs with excitement as his mother approached and reached up his arms to her. Kate would have taken him but Amelia held him fast on her lap, preventing her from removing him, stayed her with a gentle touch of her hand.

'Eliot says you are willing to allow us to adopt him. Is that correct?'

'It's a mad idea. The daftest I ever heard.'

A small frown puckered Amelia's smooth brow. 'I can see that it would be hard for you to part with him. When he first put the notion to me, I asked Eliot what kind of mother would give up her child, but I can see you have no wish to do so, not deep down. You love him too much to give him up, is that not so?'

Kate dropped her hands to her side, not knowing what to do with them since the urge to snatch up Callum and run from the house was almost overwhelming. 'I want a better future for him, 'tis true. I'd got no further than that,' she said, speaking so quietly that Amelia had to lean forward slightly to hear the half whispered words.

Amelia again smiled into the grubby face of the child. 'And doesn't he deserve it? He's a delight, and healthy?'

'He's never ailed a thing, by a miracle, praise be.'

'All the more credit to you as his mother that you have kept him so fit and well, particularly considering the circumstances you must have had to endure.'

'Life is never easy for the likes of us, ma'am.'

'I'm quite sure that it is not.'

'And after me husband was drownded, I'd no choice but to manage on me own.' Wanting to make her son's status quite clear, yet the bitterness in Kate's tone spoke volumes, implying the additional, unspoken thought – what would you know of dire poverty?

But Amelia seemed unaware of it. 'You have done a grand job, Kate.'

Neither woman spoke for some moments after this little exchange, as they both watched the child. He was playing with Amelia's beads now, jiggling and sucking on them, making her laugh all the more. And then Amelia suddenly gasped. 'I've had a marvellous idea. There's no reason at all why you should give him up, not entirely.'

'Begging your pardon, ma'am?'

'We shall adopt him, as Eliot suggests. We'll bring him up as our very own son to be a fine gentleman, and won't we be proud to do so,' she said, rubbing her nose against his in just the manner Kate herself was fond of doing; a gesture which brought an ache to her heart. But then smiling up at Kate, Amelia added, 'And you shall stay and care for him too. You shall be his nursemaid, his nanny. How would that suit? Isn't that the perfect solution?'

Kate stared at her, unspeaking. Was she truly being asked to give up being the mother of her own child to be his nursemaid instead? This seemed to bring a whole new twist to the judgement of Solomon. But what was the alternative? To take him back to Poor House Lane, or up to the Union Workhouse where they'd take him away from her anyway. Kate shuddered at the thought. Or he could very likely take sick and die in Poor House Lane. And she had to admit this was an unbelievable offer, a marvellous opportunity for him. Had she the right to deprive Callum of it because of her own oversensitivity? Kate knew she could not. She loved him too much for that.

'Your background, or lack of it, will not be a problem. Maids are treated well here, so long as they are willing, good-tempered and honest.'

'I'm sure they are, ma'am.'

'Are you a regular churchgoer, Kate? Ah, perhaps you're a Catholic, because we would expect you to attend family prayers. Would that be a problem for you?'

Kate stared at her, her mind in a whirl. This woman was asking her to give up her son, and yet was fussing about family prayers! 'I'm sure it would not, ma'am, so long as I had time off to go to mass.' Kate, who had never been much of a churchgoer in her entire life, managed to give the expected answer. Her gaze, and her thoughts, were fixed on Callum. The way his bright little eyes roved about the room, seeking mischief, his hands reaching out again for the bag of peppermints on the nearby table.

'Perhaps you'd like time to consider the offer,' Amelia kindly suggested.

Kate swallowed, cleared her throat as if about to speak but still no sound came. Her eyes were still fixed upon her child, drinking in the sight of him as if she were dying of thirst and he alone could quench it. Yet what she'd seen of Eliot Tyson's wife had impressed her. Amelia Tyson may be a woman of her class, sheltered and pampered, very moral and proper, no doubt with strict rules on etiquette and fussy about how he must hold his knife, how he must say please and thank you and learn to share and take his turn. But was that a bad thing? If Callum was to make his way in the world he'd be much better equipped if he knew all about such niceties. And she'd give him book learning, and figuring, no doubt put him up on one of them fine horses they kept in the stables. Wouldn't it be cruelly selfish, a crying shame in fact, to deprive him of such a grand chance in life?

And this fine lady was even offering her the chance to stay with him.

Kate found her voice. 'I don't need no more time. 'Tis very thoughtful of you to consider my feelings, and I'd be pleased to accept.' Not for a moment had she considered the effect of this decision upon her own life, Kate's one thought being for the well-being of her son, and of course eager to grasp at any opportunity to stay close by him.

When Eliot Tyson returned, some twenty minutes later than he'd promised, all the details had been finalised. Kate was to occupy the nursery landing, close by his side at night, and entirely responsible for his day to day care except for the hours each afternoon and evening he would spend with Amelia. This regime would continue at least until he was old enough to have a governess. It seemed, to Kate, like a miracle. They would both have clean clothes provided, regular meals and a warm bed to sleep in. One each, in fact. It might have seemed like paradise, save for the fact that from this day forward, he would be deemed to be the son of the house, the child of Amelia and Eliot. Callum Tyson, not Callum O'Connor. That would be hard to come to terms with, but she'd do it, for his sake.

When these arrangements were explained to Eliot, he looked momentarily taken aback. 'Then you'll be staying too?' Kate detected a note of surprise, a hint of irritation in his tone. The eyes, as brown and hard as polished pebbles, were glaring at her, as if he believed the suggestion had come from her. He clearly hadn't bargained on having the mother around, a thorn in his side, which gave Kate a surge of satisfaction as if she'd scored a small victory over him.

'I will so.'

'Better for the child, I thought, darling,' said Amelia sweetly.

At which comment he seemed to pull himself together and smiled affectionately upon his wife. 'If that is what you wish, my dear. Whyever not? Sounds a very practical, sensible arrangement.'

–

Millie was surprisingly cool when she heard the news. Kate had returned to Poor House Lane, of course, to collect her few personal possessions: the cap her father had worn when he'd first crossed the sea from Ireland, the bible he'd given her when she was a small child, and a tiny pair of clogs Dermot had made for Callum to wear when he started to walk. She gathered other things into her bundle too, scrappy items of clothing mainly, knowing they'd be thrown away, probably burned, once she arrived back at the house on Thorny Hills but her strong sense of independence making her cling on to them all the same.

Besides wanting her precious belongings, Kate naturally felt the need to explain all that had taken place that morning, to tell her friends of her good fortune. Surprisingly, their reaction was not at all what she'd expected or hoped for. She'd wanted them to be pleased for her, to wish her well. Instead, all Millie could say, over and over again, was: 'You've given away your child? You've given Callum to Eliot Tyson? How could you do such a thing?'

'For Callum's sake, because it will be better for him.' But no matter how forcibly Kate put her case, Millie wouldn't even try to understand, which left her feeling sick at heart. Was it all a terrible mistake? Had she made the wrong decision? Yet just looking at Millie's whimpering brood with their runny noses, scabs and sores all over their emaciated bodies, never mind the child who even as they talked lay in a feverish state watched over by an anxious Ma Parkin, and she knew that no matter what it cost her personally to give Callum up, it would be worth it. She would be providing her son with the best possible chance he could have. And she would be there with him, every step of the way. Where was the wrong in that?

Clem said, 'How can you trust that man after what he's done to Dermot?'

In a sudden flash of intuition, Kate realised that Dermot might see her action as a kind of betrayal, as if she'd abandoned him. It came to her that she'd been so taken up with her own concerns, worrying over whether to agree to this outrageous plan of Tyson's; whether she could bear to relinquish her son to another woman, that when she'd made her decision, she hadn't given Dermot a thought. Her brother's plight had gone clean out of her head. She must make it clear that she hadn't forgotten him, that she'd do something for him too. 'It was Ned Swainson who gave Dermot the push, not Tyson himself.'

'Aye, but from what you told us, Tyson got you your job back but left poor Dermot high and dry. I doubt your brother will see what's happened to you as quite the good news you're making it out to be. Good for Callum, happen, and for you too in a way, but it don't do much for Dermot, poor lad, now do it?'

'Tell him I'll sort it, so I will.'

Clem looked doubtful. 'I'll try, but whether he'll believe me or not, is another matter. You said that before, Kate. Isn't that why you went to see Tyson in the first place?'

'I did try but got nowhere. But I'll see it's put right, to be sure. Make him believe that, Clem, please.'

57

'I'll do me best, lass.' Though he still looked doubtful.

She went to say goodbye to Ma Parkin where she sat hunched in a chair, smoothing the child's fevered brow with a cold compress, and kissed the old lady on her sunken cheeks. 'I'll come and see you, Ma, to be sure I will. And the bairn.'

The old woman turned from the sick child to look into Kate's eyes, imparting a knowledge about his condition in the glance exchanged between them that Kate would rather not have seen. The wrinkled old hands clasped hers hard, and the faded eyes were fierce. 'Nay, don't. Once you leave this yard, lass, don't ever come back. You's doing reet by that child o'thine, hard as it might seem. Don't ever think otherwise. You'd do him no service to come back here and risk catching summat. You's med up thee mind. Stick by it. Don't come back.'

'Oh, Ma, what will I do without you?' and she hugged the old woman tight, the closest contact there'd ever been between the two of them in all the long months they'd shared the misery of this single room. In all of that time Kate had been unaware of how deep the affection ran. She'd thought the old woman senile, but her shrewd advice gave the lie to that. Even now Amelia had denied Kate's request to bring Callum with her, so that he too could say his goodbyes to Millie and the other children.

'Best he stay here with me, Kate, where he's safe,' had been her uncompromising decision. Quite rightly, as it turned out.

Kate shook Clem's only hand, then hugged him too, both aware of Millie standing close by, wringing her hands in silent anguish, pretending to be inured to the likely loss of another child, for all she never would be. 'Take care of Millie, and the childer.' He solemnly nodded, looking sad-eyed as the two young women faced each other for what each knew must be the last time.

'Ma's right. You'll not venture round these parts again. I wouldn't, if I were you.'

'We might see each other about, round town. Kendal's not so big.'

'Aye, course we will. And we can have a bit of a crack.' They both knew that if they did chance upon each other in the market place, for instance, there would be little possibility of Kate being allowed to acknowledge her friend let alone have time for gossip, not if she were accompanying her mistress on some errand, or wheeling Callum out in the perambulator as nursemaids of the nobs did. If she was on her own, mind, that would be a different matter.

'You'll always be my best friend, Millie. I'll never forget you.' And her eyes suddenly filled with tears. 'Look at me, best bit of fortune I've ever had in me life, and I'm crying buckets, so I am.'

Millie was crying too. 'Oh, but we'll miss you, love.' They hugged each other tight, made all kinds of unlikely promises, and then Kate picked up her bundle and set out on her new life.

Chapter Five

Fanny, the stuck-up maid who'd thought so little of her mucky boots, was allotted the task of showing Kate around, and supplying her with the facilities to make herself presentable before introducing her to the rest of the staff. She brought out an old tin bath, placing it in one of the outhouses because she said she'd no intention of carrying pans of hot water up three flights of stairs, thank you very much. Together the two girls filled it and then, lip curled in distaste, Fanny waited for Kate's clothes as she took them off one by one before carrying them away to put on the garden bonfire.

When she returned, Kate was still standing shivering, not quite able to pluck up the courage to put even a toe in the water. Amelia had elected to mind Callum for a while to allow Kate time to settle in, the baby having already been bathed and changed and checked over by the doctor. But although Kate had seen how splendid he looked, she was less keen to try out the experience for herself.

'Well, get on with it then. Have you never seen a bath before?'

'Course I have. We got one every month or so at the Poor House, though it was generally cold.' And the water shared with a dozen others, she might well have added.

Kate had generally avoided them, not trusting what those who went in before her might be carrying.

'Aye, and this will be too if you don't look sharp about it.' And then, looking more closely at Kate. 'By heck, you're as thin as a drink of water.'

'So would you be if you'd lived on porridge and Poor House soup.'

Fanny said nothing to this, but set about helping Kate to scrub herself clean, wash her hair and comb it free of any head-lice. Kate watched in amazement as the soap did its work. As Fanny scrubbed at the filth and the muck, little pink patches of flesh began to emerge among the bubbles and Kate was entranced. Although she'd done her best to keep clean by scrubbing her face and hands regularly with cold water, the rest of her body and hair had largely been left to its own devices, it being far too cold and damp to remove any item of clothing in Poor House Lane, even if there'd been such a thing as privacy. She'd never realised how very soft and silky was her skin, how gloriously soft and slippy her hair.

'Well isn't this the grandest way to spend an afternoon?' Kate said, unable to contain her excitement. 'I won't know meself when yer done.'

Fanny tightened her lips, staying oddly silent as she poured jugs of clean, warm water over Kate's head, splashed and scrubbed at her back and shoulders. There was none of the jocularity or good-hearted teasing one might expect from a couple of young girls set free from their labours to enjoy a little bath-time fun. She didn't even seem curious about the newcomer, not asking a single question but remaining tight-lipped throughout.

'There you are then. You'll smell a bit sweeter and be nicer to be near, at least.' Almost as if she were relieved that the task had come to an end.

Perhaps, Kate thought, she preferred cleaning out fire grates to scrubbing filthy paupers. 'Thank you so much.'

'I reckon you've left half of Poor House Lane behind you in that bath water. We could happen grow a crop of spuds in that muck.'

Kate simply laughed, not caring a jot if Fanny did make rude remarks about the amount of filth which caked the surface of the water; she couldn't ever remember feeling so wonderful in all her life. The water had been piping hot, the soap rich with frothy bubbles. Her hair felt marvellous, so clean it squeaked after being thoroughly washed and scoured with sulphur soap, and rubbed dry with a rough towel.

Fanny handed her a set of clean clothes. Fresh flannel underwear, a clean shift, then a simple, pale grey cotton frock with a belt that buckled about her waist, darker grey woollen stockings and shiny black boots that were exactly her size. Kate couldn't remember ever having boots that fit before. Fanny attached a stiff white collar about her neck, fastening it with a stud at the front. Last, but by no means least, there was a crisp, white apron which almost completely covered the dress.

And as Fanny helped her to do up buttons, tie laces and apron strings, Kate risked a few enquiries of her own, 'Are there many servants? I'm thinking they'd be needed in a grand big house like this.'

'Not that many, not enough in my opinion, and we're a motley crew. There's Askew the gardener, he's getting on a bit and should retire, only he loves his garden too much.

Dennis the coachman, he's my intended, so keep yer hands off him.' Fanny's round cheeks went slightly pink at this. 'Then there's old Jinny who comes in daily to do the laundry, and Mrs Petty. She's the cook and housekeeper all rolled into one, and a right roly-poly she is too. There's Ida, the skivvy, who helps with the veg and the washing-up, and such like. We've no butler here and Beckworth, the master's valet, recently retired, is not to be replaced, apparently. Again, to save a bit of brass, I reckon. And there's me. I'm the only maid so I have to run up and down all them stairs, clean all the rooms, answer the door, take in tea, the whole bloomin' lot. Run off me feet, I am, most of the time.'

'And now there's me.'

Fanny cast her a sideways glance as she carefully parted Kate's hair down the middle and, looping it loosely back over each ear, set about tying it firmly and tidily into a bun on the top of her head before pinning on a cap. The latter was, apparently, looked upon almost as a badge of office. It was sternly plain and stiff with starch, without any of the frills that distinguished Fanny's own cap. 'Aye, well, we'll see how long you last. Most new maids don't stop long. Too much like hard work, or they find it lonely and prefer to work in the finishing room at the factory where they can gossip with their friends. They're usually gone afore the month is out.'

'I won't leave. I'm different.'

'Oh, aye, ses who?'

'I shall stay because of Callum, my baby. Mrs Tyson is…' Kate started to explain but Fanny cut in.

'Aye, I saw the bairn when you arrived,' and giving a loud sniff of disapproval, continued: 'Lucky you had that accident with Mr T's carriage. Soft as butter, the mistress is, over bairns, since she's none of her own, more's the pity. A year or two back you wouldn't have got yer foot through t'door. So what wages will you be getting?'

Surprised by her obvious hostility, Kate quietly responded, 'I – I don't know. I haven't been told yet.'

Fanny had begun to ladle water from the bath, now she paused in her labours to look at her askance. 'Nay, that should be the first question you ask. I get eighteen pound a year. It should be twenty, by rights, being the only housemaid. But you should get less since you're new.'

Kate quickly picked up another can and began to help. 'Why is the work so hard? There's only Mr and Mrs Tyson to see to, is there not?'

'Aye, usually, though we do get visits from the two aunts, Miss Vera and Miss Cissie from time to time. Right pair they are. Create more work than a houseful of nippers would, had the mistress been fortunate enough to hang on to 'em, that is. Clever of you to win her round with the bairn, appealing to her soft side, 'cause she's been telling me for years we don't need another housemaid.'

'It's not like that at all.'

Fanny gave a half shrug and setting aside the ladling can, gave Kate's apron strings a final tweak and said, 'There you are then. All done and dusted.'

Kate twirled about in her new crisp uniform. Beaming with delight, eyes gleaming with such excitement and happiness that even the tight-lipped Fanny was moved to say, 'By heck, you look grand. A new woman.'

'I feel like one too.' Kate had never felt so fresh, so clean, so bright and shining in all of her life. It was a miracle. 'Do I get to keep all of this?'

'There's another set, for when this one's in t'wash, and work aprons, of course. Brats, we call 'em. None of it's new. These uniforms have been in the family for years. You wouldn't believe how penny-pinching they are in this household. Still, better than having to pay for it, like in most places, so mind you look after it. You're expected to keep it neat and tidy, wear yer flippin cap at all times, and don't lose owt or you'll be fined a shilling. The mistress has been a bit below par and neglectful of her duties of late, but slatternly maids give a house a bad name and if she don't sort you out, Mrs P certainly will.'

Not these dire words of warning, nor even the under-current of Fanny's disapproval and hostility could dent Kate's high spirits. She felt wonderful, so clean! Reborn.

Fanny herself was smartly attired in a well-starched print, covered by an equally capacious work apron in a matching plain blue, a frilled white cap perched precari-ously atop a mass of dark curls. She was a plump girl with boot-button-dark eyes, and had she chosen to smile a little more, might well have been pretty. 'Happen you're ready now to meet your doom in the shape of our Mrs Petty. Don't be put off, her bark's worse than her bite. Generally speaking.'

Kate would have liked to ask what was meant by this, but no opportunity was given her. They had to finish emptying the bath, wipe the floor clean, put the towels to dry, and all at record speed as Fanny had to change into her black uniform dress and white frilly apron before serving afternoon tea. And Mrs Tyson was most particular about meal times being punctual.

'Look sharp,' she said, then she was off, clattering across the yard in her button boots and Kate had no option but to run after her and save any further questions for later.

Mrs Petty was the fattest woman Kate had ever seen in her life. But then there hadn't been sufficient food in Poor House Lane for obesity to be much of a problem, so everyone seemed plump and well fed to her. Mrs Petty, in her turn, took one look at Kate, then set her hands on her ample hips and shook her head in despair, her several chins shaking with mirth.

'By heck, what have we here? Is it a sparrow or a stick insect? You're that thin, lass, one puff of wind would blow thee away. I'll have to take care not to cough too loud. Come from the pauper's cottages in Poor House Lane, I'm told. Well, no fault o' thine, I suppose. Don't you fret, we'll soon fatten thee up. Put some meat on them bones.'

Kate politely thanked her. Already her mouth was watering at the wonderful appetising smells emanating from the huge cooking range that stood in the chimney inglenook in the big kitchen. Oh, and hadn't she fallen on her feet here right enough?

'Course, you're lucky to have got tekken on. Work-house children normally only get a position with small-time shopkeepers, shoemakers and the like. Most folk don't care for the scraggy appearance of a pauper child, wondering where they come from, what their background was. You're fortunate, girl, that our mistress is a sweet, generous-hearted lady who doesn't trouble her head over such things. Play your cards right and you'll be set for life here. You could work your way up to my job, if you've a mind to it, once I retire to the Fylde Coast with me sister Annie, that is. I've told that to our Fanny here. Not that she listens. Too starry-eyed over our lovely Dennis to bother. You strike me as a different kettle of fish altogether. Good head on them shoulders, I'd say. Nobody's fool, eh?'

'I try not to be. I can stick up fer myself, for sure.'

'Aye, you do right. Many of them poor nippers, like our Ida here, were badly treated, beaten and ill-fed by folk what thought they could treat a workhouse brat like muck. You'll get none of that here.'

'I'm glad to hear it.'

Mrs Petty briskly nodded, as if she'd said her piece, then turning to Ida shouted. 'Nay, have you not mashed them spuds yet. Gerron wi' it, girl. I'm fair clemmed.'

The master and mistress had already dined, having been joined by Mr Tyson's brother Charles and his wife, Lucy. Kate had bathed Callum, dressed him in a warm night-shirt she found in a chest in the nursery, and given him his supper; delicious hot cocoa which she'd warmed over a spirit lamp, with an arrowroot biscuit. It had been wonderful to see the little boy drink every drop, smacking his lips with pleasure over the good food. Kate had been about to put him to bed in the big ancient crib which stood in the night nursery when Amelia had come bustling in to collect him, 'so that I can show him off to my dear sister-in-law.'

Kate didn't dare point out that it was already past his bedtime and meekly, if rather reluctantly, handed him over, agreeing that it would allow her the opportunity to eat with the other servants in the kitchen, on this her first night.

A long deal table ran the length of the kitchen, around which they were now gathering, taking their seats preparatory to eating supper. Kate could hardly wait, for, apart from sharing a few sips of Callum's cocoa, she'd eaten nothing all day and her stomach ached with hunger.

Mrs Petty took her place at the head of the table, grace was quietly recited in unison, and then the food was placed before her, thick slices of roast lamb, a mound of mashed potatoes, heaps of peas and carrots all drenched in a delicious rich gravy. Kate just sat looking at it in wonder, not daring to even lift her fork in case she should puncture this dream and it would all vanish in a puff of steam.

'Eat up, nobody's trying to poison thee, tha knows.'

Kate cleared her throat. 'Is this all for me?'

A bark of laughter. 'Well, I don't know what you do in Poor House Lane, but we can afford to have a plate of us own here. We certainly don't all share t'same one.'

Everyone was tucking in with great gusto, and, glancing surreptitiously around the table, Kate saw that they were casting equally curious glances in her direction. The old codger at the end with the white whiskers must be the gardener, Askew. She recognised the handsome young man with the dark brown curls as Dennis the coachman. Fanny was seated close beside him, constantly nudging his elbow and whispering in his ear. Next to her sat a snotty-nosed girl who she understood to be Ida, the skivvy. The girl smiled kindly across at Kate, revealing a mouth full of blackened and broken teeth, and Kate smiled back, sensing a kindred spirit. Perhaps she too had lived in Poor House Lane, or up at the Union Workhouse.

The ache in her stomach had turned to a dull pain now, and still she didn't pick up her knife or fork. Just looking at all this food was doing funny things to her insides. Kate suddenly knew that she couldn't eat a morsel. It was all far too exciting and terrifying. She'd bring the whole lot up again, she was sure of it. She was worrying far too much about Callum and this shocking decision she'd made. Where was he? Was he behaving himself? Was he wondering where she'd gone? Was he crying for his mam? Did he imagine that she'd abandoned him completely? 'Perhaps I should go and find Callum.' She half rose from her seat but Mrs Petty waved her down again.

'The missus is taking good care of the little lad. He's your brat, I take it, so you should be grateful for her care. She don't usually tek on girls lumbered with a bairn, with or without a father. Mind, we could do wi' a bit more help round here, so we won't complain. They're hard come by, these days, is a good housemaid. And our Fanny is fair whacked.'

Kate's first reaction to this was a fierce desire to defend her son, to insist that he wasn't a brat and that he'd had a father once, one she'd been legally wed to, but, mindful of her place and that she was a newcomer, she swallowed her pride and said nothing. Instead, just to set the record straight, she haltingly explained that she wasn't going to be a housemaid. 'It's Callum she really wants, not me. Mr and Mrs Tyson mean to adopt him, but I'm to be employed as his nursemaid.'

The silence which fell upon the assembled company at this, was deafening. Knives and forks were stilled, mouths stopped chewing as every pair of eyes turned to stare at her, bringing a stain of colour to her cheeks over the embarrassment of being the focus of so much attention. Had she said the wrong thing? Let the cat out of the bag? Not that Callum could rightly be called a cat, or kept quiet. She'd been seen arriving with him, after all, and he was all too evidently her son, a pauper's child, thin and scraggy, copper haired and pale. And Mrs Tyson could hardly keep it a secret, what she planned to do. So why were they all looking at her with this strange, condemning disapproval on their faces?

'I thought you all knew,' she mumbled, wishing Mrs Petty's clean flagged floor would open up and allow her to fall right through it. 'I – I assumed word would have got around. Or that Mr Tyson would have mentioned it.'

Mrs Petty was the first to speak. Laying down her knife and fork and rubbing a rough hand over her plump cheeks, she said, 'By heck, I've heard of some wheezes to land a job, but this one just about takes the biscuit.'

'And what would ye be meaning by that, may I ask?' Kate burst out, feeling bewildered. The tension in the room was such now that her skin felt ice cold, despite the heat in the kitchen. What was happening? What had gone wrong?

'Nay, to give away your own son in order to get a job and escape Poor House Lane, that's a bit rich that is. I've never heard the like in all my days.'

'That's not how it is. I didn't give him away. It's for his own good, not mine.'

'Oh aye? And do I look fourpence to the shilling to believe such a tale?'

''Tis so. It was Mr Tyson's idea, not mine, and Mrs Tyson just loved him on sight. Everybody does love Callum. Isn't he a grand little chap?' Kate demanded, gazing around at them all, and her eyes filled with a gush of tears. How could she even begin to explain what it felt like to give him up, so that he could have a decent future, to survive even? Nobody noticed her distress as they'd all turned their faces away from her, picked up their knives and forks again and were steadfastly concentrating on their food. Only little Ida gave her a half-hearted smile.

'I were abandoned by me mam an' all.'

'I'm not abandoning him. *I'm not!* I'm staying right here.'

For the length of the entire meal, no one spoke another word to her. Kate did her best to ignore them, and to eat the wonderful food set before her but somehow she couldn't chew the tender lamb; and the potatoes tasted like dry flour, clogging her mouth. In the end, she gave up the effort and left it largely untouched. Even the hot apple pie and custard which followed was too much for her, and she was relieved when the endless meal was finally over.

'Can I help with the washing up?' she offered, but Mrs Petty gave a loud sniff and turned away. 'Ida can manage. That's what she gets paid for. It's her job, and she at least come by it honest.'

The rest of the servants settled down for the evening, happily chatting to each other and relaxing after a hard day's work. Mrs Petty was showing Ida how to knit, Askew contentedly snoring, and Fanny and Dennis doing a bit of canoodling on the settle under the window. They all continued to ignore her. Whatever their liberal views of employing pauper girls in general, those who gave away their sons were obviously beyond the pale.

Kate crept quietly back upstairs. She wasn't sure if this was allowed, having seen the lengthy list of rules stuck up on Mrs Petty's larder door which included such items as:

No maid to go into the still room, china closet or larder without permission.

The linen cupboard will at all times be kept locked and freshly folded linen cannot be returned until it has been properly checked.

Requests for soap, oil or candles must be made direct to the housekeeper's room by seven-thirty a.m.

There were various others of a similar ilk, concluding with a lengthy instruction on how waste was an abomination, with precise details on how various items such as rabbit skins, old tea-leaves, dripping and the like, must be dealt with.

But, since no one had brought Callum down to her, Kate felt she'd no choice but to go looking for him. Perhaps the Tysons were waiting for her to collect him and put him to bed, the ways of the upper classes being a bit of a mystery to her. She was ready to go to bed herself, come to think of it. What a day it had been. She was quite worn out. Things might look better after a good night's sleep, but if they didn't, she would leave first thing in the morning, taking Callum with her, to be sure. This whole idea had been crazy from the start. She must have lost her senses to agree to it. They'd just have to take their chances with all the rest at the Union Workhouse, but at least they'd be together.

The small parlour was empty, so Kate decided to head for the upstairs drawing room, but as she passed the dining room she became aware of loud voices coming from within. Perhaps they were all still in there. She tapped on the door, hopping from foot to foot with impatience as she waited for the invitation to enter. Pressing her ear to the door panel, she tried to hear what was being said. A man's voice, loud and booming, and very angry.

'You're damned well being taken advantage of. Surely to God, Eliot, you don't seriously intend to go through with this madcap scheme?'

This must be the brother, Charles. Perhaps, after all, the two ladies had retired to the drawing room for coffee, since Eliot Tyson and his brother were apparently in the midst of one almighty row. And it wasn't difficult to guess the subject of their argument.

'For God's sake, you'd risk putting a workhouse brat in line to take over the factory, just because your own wife is barren? You must have taken leave of your senses.'

A furious mumble, which she couldn't quite make out beyond a few firm opening words. 'How dare you accuse my wife...'

'Well, however you like to dress it up, don't think, for one minute, that you'll get away with this. Father's will made no provision for such an eventuality, and I'll see you live to regret it if you insist on going through with this idiotic scheme. I'll not see my inheritance lost to some tart's bastard.'

At which point the door was flung open and, losing her balance, Kate fell into the room.

Chapter Six

'I'm sorry you had to hear all of that, Kate. Most unfortunate. My brother is not an easy man to understand. He has a different set of moral values to my own. Money is his driving force, I'm afraid, with not a charitable bone in his body. Other people are of no account to him, so long as he has what he wants: power and wealth. We operate by different standards in this household. I hope his words won't make you have second thoughts about our agreement. My wife has already taken little Callum to her heart. It would break it now, were you to remove him.'

Eliot was standing with his back to the fire, gazing down upon the top of his new maid's head. Pity for the girl had caused him to offer her a restorative glass of port, which she'd very properly refused. Nevertheless, he'd seated her on an upright chair, where she remained as still as a statue, hands clasped, head bowed in abject misery, which he did not wonder at. To be caught eavesdropping at her employer's door on her very first night was not a good beginning. Charlie, praise be, had stormed off after a few choice words on the subject of servants getting above their station, calling for Lucy, and his carriage, in one single breath.

Eliot had dealt with him calmly, as was ever the best way, telling his brother to get off his high horse, reminding him of how their own origins had been humble enough, their father possessing nothing but faith in his own abilities when he'd set about starting the business all those years before.

Nonetheless, Eliot was beginning to have doubts: to wonder at his folly, far too impulsive at times for his own good, and think that perhaps Charlie might have a point about the wisdom of taking this waif into his home and adopting an unknown child. It was a somewhat reckless act on his part, with possibly more repercussions than he had at first anticipated. And for all he knew, the infant could be carrying all manner of unknown ailments, and have a temperament quite unsuited to the life before him. Yet simply to see the joy on his wife's face told him that he'd done the right thing.

So long as he could deal with the consequences of having the child's mother live on the premises too, which was something he had not anticipated. Kate O'Connor was undoubtedly attractive; a rare beauty with that indefinable quality of sexual allure that any man would find hard to resist. Not that this cut any ice with him. Eliot felt himself impervious to feminine charm, however tempting, as he would never betray a wife he adored. If he defended the girl, it was out of common humanity because she seemed so fragile, and because, deep down, he admired her spirit. She'd displayed amazing strength and resilience in the face of adversity, for all she was at times far too quick to stoke herself up into a temper.

No, young Kate O'Connor was like a high-tensile wire about to snap, and he really didn't have the patience to deal with any histrionics on her part. Conflict over who the child truly belonged to was the last thing he needed. The boy must be entirely theirs. Eliot made a mental note to get the papers drawn up by his solicitor with all speed, and duly signed.

He was beginning to wonder if she would ever speak again when the girl suddenly got to her feet and stood before him, her face parchment pale but with her chin set characteristically high.

'I'd just like to point out that I never asked you to take my child. Nor would I *ever* give him away in order to put food in me own mouth. I'd die sooner than lose him.' Kate was still smarting from the treatment meted out to her by the other servants. It seemed excessively cruel for them to jump to the wrong conclusion, and a worse insult for Mr Tyson's brother to brand her a tart without ever having met her.

Eliot nodded. 'I understand.'

'I hope you do. Your servants have a different opinion. I want you, and them, to understand that I'm doing this for Callum, for *his* future, not *mine*. Nor is my son a bastard, and I'll not have him so addressed. I'd be obliged if you'd make that clear to your esteemed brother, among others.'

Again he quietly agreed, inwardly smiling at her use of the somewhat emotive description. It was not an adjective he would use to describe Charles. But then, sensing she had more to say, he urged her to relax and to be seated again. She ignored his instruction, treating it as a request, not an order. The set of her shoulders remained stiff, the grey eyes meeting his with a barefaced stubbornness which he knew Charlie, for one, would call insolence.

'I'm wondering what you mean to do over me brother. *If* you recall, Dermot was unjustly given the sack by your foreman, whose own practices are clearly in doubt. I'm thinking that mebbe it would be a charitable act for you to reinstate him.'

He had to hand it to her, she had guts, and the most outrageous cheek. There was more courage in her little finger than most people could summon up in a lifetime. Whether that was a good thing or a bad, rather depended on how she chose to use it. Given the wrong slant, her audacity could prove to be obstinate pig-headedness. So far, she was employing it for the good of her nearest and dearest, fighting for her son, and her brother, which he supposed must be commendable.

But however much he might privately admire her robust spirit, he'd be damned if he'd be bullied by a slip of a girl, a mere pauper from Poor House Lane. He wondered what would happen if she ever needed something for herself. What tenacity would she display then? She might have tantalising charm as well as captivating beauty, but these attributes were quite at odds with her tempestuous nature. And her brother was another matter altogether. No, Eliot decided that he'd done what he could, and that was an end to the matter.

'You were badly used by Swainson, I agree, but I've already spoken to him on the subject. The boy was blatantly cheating me. My foreman assures me that the leather he used on those boots was not of the same quality as that which was issued to him. He'd clearly sold it at profit to himself, and no doubt gambled the money away. Swainson says this is not the first time.'

'If that's true, and I'm not saying it is, I'll speak to Dermot about it. He'll have learned his lesson, to be sure. He'll not do it again.'

'I can't take the risk, I'm sorry. If I let him off everyone will see me as soft, and likewise attempt to take advantage. Then the standards, for which Tyson's are famous, will be seen to fail and I can't risk that. We have our reputation to think of. Besides, I feel our arrangement is a fair one. Your son will be well cared for, and you yourself have been given a position in my household to allow you to continue to be close to him. That seems more than fair to me.'

'But what am I to tell Dermot? I cannot allow me own brother to starve.'

'He should have thought of the consequences of his actions before he attempted to cheat me. And now, I think we are both tired. It has been a long day and perhaps you are not thinking too clearly. Go to bed.' As he turned from her, intimating that the subject was closed, Kate had no choice but to comply.

–

For Eliot, it was a long time before he felt able to retire. He smoked a second cigar and chided himself for all kinds of a fool for embarking on this dangerous venture, before he finally went to his wife's bed.

Despite the troubles in the kitchen, and her failure to secure any hope for Dermot, Kate passed a blissfully contented night sleeping beside her child in a deeply comfortable bed. She'd gone straight from the difficult interview with Eliot Tyson to collect him from the drawing room where he was again being fed sweets by Mrs Tyson. No doubt in an effort to keep him quiet, Kate suspected, because the poor little mite was worn out, his eyes big and wide and dark from lack of sleep.

'I know it must be well past his bedtime but we couldn't resist playing with him, could we not Lucy? He's so full of beans, quite the life and soul of the party. Though of course he must have a proper routine in future, as my dear sister-in-law has quite rightly pointed out.'

Kate barely glanced at the visitor, who was standing ready dressed in her outdoor attire of coat and hat and muff, evidently waiting for the carriage to be brought to the door. At first sight despite her obvious, dark-haired beauty, she appeared sour-faced, with lips as tightly pursed as a wrinkled prune. There was no sign of her bad-tempered husband, for which Kate was vastly relieved. She gathered Callum into her arms, inwardly cursing herself for leaving him so long. And for making such a fool of herself by listening at the dining room door. She scurried back to the nursery, thankful to make her escape and be alone with her child at last.

Ignoring the big, ancient crib which stood four-square in the centre of the floor, Kate took him into bed with her. The sweet, baby scent of him seemed like a miracle, as if the pair of them had indeed been reborn. Clad in a night-gown of softest lawn, she felt like a princess lying between the crisp clean sheets with her son snuffling contentedly beside her. No matter what difficulties might lie ahead, this must be right for Callum. Wouldn't he thrive in this place? Indeed, she refused to be bullied, not by prating servants nor ill-mannered brothers. She'd stick it out, for the sake of a glorious future for her lovely boy.

Until now she'd only been planning on Callum getting regular meals, a safe place to lay his head, and an education. Now Kate saw that there was much more involved, enough to make Charles Tyson furiously jealous. In a way she didn't blame him. A fine house, a business employing hundreds of people would be worth fighting for, would it not? To think of her son gaining such an inheritance, was astonishing, to say the least, more than she could take in right now. Oh, but wouldn't he make a fine gentleman one day? Strong and healthy and handsome. As she slid into sleep, a small voice at the back of her head was trying to decide how she could persuade her mistress to stop giving him sweets before the woman ruined all those brand-new teeth of his.

-

When next Eliot Tyson confronted his foreman, the man's attitude could only be described as truculent. Swainson obviously bore a grudge over the fact that his authority had been undermined by his employer speaking up for the girl and not allowing her to be sacked. Not that Eliot allowed this to trouble him in the slightest. He was anxious to know what had happened to the brother, if he really was the troublemaker Swainson had made him out to be. They went through their usual morning routine of checking on the status of the work being brought in, new orders needing to be filled and then Eliot asked, 'Did you stick with your decision not to use Dermot Flannegan again?'

'Dermot Flannegan?' Swainson could remember the name of each and every outworker he'd ever employed, particularly those who made him the most profit. His prevarication was simply to buy himself time to marshal his thoughts.

'Kate O'Connor's brother.'

'Oh, him. Aye, I stuck by it all right. Nowt but a rabble-rouser that one. Born troublemakers, these Irish immigrants. Girl an' all, if you want my opinion.'

Eliot didn't, but kept his own counsel on that one. 'She won't be a trouble to you any more, she's been given employment elsewhere.'

Swainson's bristly eyebrows shot upwards, his wandering eye seeming to cavort with fury. 'And where would that be?' If it was one of the independent shoemakers, he'd make the man sorry for taking on someone the foreman of Tyson's had chosen to dispose of. Swainson didn't care to have his authority challenged, not by the firm's competitors, nor even his own boss. He'd had every intention of defying Tyson's orders and ridding himself of the lass. A troublemaker if ever there was one, with her fire-brand temper and hair to match. Now he'd been denied even *that* satisfaction.

Not for the first time, Eliot felt a prickle of discomfort in front of this man who'd worked tirelessly for his father for as long as he could remember, and was never slow to point out failings in others. Despite being accustomed to battling against a constant sense of inadequacy after taking over the business, at great cost to himself, Eliot was keenly aware that it wasn't really his place to interfere in the foreman's duties, certainly not to the extent of publicly undermining the man's authority in the way he had.

There were times when he wondered why he persisted with this crazy ambition not only to equal his father's success but to surpass it, for all he had no family to follow him in the business. And for some reason he couldn't quite work out, despite all his efforts Tyson's was no longer as successful a company as it had once been. Proof, perhaps, that his father had been right. Eliot understood nothing about shoes and never would.

So there was the nub of it: little though he cared for Swainson, the man was a long serving employee whom Eliot's father had trusted implicitly to act in the best interests of the firm. He was conscientious and diligent and kept the outworkers up to scratch, which was no mean task. So who was he to find fault with such a man?

'As a matter of fact, Mrs Tyson has taken a shine to the girl and provided her with a position.'

'In your own household? Is that wise?' Ned Swainson's astonishment was not feigned and Eliot felt a surge of annoyance. It certainly wasn't the foreman's place to question *his* judgement.

'It may suit her better.'

'Oh, aye, I'm sure it will. Nice easy billet, and better for the bairn.'

His tone was caustic and Eliot found it a struggle not to leap to the girl's defence yet again. He didn't usually concern himself with selecting domestic staff, but this was an extremely sensitive situation. He concentrated on checking a column of figures, asking a few questions about them along the way. Even so, he couldn't resist confirming the rightness of his decision. 'Amelia certainly seems well pleased with her. Gets her out of our hair at least, eh?' And he gave a little laugh, as if this were all women's business and out of his hands entirely.

Swainson couldn't quite believe the evidence of his own ears. He was aware that Eliot Tyson's reputation as an unfeeling employer was due more to a sense of inadequacy than genuine harshness; an insecurity he hid behind a façade of aloofness typical of his class. And he was soft as putty where his wife and family were concerned, fool that he was. But this display of sympathy was excessive even by his standards. Swainson felt a raw fury kindle within that his authority had been flouted, that the girl had apparently been rewarded for defying him. Not that he gave any sign of this, but if there was some particular reason why that fool Tyson was protecting her, he'd dearly love to know what it was. She was a good-looking little filly, no denying that. Happen Tyson fancied her, although that would be a shaker, him and his good wife still apparently acting like cooing love birds. Still, you could never tell with toffs. Ned Swainson decided to err on the side of caution, for the moment at least. 'It's not for me to comment upon Mrs Tyson's choices, sir, but I'd keep an eye on that li'le lass, if I were you. Full of fire and brimstone, that little madam.'

'I'm sure she is but Amelia is skilled at managing her maids. Probably do the girl good to have a touch more discipline. But what of the brother? Has he found work elsewhere?'

By heck, Swainson thought, he's persistent. Happen he's bursting out of his trousers with need for the girl, eager to coax her into his bed. Well, Swainson knew how that felt. He'd fancied the lass himself and been annoyed to be so rebuffed, so he wasn't going to be the one to help another enjoy what he couldn't. Besides which, the leather he'd given the lad had been of poor quality from the start, but he'd no intention of allowing his boss to discover that fact. Didn't he, Ned Swainson, the man who had held this company together for so long, deserve every penny he made out of these little side-lines? He took the view that if Tyson was so green he didn't pay proper attention to what his staff were up to, more fool him. 'Nay, I wouldn't know owt about him but I'm sure it's not the first time the lad's tried to cheat you.'

'Indeed, I'm sure it isn't. But I wouldn't be best pleased if I learned that we had – shall we say – jumped to the wrong conclusion.'

'Oh, and in what way might that come about exactly – sir?'

'I simply want to be sure we aren't making a mistake in accusing him.'

'Nay, I wouldn't waste your time worrying over that scoundrel. He can easily be replaced with any number of better men. Dermot Flannegan will survive.'

Eliot detected a certain insolence in the man's tone but didn't remark upon it. Nevertheless, he held his ground. 'I would be unhappy if, following his discharge from my employ, word got about that the lad was considered untrustworthy and unemployable, yet proved to be innocent after all. We do need to be sure of our facts.'

'Are you doubting my judgement?'

'I'm saying, don't take me for a fool, Swainson, or it will be your head on the block.'

Swainson experienced a prickle of unease between his shoulder blades. There were times, he had discovered to his cost, when this apparently well-meaning and ignorant employer of his could suddenly turn into a shrewd and sharp operator. He'd spent hours on the shop floor since his father died, in what he called 'learning the trade' which had largely left Swainson to run the factory as he thought fit. Now he seemed to be taking much more notice, which was a mite worrying. And all because of some jumped-up little tart and her disreputable brother.

Swainson manufactured a look of pure innocence and mock outrage.

'Don't you fret, you can rely on me, sir, as you well know. And how is your garden looking at the moment? Lovely time of year, spring, isn't it?'

Again Eliot hesitated, not entirely trusting the man's fawning manner but finally deciding he was probably worrying unduly. Nevertheless, he did not reply to his foreman's question, not being in the mood for idle chatter, or wish it to appear as if he could be easily diverted by trivial matters. He turned to leave the workshop, satisfied that he'd done all he could for the moment. He'd made his feelings on the matter plain. Eliot felt relieved that this particular problem seemed to have resolved itself. The lad had no doubt found work elsewhere, and, as Swainson said, wasn't worth the candle anyway.

Then for some reason he was never afterwards to fully understand, he paused to make one final point. 'Should Dermot Flannegan reappear, send him to me, will you? It might only inflame him, and cause further problems, if you try to deal with the lad yourself. As I say, Amelia has taken quite a shine to the girl, and to the child. As a matter of fact, we're thinking of adopting him. Amelia sees it as her Christian duty, an act of mercy to save the little one, at least.' There it was, out in the open, and why not? Where was the shame in it? Although Eliot was careful to give no indication of their despair over ever being able to produce a child of their own. 'I'd like them both left in peace, the girl and her brother. I'd be grateful for your cooperation in this matter. Right, I'll leave you to it then. See that the Dixon order is ready by the end of the week, will you please? I'll deliver it myself.'

Ned Swainson was left standing with his mouth hanging slack with astonishment. Adopted? Bloody hell, that was a twist he'd not seen coming.

The girl must have got her feet under the table good and proper, the clever little minx, and happen already got between the sheets. She'd certainly ideas above her station. For all Swainson knew, the child could be Tyson's bastard. No wonder a humble foreman were nowhere near good enough for her. He might be a bit long in the tooth, a bit individual-looking as you might say, but many a woman had been glad of his attentions. Indeed still were. While that canny little whore had sold her body, and her son too by the sound of it. No wonder Tyson was looking so pleased with himself. Who wouldn't be, with that luscious little filly warming his bed? Not that Tyson had a reputation for womanising but this so-called happy marriage might all be a sham, a lie. Who could tell? The nobs had different standards, different ways of going about things. If that were so, then it was poor Mrs Tyson he felt sorry for, not only having her husband's by-blow foisted upon her, poor woman, but having to employ his mistress as well.

'And what will Master Charles think of this new development?' Ned Swainson muttered to himself. As younger brother and junior partner always having to play second fiddle, Charlie-boy was unlikely to be pleased that an obstacle had been placed in the way of his inheritance. It had probably quite suited him that his sister-in-law had failed to produce an heir, but this would change everything.

Swainson realised that it might be worth a few discreet enquiries to discover exactly what Charles Tyson's reaction was to this unexpected turn of events. It wouldn't pay to go barging in, mind. He'd need to play it canny but who knows, the man might be glad of a bit of help one day, and doing favours in high places wouldn't do himself any harm. First, he must make sure that the Flannegan lad didn't trouble any of them, ever again.

'Time he learned that I'm not a man to cross. I can teach him a lesson, at least. One that he's long been in need of.'

Having made this satisfactory decision, Swainson wasted no time in putting it into effect. He strolled out into the factory yard and called over a couple of his trusties. It took only a matter of minutes to outline what he needed doing, and how he would make it worth their while. The pair went on their way with grins on their faces. Dermot Flannegan would never know what had hit him. As for the rest of this puzzling affair, he'd just have to keep his ear to the ground.

–

The night they came for him, Dermot was entirely unprepared. He'd been feeling much better of late, quite pleased with himself in fact, having got a bit of work from his old master plus some repair work on the side. Cobbling bits of leather was a waste of his skills as a shoemaker but at least it was money coming in, and Dermot was beginning to think that maybe he could set up on his own account. There were surely plenty of people who'd be glad to buy hand-made shoes, and be prepared to pay the price for quality work. He surely didn't have to depend on someone like Tyson to provide him with outwork? Of course, he needed a bit of capital to buy the materials, the leather and nails, a last, and such like. He already possessed his own set of tools which he took great pride in. And he'd need to afford to pay the rent on a place. He didn't need much, a room in some yard would do nicely. Perhaps then, him and Dolly could get wed after all. He was chewing all this over in his head as he sat on the doorstep outside of Clem's place, when they came for him. Two great bruisers. One glance told him that they spelled trouble, and that it was meant for him.

'Dermot Flannegan?'

'Who wants to know?'

Everything was a blur after that. There was the sound of Clem shouting, of Millie frantically screaming and God knows how many kids crying but he barely managed more than the odd surprised grunt as they laid into him. His last memory was of them dragging him between them over the cobbles. Ahead, just across the road, was the dark glint of the river.

Chapter Seven

Charles Tyson was not a happy man. At a stroke, every-thing had changed. All Charles's carefully nurtured hopes and dreams had crumbled to dust because of one pauper child who was to be elevated above his station. *Adopted into the family, for Christ's sake!* It really didn't bear thinking about.

Younger than his brother by little above a year, and despite his cosseted upbringing, or perhaps because of it, at twenty-five he felt cheated, feeling that life owed him much more. As boys, he and Eliot had rubbed along tolerably well, largely because they'd had separate groups of friends, and mixed very little. But once his beloved elder brother had been left full control of the company, Charles had felt largely shut out, given scarcely any say in the way things were run.

He'd once accused Eliot of only allowing him on the board as some sort of sop. More to the point, his salary and profits from the business did not, in Charles's opinion, properly reflect his status as a member of the Tyson family. To add insult to injury, even Aunt Vera and Aunt Cissie earned nearly as much as he did, simply by being share-holders and doing no work at all. It really was too bad. But when he'd voiced these grievances aloud, Eliot had simply laughed them off with some droll remark about him always being a greedy little boy, and nothing ever being good enough to please him.

Why should Eliot be the one to take over the company *and* the family town house, *and* run everything without so much as a by-your-leave? No wonder the business wasn't doing well. Admittedly, Father had left him the house at the foot of Lake Windermere but Eliot still held the lion's share. He complained frequently about Charles's own spending, and yet had recently set up a scholarship for poor grammar school boys to go to university, having some outlandish notion that education should be available to all. In Charles's view, educating the masses could well prove to be the touchpaper which exploded society and brought it tumbling down around their ears. Eliot was even considering endowing some land for almshouses. The man was a liability with his philosophy that wealth was a responsibility which should be shared. How could he even consider handing it over to strangers, undeserving ones at that, while denying his own brother the increase in salary he deserved? Why should everything always be done Eliot's way? The whole caboodle handed to him on a plate.

His 'good works' were of course the reason Whineray had invited Eliot to stand for the town council. Which again was infuriating. An absolute nonsense, in Charles's opinion. Such concerns should not be the province of a gentleman at all. It was surely women's business to tend the poor and ineffectual. What else did his useless wife have to do with her time?

And why was *he* never considered for elevation in the community? Why did no one think to give *him* the opportunity to shine? Charles certainly knew how to lead and take control much better than Eliot did. And he would make rather a dashing mayor.

Charles preened himself before his dressing mirror and thought himself a fine chap. Admittedly he cut a slightly more substantial figure than in his salad days, and if he did not possess his brother's more classical good looks, there was surely power in his square, robust features. His hair was darker and more smoothly shaped about the head, and, unlike his brother who was clean shaven, he sported a neatly clipped, fashionable moustache, kept so by an excellent barber so that the whiskers did not quite conceal the noble line of his jaw or the fullness of his mouth. He also made a point of wearing suits of the finest cloth, made up in the latest style by a wonderful little Italian tailor he'd found in Manchester.

Yet it always seemed to be Eliot who got the better bargain. Eliot who had won a place at university. Eliot who was considered the more gifted of the two brothers, in intellect, and in his pretensions with his painting. His daubs, as Father had termed them even as Mama had gushed about her favourite son's prodigious talent.

Eliot also displayed an unnatural talent for gardening, seemingly fascinated by growing stupid flowers, even being able to remember all their blasted Latin names.

Furthermore, when Eliot had travelled as a young graduate from Cambridge, he'd come back able to speak fluent Italian while Charles had been accused by his darling mama of 'wasting his opportunities'. All because he'd spent months enjoying the Bohemian life with like-minded individuals on a Greek island, instead of going to Renaissance Florence. Charles was pleased to say that he wouldn't recognise a Botticelli if he fell over one.

Fortunately, their father had largely taken Charles's side, calling his elder son a useless fop, and a Mother's Pet. Which had made the division of spoils after his death all the harder to bear.

There'd been the most fearful rows of course when he'd taken to his bed following his stroke. Father yelling like a banshee, mother sobbing and Eliot storming about as grim-faced as one of his favourite Shakespearean heroes. But after Pop's death, it seemed to be taken for granted that the elder brother would take over the company as well as the family home on Thorny Hills.

Charles himself had been left the family country home, a decaying mansion by Lake Windermere in dire need of complete refurbishment, certainly in Lucy's view. Of course, he'd also been left a substantial sum of money. Quite a sizeable amount in fact, but nowhere near as much as he'd been promised. No hope of living the life of a gentleman, not with a growing family to consider. But then everyone appreciated how expensive it was to maintain a family, save for his brother who, of course, didn't have one.

Charles had felt compelled to join the firm and, refusing to sell the Windermere mansion, had bought a fine town house on Stramongate with the aid of a substantial mortgage, where the family could reside during the week. Then there was the question of decent schools for the children, and a seemingly endless array of new gowns and furbelows for his beloved wife.

More recently there was the hoped-for purchase of a steam yacht. Charles already possessed a carriage and the governess cart which Lucy used, but the roads were so dreadful one couldn't live on the lake without having the facilities of a private yacht. He intended to have it all rigged out in polished mahogany with monogrammed cushions and china crockery, together with the customary Windermere kettle which would boil tea for them over the steam boiler. Lucy had a fancy for weekend picnics on the lake. Delightful social gatherings with friends. And why shouldn't she? While he could enjoy his favourite country pursuits of sailing, riding, shooting and fishing. But all of this cost money and Eliot absolutely refused to increase his salary, saying he should sell the Windermere mansion if he couldn't afford to keep it, which was grossly unfair.

Charles scowled as he adjusted the pearl studs of his dress shirt. He could hear Lucy scolding her maid, telling her that if she didn't buck up her ideas, she'd be out without a character come Monday morning.

It was alarming how much servants cost these days, and did one get value for money? Not according to Lucy. And if Charles sometimes worried about his growing commitments, he did not allow his wife to guess as much. Lucy believed in always buying the very best. She'd once picked up a Constable at auction which had practically bankrupted him, and worse, doubt had been thrown upon its provenance. He'd returned it, of course, which had left her in a sulk for days. Nevertheless, he enjoyed the kudos of being able to acquire decent stuff: the kind of bric-a-brac which gave some indication of their status in society. Garden statues, Chinese pots, gilt vases and marble busts being among his favourites. Their town house was a harmony of fine rugs and classical furniture kept immaculate by the substantial and overpaid staff they employed.

But didn't he deserve to live in a decent style, commensurate with his position in the community? He was, after all, an Edwardian capitalist, if not quite as rich as he needed to be.

Lucy stormed into the bedroom, and stamped her foot in temper. 'That girl will have to go. She's broken one of my best vases. She's weeping about her mother needing the money she brings in, but I've told her she should have thought about her mother before she dropped it.'

Charles wasn't interested in the plight of his wife's maid. He looked at his beloved wife and helpmeet, and his heart sank just a little. 'Is that a new gown, Beloved?' he mildly enquired, because Lucy was just as likely to fire off at him too.

'Is that some sort of criticism? You surely don't expect me to wear my old one. The Cowpers are practically aristocracy. Her father was knighted, don't you know?'

Charles sighed. 'Yes, I do know, my love. But I am still at a loss to understand why that should require you to buy a new gown every time we have dinner with them.'

'Don't be peevish!' Lucy marched over to her long mirror and began to tweak the frills of her gown and fiddle with her coiffure. 'The girl never did manage to do my hair right. I shall get a French maid next time, far more skills in their smallest finger than a Westmorland girl. And so much more stylish.'

'I'm not sure we can afford a French maid, my love.'

'Oh, do stop complaining about money. I hear nothing else from you these days. You're getting to be quite a bore on the subject, Charles, every bit as mean as your brother. I suppose you'll be saying next that I can't have the new drapes for the dining room.'

'No, I wouldn't dream of interfering with your plans, Beloved, I only wonder if they have to be Chinese silk. And I thought the peacock blue gown you bought last week looked superb on you, and has been seen by only a very few people.'

'How parsimonious you are of a sudden. It's so upsetting. Don't you like me to look well? And I feel so fat and weary in this particular pregnancy.'

And to his utter dismay, she burst into noisy tears so that it took fifteen long minutes before he could calm her again, along with a promise to take her to Italy, once her confinement was safely over. Not that he minded too much. He liked Italy and was really rather in need of a rest himself. Eliot might place unnecessary restrictions upon his power in the company, but he certainly didn't hold back on the work he piled on to him.

Besides, Lucy was a fine, handsome woman with her ebony hair and violet eyes, a startling beauty in her day – still was, he supposed, despite the plumpness due to her delicate condition, and a certain discontentment about the mouth. She deserved a treat now and then, to cheer her. This pregnancy had distressed her more than the other two, claiming it was too soon, and blaming him for that, though he needed only to tip his hat on the bed and she was off. Secretly, it gave him enormous pleasure that she was *enceinte*, proving himself to be virile, and his wife fertile. Quite unlike poor Amelia, who still showed no sign of producing. Why didn't anyone appreciate what a credit his darling Lucy was to this family by keeping the blood line going?

He had rather hoped that this would be to his advantage, that the aunts would see that he deserved decent prospects, in the fullness of time of course. But they had bluntly informed him that they had not the slightest intention of leaving him a single penny in their respective wills; insisting that as a man, with youth and vigour on his side, he was perfectly capable of making his own fortune. Aunt Vera had declared she would leave all her money to the Church, and Cissie would no doubt bestow hers upon some animal charity or other. Surely, he thought, family was far more important than any religious establishment or stupid dog's home?

Moreover, Lucy had never enjoyed the same advantages or opportunities in life that his brother and Amelia so took for granted. Lucy's parents had been simple country folk, nothing but an ordinary farmer, land rich but cash poor, most of which would pass to her elder brothers, leaving little for her sisters, or for Lucy herself. But then didn't they both suffer from being the youngest in the family, with little hope of a decent inheritance from any direction?

Completely in tune with his mood, as ever, Lucy broke into his thoughts. 'Has Eliot agreed to give you a more prominent role in the company, now that I'm expecting again and our commitments will increase? Perhaps even permit you to take it over completely and be given the lion's share of the profits, since you are the one with a son to follow on, possibly with a second on the way.'

'I do agree that this makes perfect sense, Beloved. Unfortunately, Eliot views the matter rather differently.'

Charles felt a spurt of irritation that his wife had raised the matter while it remained unsettled, had in fact become a bone of contention between them. Eliot had laughed out loud when Charles had put the suggestion to him, baldly stating that feeding his family was Charles's own responsibility and not that of the company. There was also a great deal more about not believing everything their father had told them, of cutting his coat according to his cloth, and other such nonsense which Charles preferred not to reflect upon.

'In any case, from what we learned last evening, it would seem that he means to get himself a son, after all, one way or another.'

A quick, indrawn breath from Lucy. 'You mean the adoption of that pauper child? Surely, you don't seriously believe that will take place, do you? I assumed it was some stupid fancy on Amelia's part, and would quickly die a death. Eliot will surely put paid to such nonsense.'

Charles looked grim. 'I very much fear that Eliot means to go ahead with it, and with all speed. He is as much besotted by the boy as his pathetic wife.'

Lucy put a hand to her throat and her cry of dismay rose in pitch to a frightening level. 'Then how will we manage? Didn't you tell him about the planned refurbishments to the Windermere house for the sake of the children?'

They'd both convinced themselves that the planned addition of a nursery wing, plus a new conservatory, not to mention the steam yacht, would be for the children's benefit and not their own pleasure at all. That they needed to keep this exceedingly expensive property on the lake for the health of their growing family. Nevertheless, inwardly Charles squirmed. He'd made a point of not mentioning these plans to Eliot, knowing what his reaction would be. The mortgage on the Stramongate house was already straining his bank account to the limits, a further loan for the improvements could buckle it entirely.

'Time enough for such details later, Beloved, when the work begins.'

'But if he does adopt this child, where will that leave our own precious darlings? Without any inheritance at all, that's where.' Once more the tears spurted. 'We'll be the paupers then. Oh, what are we to do? We are ruined, ruined!'

'Not at all, my sweet. No, no, indeed not! Do not fret yourself.'

'Oh my, I fear I am about to faint. Please, Charles, bring my *Sal Volatile*. Hurry!'

At his wits' end, Charles hurried to carry out her order, as he always did, endeavouring to keep his wife calm, reminding Lucy of the child she carried, of making her face all red and blotchy, of ruining her hair, and when all of that failed, of their dinner date with the Cowpers, which rapidly brought her back under control.

'There's my girl. Chin up, we'll find a solution to the conundrum, make no mistake. I'll not see our little treasures pushed out into the cold, as I was. Oh, dear me no. Now, my dear, go and freshen your pretty face with a little cold water and we'll be on our way. You know how you always like to be punctual, and you do look charming, quite delicious, the new gown was worth every penny of whatever it might have cost. I am a most fortunate man, most fortunate indeed.' And pulling her into his arms, kissed her heartily while fondling her breasts. That was another thing he enjoyed about Lucy, her full breasts, ripe as plums. But then pregnancy always suited her.

Blushing bright pink, Lucy slapped his hand playfully away. 'Shameful man.' But he could see that she was pleased by the attention. Perhaps he'd be able to talk her out of the Chinese silk drapes after all, on the grounds that they were about to restore their other house, and must save every penny for that. If not, then he'd just have to bring his dratted brother to heel, one way or another.

-

Kate was up with the lark every single morning, marvelling at the clear view of the distant mountains she could see through the bars of the nursery windows, their peaks dusted with a frosting of snow against a clear blue sky. Closer to hand she could look down upon the river; sluggish this morning as it slid quietly along past wide, grassy banks, most unlike the raging torrent which had swept away her lovely husband. Beyond the church, which she could just see if she strained her head to one side, lay Poor House Lane and the yards where she had spent her youth. In crossing the river, she seemed to have crossed a Rubicon in her own life, just as the bible stated. She'd made a decision and Kate rather thought there would be no going back, even if she wanted to.

She meant to write to Dermot, tell him that she'd tried, at least, and that she wished him well. Sure and it was vital that they kept in touch.

The door opened and Fanny entered, a pail of hot water dangling from one arm, and a tray of breakfast in her hands. Kate could see boiled eggs, tea and toast, and her mouth began to water. Would she ever recover from this perpetual feeling of hunger, she wondered. Fanny set both down in tight-lipped silence, as always not responding when Kate thanked her. She hadn't spoken to her since that very first meal in the kitchen, nearly a week ago now. None of the servants had. It had been a depressingly silent week. On this occasion, it was only when Kate offered to fetch it herself in future that the girl was finally driven to speak.

'You's not allowed to leave the bairn unattended. Instructions from the mistress. Otherwise, I wouldn't be waiting on you, you can be sure of that. Oh, and the mistress says when Baby is dressed, would you please go down to the small parlour. She would like to talk to you about proper arrangements for his routine.'

'Of course. And thank you again for bringing breakfast up for us, Fanny. If you've not the time, we'd be happy to eat in the kitchen instead.'

Fanny looked shocked. 'Nursemaids stay in the nursery, with the bairn, for everything, including meals. That's how it's done.'

It had already been made clear to Kate that she was not expected below stairs. A state of affairs which made her thoroughly depressed and quite at a loss. It was going to be very lonely indeed if she was never allowed below stairs with the other servants, and they didn't speak to her if she should happen to go down. Clearly, there were all kinds of pitfalls ahead, all manner of rules and regulations she needed to learn and understand. Even so, she persisted in her attempts to be friendly, thankful that Fanny had at last responded, and so she eagerly addressed her departing figure.

'Perhaps you and I could come to some arrangement then, whereby I could help you with some of your chores in return?'

But Fanny simply gave a loud snort and stalked out of the room, head high, closing the door with a sharp click behind her. Kate felt certain that had it not been for the close proximity of her mistress taking breakfast in her own room nearby, she would very likely have slammed it.

'Ah, Kate. I hope you are happily settled in. I've left you in peace till you felt quite at home, but now I think it time we sort out essential arrangements. Sit our little cherub down on the rug, there's a good girl, while we chat. We've a great deal to discuss.'

She did not invite Kate to sit.

Every morning during this last week, the mistress had visited the nursery, cooing and gurgling over Callum for so long that getting him up and dressed had frequently been delayed by a half hour or more. At first, Kate had been at a loss to know what to dress him in as his old clothes weren't even fit for the rag-bag, but inspection of the chest of mahogany drawers revealed many items of baby wear, mainly undergarments and old fashioned dresses, of the finest materials and beautifully clean. Some of them she considered to be rather girlish and at times struggled to find something that was just right for him. This morning, she'd chosen a dress with pleats and a sailor collar, and a matching set of pants to go underneath, so today he looked a fine little chap, sitting happily on the rug playing with a wooden engine Kate had found in a toy cupboard; his cheeks all pink and surely plumper already.

Amelia said, 'While you've been settling in, I have not been idle but busily taking advice. Now I've made a list which I'd like you to peruse with care, at your leisure. Oh dear, you can read, I trust. I quite forgot to ask.'

'To be sure ma'am, Daddy taught me fine how to read. And Dermot can read too, so he can.'

'Excellent, and most commendable of your father. Well then, I shall run quickly through the bare essentials and if you see any problems, you have only to say.' Hardly pausing to draw breath, she proceeded to read from the paper. 'The nurseries must be painted and redecorated according to the dictates of *Doctor Barker's Advice to Mothers*, a copy of which I have here, loaned to me by my dear sister-in-law who has two children of her own and a third on the way. It must be quite plain and unadorned with a table and a couple of chairs. A rocking chair, a shallow bath on a stand for baby, and a place to store his clothes, most of which we already have. There is also a toy cupboard, and the crib which has been in the family for generations and will serve him well, of course. But he is to have no pillow, as that would make him round-shouldered, and the mattress must be changed to one of straw, which is healthier, I am told.'

'Very good, ma'am.' Kate couldn't help wondering how it was that so many babies and children who slept on a straw mattress in Poor House Lane and had never seen a pillow in their lives, grew up round-shouldered, bow-legged and very far from healthy.

'He will take breakfast at eight with porridge and an egg. Luncheon at one, upon which I have given full instructions to Mrs Petty. Generally chicken or fish, perhaps boiled mutton on occasion, and plenty of fresh vegetables, rice pudding and fruit jellies. Tea with jam and bread and cake at four, then milk or cocoa and biscuits before going to bed. He must also take a little fruit each day.'

'And not too many sweets, ma'am.'

Amelia gave her a sharp look. 'Indeed not, of course. His diet must be healthy. And he needs lots of exercise and fresh air.' And so the list and its accompanying instructions went on till Kate felt dizzy with trying to remember it all. How on earth would she cope?

Chapter Eight

Kate might have been taught the rudiments of domestic labour by the Poor Law Guardians, but the finer, more delicate work was quite beyond her, and she discovered she had much to learn. She must remember to keep Callum's play clothes separate from his walking-out clothes, for the sake of hygiene, and Kate herself was personally responsible for laundering and ironing all his garments. For all he was now a sturdy toddler who loved to play and get grubby, as children did, he must be presentable at all times, and since his clothes were generally pale in colour, showing every speck of dirt, much frilled and beribboned, this was no mean feat.

There were a multitude of rules to be learned which Amelia would explain to her with endless care and tact: that she must always keep her hands still when being addressed by her betters, and not fidget. She must look at a person directly when being spoken to. Should she be required to walk out with Amelia, or her master, on some errand or other, to always walk a few paces behind.

And most startling of all, she must address her own son as *Master* Callum. Kate found this dreadfully difficult, as well as oddly distancing and unfeeling, so she only obeyed this rule when Amelia was present.

There were, of course, difficulties and differences of opinion. Kate thought the bath on the stand too small for Callum, and would have preferred to use the bathroom, from where taps jetted streams of hot water. This, however, was not allowed. It was the only bathroom in the house, servants having to make do with the old hip baths, and kept for the exclusive use of the master and mistress. Amelia considered it far too dangerous a place for a child of such tender years.

'What if he were to slip and drown in that great bath?'

'I wouldn't let him slip, ma'am.'

But it was forbidden.

Kate maintained that he was often overdressed, with so many layers of clothing that at times it restricted his movement and he would become frustrated in his play.

'I will not hear of a single layer being removed, not until May is out, at the very least,' was her mistress's stout response.

Putting all the new information and instructions she'd been given into effect seemed fraught with pitfalls. The contents of the nursery medicine cupboard alone were difficult enough to understand, with strange names such as Gregory Mixture and Godfrey's Cordial, Daffy's Elixir for Colic, and something called Dr James's Powder which claimed to be for ailing infants and looked highly suspect. Kate felt certain the box must have been in that cupboard for fifty years or more. Nothing would induce her to give Callum even one grain of it, though she did administer the prescribed regular doses of castor oil every morning, and as the days slid past, thanked her lucky stars for his robust health.

There was one occasion when Amelia was quite certain that he was starting with a cold and instructed Kate to give him hot blackcurrant tea at bedtime. He was only teething, but enjoyed the juice and perhaps it did help him to sleep a little better.

The routine continued assiduously with twice daily walks, morning and afternoon. There were set times for play and he must be rested on the nursery sofa to strengthen his back, bathed in salt water to keep his strength up. After his afternoon nap he was changed and allowed downstairs to see Amelia in the parlour where he was allowed to colour in pictures, or stick scraps in a book while she read extracts from Sir Walter Scott to help form an appreciative mind. Eliot would come in later and play more boisterous games with him, declaring himself to be looking forward with pleasure to tutoring the boy in backgammon and draughts. Kate thought that her son might turn into a little adult before ever he reached his second birthday.

And each and every bed time, Amelia would come to kiss him goodnight. Kate found this the hardest part of the day. She would stand some distance away with her hands firmly clasped behind her back so as not to be tempted to interfere, watching with an aching heart as Amelia dandled Callum on her knee, kissing and cuddling him, before settling him in the great crib with many soft words and yet more kisses.

-

It was a week or two later that, quite by chance, or so Charles assumed, he discovered Ned Swainson still in the office one evening long after his shift should have ended.

'No home to go to, Swainson?'

The foreman had lingered on after work on numerous occasions recently, and was delighted that, at last, his patience had been rewarded. 'I was hoping to have a private word with you, as a matter of fact.'

'Problems?'

'You could say so.'

'Then perhaps you should discuss them with my brother. He's the one with power round here, as you well know.' Charles's tone was bitter and he did not pause as he made for the door. He, for one, didn't care to spend any extra hours, minutes even, in this place since he didn't consider that he received proper remuneration for his work. It shamed him to have to admit to needing to earn money at all. He was anxious to get home, pour himself a large brandy and relax. Besides, the foreman was an odd cove with that permanent leer and his wandering eye.

'It was about your brother that I wished to speak to you.' Swainson announced to Charles's departing figure. 'And this new addition to his family.'

Charles paused, his hand sliding from the brass door knob as he swung back into the room. 'How do you know about that?'

'Mr Tyson himself told me that he was going adopt the child. Pardon my presumption, but I thought it were a rum do, like, and it crossed my mind that such an eventuality might put your good self into a tricky position. And I wondered – I wondered what you intended to do about it.'

Charles considered the man with fresh interest, eyes narrowed into a speculative gaze. What was he getting at?

What point was the fellow trying to make? 'What's it to you?'

'Nowt, save fer the fact that lass, the mother of the brat, and her ruffian brother, did their level best to besmirch my name, and I don't care for that, not one little bit. They nearly had me sacked, with the accusations they were making. If Tyson's isn't run quite as it used to be, the fault isn't mine. I've had to learn to look after me own interests, and so should you. I were thinking like, if'n you were needing someone on your side; someone who could keep his ear to the ground and didn't mind getting his hands dirty, so to speak, we might be able to do each other a good turn. That's if it should prove necessary like, for you to stand up for your rights, or should you fancy feathering yer own nest a bit more, if'n you catch my drift.'

There followed a short, thoughtful silence, and then Charles said in low urgent tones. 'Is there somewhere we could enjoy a drink without interruption? I'd like to hear more.'

–

There was no doubt that Amelia doted upon her adopted son and spoiled him dreadfully. Amelia devoted hours to playing hilarious games with him: tiddly-winks, old maid and snap. The little boy would shout out so loud, whether or not he had successfully matched two cards, that Amelia would hold her sides through laughing so much.

And if having two mothers sometimes caused confusion for the little boy, there were other occasions when he took advantage of the situation. Kate would recognise when he was 'playing-up' and attempt to firmly control his temper. Amelia, however, did not have the heart to chastise him or listen to his tantrums, and would dash to pick him up for a cuddle, despite Kate's protests.

'That does him no good at all, ma'am. He has to learn that he doesn't get his own way in everything.'

'Oh, but he was so distressed. Look at his scarlet face.'

'That's temper, not distress. He must learn manners if he is to be a proper little gentleman.'

'Oh, he will, he will, but he is so small yet, and still much too thin. Come along now Callum, Mama will find you a nice peppermint, if you promise to be a very good boy in future,' and off she would go, leading a triumphant Callum by the hand and Kate would sigh with exasperation.

One evening, towards the end of the first month, Callum was not being quite so cooperative as usual, resisting all attempts to make him lie down and be still. He kept sticking his legs in the air to push off the blankets, and waving his arms about. Then of a sudden he rolled over and pulled himself to his feet by the rim of the crib, beginning to shake it vigorously, making it rock. Amelia grew quite frantic, certain he was about to turn it over, but paying her no heed he suddenly spotted Kate doing some mending in the rocking chair in the far corner of the room, and cried out to her.

'Mammy!' When she didn't come to him immediately, he cried out again. '*Mammy, Mammy. Want Mammy!*' And as Amelia hushed and shushed him, he refused to be comforted and began to cry.

'Kate, you'd better see to him tonight. He's perhaps teething and feeling fretful.' So, on this occasion, Kate was allowed to put her own son to bed.

Afterwards, when he was happily settled and drifting into sleep, Amelia turned to Kate, a smile on her face which looked somehow stiff and awkward, and very slightly embarrassed. Kate was soon to discover why.

'I know it can't be easy for you, my dear, but I think it's time we settled one little matter between us. I believe it would be best in future if Callum were to learn to call you Nurse. I am his Mama now, after all. Could you please see that you teach him to do this. Better to start as we mean to go on, don't you think, and that we do things correctly in order to avoid confusion later. You do understand that I'm not trying to shut you out? It is Callum I am thinking of, and his future.'

'Y-yes, ma'am. Of course.' Kate was startled. She knew she should have expected this, but somehow it came as a shock, like a bolt from the blue.

'It wouldn't do, would it, were you to meet up with the other nurses when out on your walks, if he were to call you by the wrong name.'

'I – I understand.'

'Good, good. I believe we will suit very well.' And having settled this most sensitive matter, she swept out of the nursery, leaving Kate to sink into a chair and quietly sob into her apron.

As spring changed to summer, Amelia began to take him out on railway trips to Grange-over-Sands or Arnside, with foot-warmers and waterproofs in case the day turned inclement, once as far as Morecambe where, armed with bucket and spade, shrimping net and sailing boat he was indeed as happy as a sand-boy. At home he was allowed to run about the house and garden in plimsolls and with bare legs, teasing Amelia to chase him and giggling ecstatically when she succeeded in catching him.

Sometimes the entire family would visit Charles and Lucy's mansion on Lake Windermere, where they would take a picnic on a steamer trip, and find a quiet cove to enjoy it.

'We really should have our own private yacht,' Lucy would frequently be heard to declare. 'Then we would no longer be obliged to endure the proximity of all these other people, the riff-raff.'

'Oh, but that's part of the fun,' Amelia would maintain.

They would boil tea on a spirit stove, enjoy jam and bread and an assortment of delicious cakes which Mrs Petty would make up for them. Kate had never known so many treats, or such contentment. Every day brought new pleasures, and was a wonderful journey of discovery for her. And if sometimes she thought herself overworked, being left to mind Lucy's two offspring on these occasions in addition to Callum, a mischievous duo to say the least, she shouldered the chore with goodwill and gratitude. Wasn't she the lucky one?

The weeks and months flew by and Kate grew used to the nursery routine, discovering in it a security she'd never known before. She took increasing pride in the newly painted nursery, keeping it immaculately clean and tidy, and came to love living in this fine house, revelling in her new status. And if what Mrs Petty said was true, that other girls were starting to look down upon domestic service and wish for more freedom, Kate thought them wrong. To her it felt like paradise.

Dermot was the only blot on her horizon. She worried about her brother a great deal, had written him several letters but received not a single reply to any of them. Once, she asked Amelia if she might call upon her friends, Millie and Clem, in order to make proper enquiries about him. But her mistress wouldn't hear of it.

'Who knows what diseases might be lurking in those yards? I'm surprised you even ask, Kate.'

And because Amelia was so kind and showed the patience of a saint in every other way, Kate felt obliged to let the subject drop. She would simply have to trust in Dermot's ability to survive on his wits, as he'd certainly done thus far.

Mrs Petty's attitude remained obstinately immovable, and, faced with the stone wall of her resistance, Kate wisely decided not to make a fuss, as she felt sure this would only make matters worse. If the woman chose to think the worst of her, then there was little she could do to change her mind.

Following the housekeeper's example, the servants held fast to their unwillingness to speak to Kate and the atmosphere, whenever she ventured into the kitchen, remained cold and strained. Kate resolved to deal with the problem by tackling each of them one by one.

She first approached Ida, who was only too eager to make friends and tell her own sad tale of being ill-treated; a far worse story, Kate felt, than her own, as the girl had been frequently locked in a cupboard for hours at a time and kept on starvation rations. She was saved one day when the local vicar called and heard her crying. The woman of the house was prosecuted but, following her dreadful experience, Ida had been too scared to venture out of the workhouse again until Mrs Tyson personally called while carrying out her charitable duties, and taken pity on her.

The gardener, old Askew, Kate found to be no trouble at all. He hadn't so much sent her to Coventry, he assured her, as not realised what was going on. She needed only to show a little interest in his tomatoes and he was her instant friend.

Fanny was more tricky, blowing hot and cold, some days willing to exchange a few chill words, generally comprising the relaying of instructions from Mrs Petty or the mistress; at other times her mouth would be pursed so tight it looked as if she'd swallowed a lemon. Kate just kept smiling and agreeing with her, hoping for the best. And she kept a wide berth from Dennis who was only too ready to smile and wink at her at every opportunity. He'd once caught her on the back stairs, told her what a pretty little bird she was and how about a kiss. Kate had made a joke of it, managed to wriggle from his grasp and fled.

He was a pert, cocksure sort of fellow who knew everything there was to learn about the workings of the internal combustion engine and was evidently hoping to persuade his employer to abandon the carriage and buy a motor. He also appreciated the value of polished brass and shining paintwork and was frequently heard to declare that if he didn't get proper treatment and promotion with the Tyson's, he would move on somewhere more forward-looking and amenable, and of course take Fanny with him.

According to his adoring fiancée, he would easily pass muster as a gentleman's gentleman, since he knew how to be discreet.

'Not that our Mr Tyson would ever stray, any more than my lovely Dennis would, so don't you cast an eye in that direction either, madam.'

'Huh, as if I would,' Kate tartly replied, but the comment made her consider her employer in a different light, and if he passed her on the stairs, or was reading at his desk when she took Callum into the drawing room before dinner, she would cast covert glances in his direction and wonder what kind of man he was, what sort of husband he made. Was he loving and kind, or firm and dictatorial? Kate knew very little about marriage, not having any memory of her mother, and her own had been too short-lived to teach her anything save that men had their own view of the world, their own way of looking at things which wasn't necessarily the same as a woman's. This meant that they were not always easy to understand, or bend to your own will.

But she remembered also, from those few blissful short weeks that a man and woman could have a deal of fun together. And so Kate would look at Eliot and wonder what kind of bed-mate he might make.

Eliot Tyson had certainly turned out to be very different from Kate's expectations. Far from being the unyielding tyrant she'd been led to expect, with his quiet brown eyes and winning, slightly diffident smile, he'd proved to be a pleasant, easy-going sort of employer who was prepared to discuss matters with his servants as if he truly valued their opinion. Kate had personally witnessed him thanking Dennis for keeping the harness and other trappings clean and neat. He would ask the gardener if he would mind feeding the pigeons, or politely request a sandwich from Mrs Petty, should he feel hungry after an hour or two of work pruning his trees, or if he'd come home late from the factory.

He was liberal in his views, a definite individual, and not in any way a man to ignore.

If he had a fault it was that his approach to life, and to business, was perhaps a touch too casual. In Kate's humble opinion he seemed to spend less time at the factory than he properly should, spending hour upon hour with his beloved wife and with Callum, much of it in the garden. Kate thought all of this rather strange, for how could he possibly manage to keep a proper eye on things when he was so often absent from the factory? No wonder the likes of Ned Swainson got a bit above themselves and took advantage, with a largely absentee boss.

When once she dared to tentatively ask him if he was perhaps neglecting his business, he'd laughed and asked if she wasn't pleased that he was proving to be such a diligent father.

'Haven't I wanted this all my life, Kate? Where is the harm in spending a little time with my son? And here, in the garden, is where I find the peace and solace I need, a time which welds us together as a family. Doesn't that have equal value to making money?'

Kate could not deny it, yet experienced great pangs of jealousy watching the three together. He was planning a new design for the garden, and worked happily side by side with old Askew, re-shaping it to a scheme he had drawn up with meticulous care, describing it all to Callum as if the little boy could possibly understand.

'It is not in any way to be a grand design, you see,' he would explain to the child, who would gaze up at him with wide-eyed adoration, 'But a series of small, intimate, outdoor rooms, linked together to form a composite whole. Won't that be nice?'

'Me like pretty flowers,' Callum said, nodding vigorously, clearly enchanted with the garden.

In the weeks following, Kate too grew to love walking there, admiring the fruits of her employer's labours. There was always something new to see, perhaps an unexpected artefact at the turn of a path, the minutia of a mosaic patio laid by his own hands, or a showy, exotic plant to delight the eye. He was a collector, a creator, and, like all good gardeners, a patient optimist, content to plant trees he would never see mature in his own lifetime.

Master Eliot, as old Askew insisted on calling his employer, displayed a fine eye for detail, with which Kate could only agree.

And a winning way with her child.

On one particular morning in early autumn, she discovered him planting a dozen young saplings, whips as he called them.

'Haven't you enough trees already?' she laughed, looking about her at the gracious line of beeches along the drive, the woodland copse of ash and rowan that stood behind the house, shielding Tyson Lodge from the terrace of fine houses beyond, and the high school from which each afternoon burst forth a chattering mass of giggling girls.

'One can never have enough trees. We must plant for the next generation,' he explained.

'For Callum, you mean?'

He gave her a wry smile. 'For Callum, and for his children, and for all future generations to come.'

'Then will you tell me why you don't take the same care over the business that you do with your blessed trees?'

He paused in his digging to glance up at her in surprise, a frown puckering his brow, perhaps affronted by her impudence. 'Dammit, I do. I always have taken proper care of the company. I run the factory with great care and attention to detail.'

'Not recently, you don't. Not since you got Callum, which seems odd to me. Doesn't he, and these future generations you talk about, deserve to have some money coming in, so that they can carry on living in this grand house and enjoy this wonderful garden that you've made?'

Kate thought for a moment that he was going to be angry, though she'd never yet seen him lose his temper. Nor did he on this occasion. Instead, his frozen expression was finally warmed by a lazy smile. 'My word, you have a way with words, Kate O'Connor; a happy knack for cutting to the heart of a matter. But it is a justified criticism. I should spend more time at the factory, I don't deny it. I've been enjoying my new son.' He glanced fondly down at the boy, digging beside him in the rich earth with a small trowel.

'Well then, what are ye going to do about it? Or this little chap could suffer and then I'd have given him up for nothing. Why don't ye get back to work?' She seemed to be growing more daring by the minute. Surely to God he'd bite her head off for such bare-faced cheek?

Frowning, Eliot leaned on his spade to give the matter closer attention, just as if nursemaids questioned his judgement every day of the week. 'I suppose because I'm not a greedy man and would much rather spend my time here in the garden, or with my wife, than in the office. Amelia is so much improved now that she has Callum, and you to help her. Am I not the most fortunate of souls, with all that a man could wish for? With sufficient funds for our needs, I am content.'

'But will you continue to be so if the money runs out? Will there be sufficient funds, as you call them, if you carry on in this fashion? Sure and I'm no expert but if you neglect the business too much, and leave it in the hands of that nasty Ned Swainson, then may the Good Lord save you!'

He shook his head sadly. 'Oh Kate, I'm well aware of your dislike of my poor foreman. Spare me further complaints about him, I beg you, on such a golden autumn day.'

She was not to be distracted. 'Why not let Mr Charles run the company for a while then?'

At this, Eliot Tyson put back his head and laughed, a harsh, brittle sound with little humour in it. 'Because he'd have us bankrupt in a matter of months. Fortunately, I've an accounts clerk to keep an eye on the financial side of things. Charles has his place in the company, as junior partner in charge of overseas orders. Plus, of course, whether you approve of him or not, I do have a most able foreman to deal with everyday matters.'

'Saints preserve us, I wouldn't trust the little toad as far as I could throw him. Begging your pardon, sir, but the man's nought but horse shite, so help me God.'

Eliot let out a great shout of laughter, a genuine, heart-felt emotion, which went on for so long that Kate found her own lips twitching into a smile. 'Begging yer pardon over me language, sir.'

'I wouldn't ever let Mrs Tyson hear you use such words, Kate. She'd faint clean away.' He took out a linen handkerchief and wiped tears of mirth from his eyes, blew his nose then tucking the handkerchief away again, a smile still playing about his mouth. Kate found her gaze fixed upon that mouth, upon the wide, upward curve of the lips, wondering what they might feel like pressed against her own. Cool? Firm? Or warm and soft and persuasively seductive? She pushed the thought away and concentrated on what he was saying to her. 'While I don't share your harsh opinion of Swainson, in other respects, Kate O'Connor, your criticism is justified. I should, *and will*, strive to be more assiduous in my duties in future. You are quite right that I have a son to think of now, and Callum's future should be made secure. I promise I will be more assiduous in that respect. I shall even go in tomorrow and check that everything is in order. There, does that suit?'

And they both smiled into each other's eyes, aware of the incongruity of the exchange, and yet both well satisfied with it.

Nevertheless, Kate couldn't help wondering if, despite these fine words, he would keep his word. Why would someone who'd never needed to think too much about money in their life, struggle to find rent, or worry about where the next meal was coming from, trouble himself over how or why it arrived in their pocket?

The next morning he left for the office at six. Admittedly he was home again by lunch-time, after which he took himself off to the summer house where he set up his easel and spent the rest of the afternoon teaching Callum how to paint his beloved trees. The child was soon plastered with the stuff, daubed in green and gold and yellow from top to toe by the time they were done for the afternoon. Drat the man, he was too relaxed and easy-going for his own good, allowing the joys of fatherhood to cloud his judgement over the business. A flaw in him, to be sure, but, in Kate's opinion, understandable, and his only one. In every other respect he seemed to her quite perfect. So perfect, she was having trouble getting him out of her mind.

She'd go to mass on Sunday, so she would, without fail.

Chapter Nine

Lucy looked on events with increasing alarm and despondency. Despite Charles's promises that he had the matter in hand, nothing had changed. The workhouse brat had indeed been adopted and accepted into the family, papers duly signed, and her own expertise as a mother was frequently called upon to supply advice to Amelia. Admittedly the woman followed every word of it to the letter, using that stupid book of Doctor Barker's that Lucy had given her as some sort of bible.

What Lucy really longed to say was 'put the dratted infant back where he belongs,' but dared not. Amelia could be remarkably stubborn, and so could Eliot, and relations between the two branches of the family had never been easy since Eliot simply didn't appreciate Charles as he should, nor provided proper recompense for the hours he put in at the factory. Lucy had hardly seen her husband lately. It really was too bad.

For Lucy, nothing was certain, nor quite as it should be. She still felt bloated and tired after her latest pregnancy, another boy whom they'd named George after his grandfather, needing to make a point. She'd wanted to do this with their first born but Charles had been so furious with his father for not leaving him a proper share in the business, he wouldn't hear of it. He'd regretted it ever since, of course, particularly as Eliot refused to share the task of running the company properly with him, claiming that he had no real head for business. Arrogant nonsense. Eliot never had appreciated Charles's virtues, his ambition or his drive, not to mention his clever way of looking at things, Lucy thought admiringly, if with no small degree of prejudice.

Now it looked as if their precious children were to be deprived of their heritage as well. It really was too much. She mustn't let it happen. Nor would it. Not if she had any say in the matter.

-

One day in late Autumn, with the first crispness of winter in the air and Callum having celebrated his second birthday, Amelia declared her intention of taking him shopping. 'He is no longer a baby. Now that he is grown so big, our little man should have some new winter clothes, don't you think? You must come too Kate, to help me choose, and to wheel his pram.'

They walked him out the very next morning in the big, black perambulator which, to Kate's mind, resembled nothing so much as an invalid carriage in every respect, save for its size. As always, she felt hugely conspicuous as they strolled in leisurely fashion across the new Victoria Bridge which her own father had helped to build, opened only a few short years ago to celebrate the Golden Jubilee. Then along Stramongate and up into town, Amelia stopping frequently to chat to ladies she met along the way as she so liked to do.

When they had first come into town with the baby, she had been delighted to show off the new addition to her household. Several ladies had expressed surprise, saying how they hadn't even known a 'happy event' was due, nor remarking on the unlikely size of this new baby. Amelia did not enlighten them on the truth of the situation, merely smiled and looked suitably proud. Today they agreed what a fine boy he'd grown into, and if privately they understood more of the situation than had been officially revealed, they were certainly not letting on. Kate, naturally, said not a word.

On this particular morning, they called at Blacow Bros on the corner of Finkle Street and Branthwaite Brow to collect a new hat which Eliot had ordered, and then progressed on to Musgrove's where, comfortably seated on a chair, Amelia proceeded to buy outfits for Callum, an event which seemed to take most of the morning, putting to the lie Fanny's insistence that the family was parsimonious to a fault.

The ubiquitous 'Jack Tar' suit was the first selected item, which all little boys possessed and made them look like sailors. A kilt was chosen next, in which Kate thought he looked a 'right little doat', to use an Irish expression she'd learned off her daddy. A cream woollen coat with a broad blue silk collar, with shorts that almost reached his ankles to allow room for growth suited him better. It even had a matching waistcoat so that he could be a 'proper little man'. Kate thought he looked rather fine in it, though how she would manage to keep it clean was another matter altogether.

Several other items followed, including nightgowns, smocks, shorts, shoes and socks, so that Kate marvelled one small child could need so much in the way of clothing.

'Oh Kate, what do you think of this?' She had him rigged out in a Tyrolean style short jacket with a round hat with ribbons, which Amelia declared was 'quite perfect for sporting occasions.' Kate kept her opinions to herself.

Last, but by no means least, came a blue velveteen suit with girlishly pointed-toed shoes for parties.

'Is this what your Doctor Barker, the author of your book recommends that you buy?' Kate dared to ask.

'Indeed no, I'm sure it is not, Kate dear, but I simply can't resist it. Doesn't he look heavenly?'

Kate almost burst out laughing on the spot, saying he looked like a miniature Little Lord Fauntleroy. All he needed was a white lace collar since he already owned the flowing locks, albeit in bright copper. But she managed to restrain herself just in time. 'Doesn't he just!'

Callum was, in fact, beginning to grizzle and complain from all the tryings-on and fussing he'd been subjected to for the entire morning, and having instructed the shop assistant to deliver the items, a service carried out by a porter on a bicycle who would pedal about town with the boxes perched on the handlebars, Amelia told Kate to wheel him home, as she intended to meet up with Mrs Dawson for lunch at the Rainbow Hotel.

'You may walk him back the long way, down High-gate, through Kirkland and across Nether Bridge and back along by the river, so that he has plenty of fresh air. But please do not make any detours into any of the yards along the way, the air is unsanitary in those dreadful places. No visiting old acquaintances, Kate. Remember our agreement.'

'Very good, ma'am.' Kate gave a wry smile, and could only marvel that her robust son had survived the unsanitary air for as long as he had, living in 'those dreadful places'. Even so, she was equally unwilling to jeopardise his health and didn't in the least mind giving her promise. Much as she longed to see her old friends again and discover what had happened to Dermot, she wouldn't take the risk. She'd kept her word to stay away.

But then on her way back through Kirkland, just close to the Parish Church, she ran into Millie. Her friend was so surprised to see her that for a moment she was too startled to move an inch. All her children were gathered about her, clinging to her skirts or to each other like a brood of raggedy-eared puppies holding on to each other's tails, the youngest cradled in the arms of the eldest girl since Millie herself was loaded down with kindling she'd collected down on the river bank. Dropping it all to the ground, the next instant the pair were hugging and laughing, thrilled to be reunited.

'By heck, you look a right toff all dolled up in that rig. Well, I never! And what about young Callum in his knitted pram suit? Doesn't he look the cat's whiskers?'

'Oh, Millie, you've no idea how pleased I am to see you. You must tell me everything. How is Clem? And Ma? And little Ruby?' referring to the little girl who'd been sick when she'd left Poor House Lane. Millie simply shook her head, saying nothing, putting up a hand to prevent Kate from saying anything either. Kate swallowed, squeezed Millie's hand. 'And our Dermot? I wrote him so many letters, but he never replied to any of them. I did what I could you know, but got absolutely nowhere. Will you tell me how he is managing before I burst?'

'Hush, hush. One question at a time. To tell the truth, we're all fine, well, much the same as ever, if I'm honest.

Clem has still had no luck with finding work but he scratches a living, and we muddle through as best we can. Ma misses you, and speaks of you often. But the news about Dermot is not so good. Oh, Kate, how can I tell you. Someone came looking for him one dark night, beat him up and took him away. God knows where to, we've not seen hide nor hair of him since.'

Kate was devastated, asked a dozen more questions; wanting to know who was responsible but Millie could tell her nothing more. 'Sorry, Kate love. Two men came for him. I don't who they were, or where they took him.'

'Ach, don't ye worry, I reckon I can guess.'

'I thought mebbe they were some of his gambling cronies, they were so nasty. They frog-marched him away, holding fast to his arms like he were some sort of drunk. The poor lad didn't stand a chance, and we could do nowt neither. Our Clem was real cut up about it. Waited up half the night for him, then gathered together some of his mates and they all went out searching for the poor beggar, but, like I say, they found not a sign.'

Kate felt sick, not wanting to think too closely about what fate might have befallen Dermot. But, as always, this was swiftly replaced by anger. Oh, she knew who to blame right enough. The rotten, nasty, no-good piece of work. And wouldn't she give him a piece of her mind, so she would. The temper was rising in her, as it so often did, and before she knew it, she was saying, 'Here, take care of Callum for me for ten minutes while I go and have a word with that Ned Swainson. The nasty, rotten, no good piece of shite. He's not getting away with this.'

'Swainson! Nay, lass, don't be daft,' Millie protested. 'That'd be too dangerous. Here, come back,' she yelled, as her friend picked up the skirts of her best grey uniform dress and set off at a run. 'Kate, come back!'

But Kate didn't pause except to half turn, wave and call out: 'Just walk him up and down for a bit by the church, I'll be back in a jiffy. So help me I'll flay the rascal alive if he's hurt our Dermot.'

Ned Swainson, not unexpectedly, met her accusations with bland indifference. He knew nothing about any assault, he assured her. Why should he trouble himself about some ruffian of an Irishman? Hadn't he worries enough with all the work he had on his plate on Mr Tyson's behalf.

'I swear if you've hurt him, I'll...'

'What will ye do, Kate O'Connor? I'd heard you were nicely placed up at the big house, so I'd think before you speak, if I were you, lass. I don't take kindly to threats, not even idle ones.'

'Oh, it wouldn't be idle, so help me.' Kate was spitting mad, hating the way he avoided looking at her, even with his good eye, and wanted to throw something at him, to wring his scraggy neck. But where would that get her?

'Have you searched the river?' he blithely enquired. 'Happen you should fetch t'police and have them drag it. If the lad was drunk, he could easily have fallen in, and his body be lost. A man can drown in seconds in that cold, deep river, as you well know.'

Kate stared at him, the only sound in her head being the hammering of her heart in loud, frantic beats. She surely couldn't lose a brother as well as a husband to that flaming river? That would be too cruel. And then she realised that if this had been the case, his body would have been discovered long since. 'He's alive some place, I know it. No thanks to you. I'd not find a nastier piece of work than you, Ned Swainson, in all the muck at the bottom of a dozen rivers, so help me. If you think you can frighten me, then I'll have to disappoint you for I'm not so easily scared. But I will just nip into the finishing room, and ask around among the girls, if ye don't mind. Somebody has mebbe seen him around.'

Swainson looked affronted. 'You can't go in there without my permission. Them lasses are working and mustn't be disturbed.'

Kate gave a snort of exasperation and went in anyway, running in quickly before he had time to stop her. The huge, brightly lit room was packed with girls and women, all busily stitching the separate pieces together that comprised the uppers of a shoe or boot. They fashioned these with considerable care and skill, and with enviable speed. Kate moved up and down the lines of workers, stopping to ask anyone she recognised who she knew to be acquainted with her brother, if they'd seen him lately. Heads were shaken, eyes taking on a sad and sorrowful expression, as if they knew something she didn't. But Kate couldn't bear to acknowledge what this might be and obstinately pressed on with her questions. She couldn't even find Dolly, the girl Dermot had been hoping to marry. Within minutes she saw the foreman bearing down upon her with a couple of his trusties in tow.

'I'm not going, so don't you dare put a finger on me. I need to ask these girls if…'

She got no further as one of the men grasped her arm, while the second snatched her other wrist and twisted it up her back. As she squealed, a gasp of horror went up from the girls all around, though not one made a move to help her, too afraid of losing their own job to risk it. Swainson was smirking, which provoked Kate's temper all the more and she lashed out at him with her foot, catching him on the shin with the toe of her boot.

'You little bitch! I'll have you for that.'

'If you've done anything to our Dermot, I'll see you hang fer it, so I will.'

Now it was Kate's turn to be frog-marched away, in this case not only out of the building but out of the factory yard altogether, the sound of the foreman's threats ringing in her ears as the big gates clanged shut after her. But instead of this having the desired effect of scaring her into submission, it only served to inflame her fury all the more, for it convinced Kate beyond any doubt, that he did indeed have something to hide. Whatever had happened to Dermot, Swainson was involved, she was sure of it.

—

'You're late, Kate. Where on earth have you been? And why is your hair mussed up, and there's mud all over the hem of your uniform? This is too bad. What have you been up to? You should have been back nearly an hour since.' Amelia swooped Callum up into her arms, hugging him close as if to reassure herself he was unharmed.

She'd been sitting at the parlour window waiting for her nursemaid's return. Kate had seen the lace curtains twitch and knew, with a swift sinking of her heart that she would have to lie. She could hardly tell her mistress the truth, that she'd left Callum with Millie, who'd then taken him back to her hovel in Poor House Lane and fed him on watery gruel with the rest of her brood while she,

Kate, had gone off to accuse their foreman of assaulting her brother, ended up attacking him in the finishing room of the factory, and then been thrown off the premises. Indeed, if she told such a tale, she really would be out on her ear, and all Callum's chances of a good future would go up in a puff of smoke.

Kate made some excuse about playing a game of ball on Gooseholme and quite forgetting the time. 'I'll take him up for his tea and a wash now, shall I, ma'am? And then bring him down to you in the parlour, as usual.'

'Yes please, Kate. I'm sorry to fuss, but he is so dear to me, I got into quite a panic when I saw he wasn't here. The shop has delivered our purchases and I rather expected you would have unpacked them by now.'

'I'll get to them right away. Would you like him to wear his kilt ma'am, or the yellow silk, knickerbocker set?' Another creation she'd bought that morning.

'The blue cotton smock and shorts, I think. It is only tea with his dear mama, after all. What a fright you gave me. Parenthood is so – so taxing. Dear me, my nerves are quite in ribbons.'

Kate could see that Amelia wanted to say a great deal more but was too relieved to have Callum back so was allowing the incident to pass. She was still jiggling him up and down, smothering the wriggling child with a flurry of kisses and Kate suffered an overwhelming urge to rip him from the other woman's arms and scream at her to leave him alone; to say that he was *her* son, and not Amelia's at all. Wasn't it enough to lose the rest of her family?

Instead, she smiled and offered to bring her mistress's tea through for her, once she'd got him properly dressed and presentable for visiting his dear mama. Three days later, the fever began.

It began as a sniffle and a little shivering, but within hours had developed into a raging headache and by then the fever was all too apparent. Callum lay in his crib fretting and crying and burning up. Fear struck at Kate's heart. It was *her* fault entirely. She should never have left him with Millie. It hadn't seemed odd at the time because Millie had often minded him for her. But things were different now. She should have realised that her friend might ignore her instruction just to jiggle the pram or walk him around, and take him home to Poor House Lane. And he wasn't simply her lovely Callum any longer. He belonged to another woman, to Amelia. Kate had never seen her so angry in all the months she had known her.

Amelia demanded to know how her precious boy could possibly have caught a fever when they took such good care of him, and Kate confessed the whole sorry story. 'I just chanced to meet Millie and she told me what had happened to my brother. I was bothered about our Dermot. He's all the family I have left, after all.'

'Kate, how could you? I've even given up my own charity work for the moment, to keep my boy safe. I trusted you, and you have let me down badly. Because of your rapscallion brother you've risked the health of my child.'

Kate's instinct was to protest that Callum was *her* child, but she didn't dare. They'd made an agreement, after all. Papers had been signed, a day that would live forever in her heart. Kate had sat in the solicitor's officer and later before a judge in a big room he called his chambers, and she'd agreed to hand over all rights to her child, for the sake of his future. Everyone had been very brisk and businesslike, quite unaware of the fear and misery beating in her heart. The judge had glowered at her over his spectacles and told her what a sensible girl she was, how fortunate for her son to be taken in by such a fine couple as Mr and Mrs Tyson. He'd pushed a piece of paper in front of her and instructed Kate to make her mark, expressing surprise when she'd signed her name instead.

And so Kate had no say over her son now, no rights at all, and no matter how beneficial to her child in the long-term, for Kate this was a hard enough fact to live with. Losing her position would make it a thousand times worse, as she might then never see him again.

Now she faced a further danger. There was no denying that Callum had an infection of some sort and the doctor was called immediately. He seemed quite unconcerned and, ignoring Kate completely, addressed himself directly to Amelia.

'No rash, no swellings, no sign of anything sinister. But the boy should be carefully watched. He could simply be teething or it may be the start of influenza. There have been a few cases about, a quite nasty strain in fact. As I say, it might be nothing at all. Give him plenty of fluids, try to bring down his temperature with a cold compress, and keep him free from draughts. Children are like this, dear lady, sick one minute and bouncing around the next. There is nothing for you to fear.'

Amelia was unconvinced but his instructions were carried out to the letter, and more besides. Blankets soaked in vinegar were hung at the doors to the bedroom, gallons of home-made barley water laced with lemon juice were brought up by the jug-full from the kitchen, Mrs Petty doing her bit for the little master, despite her disapproval over this scandalous adoption.

'Did he see a gypsy woman, or a mad dog perhaps when you took him around town?' she enquired of her mistress, her voice fearful. 'They do say as that can bring on a fever.'

'I don't think so Mrs Petty. And you'd be much better off not listening to such superstitious nonsense.'

'Nay, 'tis true, you mark my words. No matter what you do in life, you has to take special care of the all-seeing eye of God. If he notices summat is not quite right, he takes his revenge.' Glaring hard across at Kate.

Amelia gave a snort of impatience. 'That will be all, thank you, Mrs Petty.'

And then the vomiting and the diarrhoea began.

Now, even old Doctor Mitchell frowned and looked troubled. 'I'm afraid the poor child has colic or gastro-enteritis of some sort. It's a common enough complaint with young children, though more usually found in poorer families, and can become pernicious if we can't stop the purging, or keep sufficient fluids inside him.' He left careful instructions for the little boy to be given an infusion of strawberry leaf tea to stop the dysentery, feverfew for the headache and colic, and goldenrod to stop the violent sickness. 'He must have nothing at all to eat but give him plenty of boiled water, and let nature take its course.'

It seemed far too inadequate a remedy for such a precious child.

Amelia absolutely refused to leave Callum's bedside, despite Kate's protests and the concerns of her husband that she mustn't tire herself. All day and night she bathed his hot little head with a cold compress, struggling to persuade him to sip the boiled water and getting upset when he absolutely refused to take it unless Kate held the feeding cup. No amount of signed papers would change Callum's mind on who his mammy was, and Kate couldn't help but nurse a secret delight over this.

But then after a while he became so ill that he neither knew nor cared who was at his bedside and from then on Amelia insisted on taking the lion's share of the nursing. Much of the time she permitted no one else to come near him and Kate found herself demoted to emptying the chamber pot and changing sheets, when all the time she longed to hold her sick child to her breast.

Chapter Ten

The stink of sickness seemed to permeate the entire house. Early on the third morning, Kate was carrying an armful of soiled linen down the stairs, hurrying so that she could quickly return to the sick room, when she almost ran into Eliot. He grasped hold of her, steadying her when she might have lost her footing and fallen.

'Kate, is he no better?' The concern on his face was unmistakeable and Kate felt a constriction of fear block her throat. So far she'd refused to believe that Callum was in any real danger, that so long as they did exactly as the doctor instructed, in no time at all he would be well, beaming his toothy grin and up to his usual mischief. Now, for the first time, she faced the reality that he might not get better at all. Quite unable to voice these fears out loud, she could do nothing more than shake her head.

'Oh, don't cry. I'm sure he will recover. He's a strong child, a fine boy.'

Kate hadn't realised, until he said those words, that she was indeed crying. Now she became aware of tears running down her cheeks unchecked. The next instant, Eliot Tyson, her employer, master of this household and a substantial shoe empire, was rocking her gently in his arms while Kate sobbed out her anguish on to his shoulder. It felt so good, so safe, such a wonderful comfort that she wanted to stay there for ever, feeling the strength of his arms about her, the power of his broad shoulder beneath her cheek.

He took out a clean, linen handkerchief and began to dab at her tears. 'There, there, that's right, let it all come out. It's been far too much for you to bear. I've tried to do a couple of hours work each morning but can't seem to settle at the factory. Despite there being matters needing my attention, I keep coming back to see how things are here, find out if the doctor has called again.'

This morning, Eliot had spotted a set of accounts which troubled him greatly, but he couldn't seem to concentrate on them through worrying over the child. He hoped that when he went back later in the day, he'd find that he'd mistaken the figures in his anxiety, and there was really no problem at all.

Kate was thinking that she could tell he'd been out by the scent of leather on his skin, mixed with the cold, clean damp of a Lakeland wind. It was utterly intoxicating.

'You must be quite worn out, probably haven't had a wink of sleep for days on end.'

Kate tried to protest that lack of sleep really didn't trouble her in the slightest but then met his gentle gaze, and the words vanished from her mind. She could see a reflection of her own image mirrored in the pupils of his brown eyes. It seemed right, somehow, that it should be there, almost as if it belonged. She also saw concern and sympathy, although really she was seeking something more, something far more personal.

Finally, he spoke, a rough, croaking sound, barely above a whisper. 'And what of my wife? How is she coping?'

It was the mention of Amelia which brought her to her senses. The power of this moment of sharing was over and Kate took a step back, releasing herself from his grip. She put a hand to her face to wipe away the tears, tucked a strand of hair behind an ear as thoughts cascaded through her brain with neither clarity nor sense. What was she thinking of? She was behaving like a fool. He was her master, a married man. Quickly, Kate bent down and gathered up the discarded laundry.

'I must get this down to the wash room right away, grab a bite to eat so that I can hurry back and take over for a while. The mistress needs rest more than any of us. You should tell her to take a nap. She might listen to you, sir. She won't take it from me.'

As Kate ran down the stairs she didn't look back, aware that his eyes followed her, every step of the way.

As if Eliot didn't have enough anxiety over Callum, and the health of his dear wife as a result, he was growing increasingly alarmed about the state of the business. Something was most definitely wrong. He'd been planning to buy new machinery for the finishing room, some fancy new sewing machines from America, and now his accountant was telling him the company didn't have the finance to carry out these plans. This came as a nasty shock. He may not enjoy the travelling and touting for orders which had been the mainstay of his father's approach to business, but Eliot prided himself on having a good head for figures, and on keeping a finger on the financial button.

He considered postponing the purchase of the new equipment. What did it matter anyway? Callum, whom he now thought of as his son, was seriously ill, and there was even a possibility that he might not recover. All he really wanted to do was to stay at home and be with the child, and to support Amelia. She was looking so tired and wan, so frightened of losing him.

Yet simply because the boy was sick, somehow made it even more important that the business be kept safe and secure, otherwise it would be tantamount to admitting that Callum might not survive. Not that there was anything Eliot could do at home in any case, Amelia having banned everyone but herself from the child's room. So he buried his fears deep and set about ensuring that the company would at least still be there for him, whenever he needed it in the future.

Eliot had always taken great care that the costings for the manufacture of the shoes were correctly done, and that all accounts were properly audited; unlike his father who had never troubled himself on that score, working purely on instinct rather than mathematics, being far more obsessed with fussing over every detail of work in the factory. And his brother's principles of economy appeared to be that if he had a penny in his pocket, it was there to be spent. Would Charles go so far as to cheat on his own brother in order to get his hands on more money? Surely not! Yet capital was leaking away and Eliot intended to discover the reason.

Could Kate perhaps be right about Swainson? Was he feathering his own nest? Or was it one of his other employees? He had to find out.

Eliot closeted himself in his office with the books and spent hours poring over lines of figures, balancing outgoings against income, searching for any unusual discrepancies or a mistake in the arithmetic. He was still there when everyone else had gone home, barely noticed Dennis who crept in late in the evening with a plate of sandwiches, courtesy of Mrs Petty. It was some time in the early hours of the morning that his fears were conclusively proved to be justified. Eliot sat staring at his findings, unwilling to believe his own eyes, even as alarm was changing slowly to a deep, burning anger.

Someone was carrying out a meticulously perpetrated fraud. And he rather thought he knew who that someone was.

He went home to quickly bathe and change, though sleep was impossible; checked on Callum, soothed and comforted his wife. Kate was optimistic that Callum was over the worst. His temperature had apparently dropped and the loss of fluids had reduced somewhat over the last twenty-four hours.

'He's on the mend, sir, so he is. Look at that bright, cheeky face. By this afternoon, he'll be shouting for his boiled egg and toast soldiers.'

Eliot clung to her optimism like a lifeline, feeling it incumbent upon himself to hold faith in the child's ultimate recovery, otherwise where was the point in anything?

The moment the bank opened, he set about his enquiries. Eliot asked pertinent questions about the financial affairs of various members of his staff, including his own brother but the manager was completely uncooperative, pleading confidentiality of client interest.

Later that day as he was studying the order books, Eliot noticed that the firm who supplied them with the dressed leather had recently changed hands, bought out by an unknown buyer. This was just the breakthrough he had been looking for and he spread his net wider, asking a number of judicial questions among business colleagues, until finally the facts emerged and a picture began to form.

At this point he called an extraordinary general meeting of the board for the very next day.

They all came: the entire family, not surprisingly since most of them were largely dependent upon the business for their income. Charles, of course, looking thoroughly peeved and disgruntled; one or two cousins and elderly uncles; and the two aunts, his father's unmarried sisters. Cissie, who hated to miss out on any fun, and Vera, a stickler for everything being just so, pin-neat and absolutely correct. Heavily involved in church affairs and the local community, she took her responsibilities very seriously indeed.

So did Eliot. Nothing was more offensive to his trusting nature than fraud, particularly when it appeared to spring from within the company itself, possibly within the family.

He'd requested a private interview with Charles before the start of the meeting proper, and while the rest of the Tyson family enjoyed coffee and a little chit-chat, the two brothers stood facing each other in the office. Eliot came straight to the point. 'I'd like to know why, exactly, you have chosen to undermine my business?'

Taken aback by the unexpectedness of this assault on his integrity, Charles coloured up, his be-whiskered cheeks turning to a fiery red. 'I don't know what you're talking about.'

'I think you do, Charles, so you can stop the blustering act of outraged innocence. Come on, tell me. I'm waiting to hear.' Eliot's attitude towards his brother had always been one of resigned tolerance. He knew Charles wasn't driven by ambition, as their father had been, but by greed. He was selfish and profligate, a spoiled child who'd been brought up to expect everything in his idle life to be handed over without any effort on his part.

Eliot had no intention of making excuses for Charles, nevertheless much of this attitude was their father's fault. Having endured a long, tough climb up from the gutter, George had been insistent that his own sons would never need to struggle so hard, or sacrifice so much. Success had been all-consuming, although sadly he'd allowed these ambitions to run out of control and a genuine desire to create a better life for the family had finally split it apart. This had affected George so badly, it made him even more determined to keep his sons out of trade. By the end of his life he'd done a complete about-face and turned into the kind of snob he'd once ridiculed and loathed.

There was a warning there, certainly, but perhaps, Eliot thought, he'd protected Charles from reality too well. He should be more honest with him and make him see things as they really were; the true legacy that George had left his sons.

'Haven't I always been fair with you, seen that you were provided with well-paid employment as junior partner, plus a handsome share in the profits?'

'I should have got my cut of the profits, as the aunts do, without needing to work.'

'Don't be childish, Charles. Everyone needs to work, even you. How else could you afford to finance your extravagant lifestyle? Despite your laziness I did my best for you and yet you've cheated on me like any common-or-garden thief. What is your reasoning behind this attempt to defraud my company?'

'There you have it!' Charles burst out. 'Listen to yourself. *My* business! *My* company! If I were guilty as charged, and I do not admit – not for one moment – that I am, wouldn't that be the reason? Your constant reference to Tyson's as if it belonged exclusively to you.'

Eliot frowned. 'It does belong exclusively to me. Like it or not, that is the situation. The company *is* run by me, and I bear sole responsibility for it. Perhaps I didn't do the job particularly well in the past while I was learning the ropes, but then Father gave me little enough training. Nevertheless, it has provided you with employment, and profit, from the few shares you own in it, as it has for several other members of the family. Now, I ask you again, Charles, and I recommend you measure your words carefully before you reply – why are you attempting to steal my profits? Do not lie, or prevaricate. It's too late for that, since I'm in full possession of the facts.'

'Then why ask?' Charles said, sounding at his most disgruntled while still endeavouring to give every impression he wasn't in the least concerned. He sensed a prickle of sweat between his shoulder blades as he began to worry about where all this might be leading.

'I am aware of your need to borrow, Charles, in order to finance your overblown lifestyle. But I hoped to see an improvement in that direction, thinking you might become more sensible with a growing family to consider. That is, until I examined the company accounts more closely. I must say your bank has been most discreet, although the manager did hint that he'd advanced you funds recently. What is it for this time? Racehorses, or that damned steam yacht your wife is obsessed with?'

Charles spluttered with fury. 'Don't speak of Lucy in those disparaging tones. What exactly are you accusing me of, because if you think I've come here to be insulted, then...'

'Shut up, Charles, and listen, for once without interrupting.' Eliot leaned back comfortably in his leather chair and waved his brother to a seat with a gesture of barely disguised impatience. Charles ignored the offer, preferring to pace back and forth on the office rug, fighting for control, putting his hands in his pockets rather than wringing them as he itched to do.

Eliot was saying, 'The facts are that not all of the profits have been put through the books. Someone has been siphoning them off. My suspicions were aroused to such an extent that I set in motion numerous enquiries, and didn't much care for what I discovered. In short, some person or persons unknown, or at least as yet unproven, have set up their own currying business, using my profits as capital to fund the enterprise. This – anonymous individual – has taken over the old firm we used to use, Marshall and Stone, and are rapidly expanding and modernising.' A slight pause as he met his brother's troubled gaze. 'Now, who do you think that might be, Charles? Any ideas?'

'Damn you to hell, Eliot.' Charles was running a hand through his hair in a most agitated fashion and sweat was pouring down his face.

'Do I take that as a confession?'

'Take it as you damned well please. I owe you nothing. Not a damn thing. I've worked my guts out for you, and you've paid me a pittance in return.'

'I don't recall you ever sweating quite so much toiling over your desk, Charles, as you are doing now. Why is that?'

Animosity crackled dangerously between the two men. Enraged by the calm in his brother's tone, Charles slammed a fist down on the desk between them. 'That's because you shut me out, drat you! You tell me nothing of what's going on. I'm never consulted on matters of policy, changes of style, new designs or anything.'

'Good heavens, it never occurred to me that you might have the necessary flair, Charles. Perhaps it is somewhat remiss of me, but I don't see you as an expert on fashion, however much of a dandy you might consider yourself.'

'Don't use your blasted sarcasm on me.' Charles was shouting now, and Eliot flapped a hand at him, warning him to lower his voice if he didn't want the whole works to be made aware of their quarrel.

'I don't care who hears, the more the better so far as I'm concerned. I did what I had to do and...' Charles stopped, having the wit to see that he was cornered. He'd damned himself from his own lips. He was furious that in trying to protect his family's future from what he perceived as a very real and dangerous threat, he'd left himself open to the accusation of fraud. He should have denied it all, kept quiet. It was doubtful Eliot would have been able to prove a thing. Hadn't Swainson assured him of that when they'd conceived the whole scheme together? He shuddered to think what Lucy's reaction would be when he explained that the purchase of the yacht, let alone the motor car they hoped to buy to drive them back and forth to the Lake Windermere house, was well and truly off. 'Dammit, I'll not see my family impoverished.'

Eliot got briskly to his feet, beginning to lose patience with this grasping, obstinate brother of his, and deciding to take a firmer line. 'The point is, Charles, I cannot allow you to bleed the company dry. If you were short of money for good reason, you should have asked me for help. If it is simply to maintain the house by the lake that you neither need nor can afford, then you are nothing less than selfish and avaricious. Wouldn't we all enjoy such a treat, but we have to be sensible. The business is not as strong or as healthy as you might imagine. Father lost his touch at the end, took on too many orders which couldn't be properly fulfilled because of too few staff and inadequate administrative control. The result was damaging to the company. He made a mess of things at the end because he simply wasn't well enough to cope. I inherited a mass of problems.'

'So you say.'

'Oh, for goodness sake. There's no talking to you. I still don't understand *why* you would choose to steal from me in that underhand way. Why not discuss your problems in a mature way? Despite our different temperaments I thought we rubbed along well enough and I do believe you've been paid a proper rate. There are certainly plenty who would be glad of such an excellent income. The fact you can't control your expensive wife is your problem, and not mine.'

'How *dare* you insult Lucy? At least she has given me a son who is legitimately mine, and not a by-blow from some cheap little tart!'

Eliot jerked as if he'd been struck and it was a mark of his supreme self-control that he managed not to plant one furiously clenched fist on to his brother's arrogant

145

nose. He drew in a long, steadying breath though his tone was glacial. 'I shall choose to ignore that most offensive remark on the grounds that you are angry and upset, and not thinking clearly. Had anyone but my own brother said those words, the outcome might have been very different. As it is, I suggest it would be for the best if you tendered your resignation forthwith, then we'll say no more on the matter. No doubt you would prefer to devote your time to this new project of yours in any case, and I'm sure neither of us has any wish to call in the police. Will you explain all of this to the board, or shall I?'

'The police?'

'You have committed fraud, Charles, and that is an offence.'

Charles was flabbergasted. This was all getting quite out of hand, the last thing he'd expected. To be so peremptorily dismissed, threatened with the *police* for God's sake? It was unthinkable. 'If I'm not given what I rightly deserve, why shouldn't I help himself?'

Eliot sighed heavily. 'Because it was never yours in the first place.'

'But it should have been. Tyson's Shoe Manufactory should have been ours equally, or it should have been sold to provide enough money for us to live on for the rest of our lives, as Father promised. Instead, you stole the lot. Robbed me of my rightful inheritance.'

Eliot had heard enough. 'For Christ's sake Charles, our father didn't *leave* the company to me either. You know damn well that he didn't want either of us to have it. Nor, if it had been sold, would it have brought in sufficient funds for us to live in idleness for the rest of our lives. Wanting us to be *gentlemen* was a foolish fantasy. Father was living in a dream world. There was never enough money for that. Funds would soon have dried up.'

'I don't believe you.'

'It's true! I wasn't left the company at all. In effect I bought it off him. He said if I wanted it, I would have to pay for it. I had it valued, worked for nothing for all the three years he was ill, and the money I should have earned, plus the sum of money I was meant to inherit on his death, every last penny of it, was used as part payment for the company. The rest I borrowed from the bank. You had the Windermere mansion and a sizeable chunk of father's money. I got Tyson Lodge. Everything else, the company, the machines and goodwill, the very land the factory stands on, I've had to pay for, am still paying for in regular payments to the bank. So, in effect, your inheritance was far greater than mine. Yes, Father did finally agree to let me have the business, but not till he'd bled me, and it, nearly dry. That's the kind of man he was. Obsessive, utterly selfish, and jealous. You had to do things his way or pay the price.'

Charles's mouth twisted into a vicious sneer. 'I don't believe a word of it. More likely you bullied and bribed Father into leaving you the business, not actually paying a penny for it. You just wanted it all for yourself.'

'Oh, for God's sake, what is the use of talking to you.'

'I'm damned if I'll make things easy for you, Eliot. The board needs to be told how you mean to hand over Tyson's to some pauper child you've adopted on a whim. The child of your mistress, dammit!'

Eliot's tone took on a hard, cutting edge. 'I warned you, Charles, to think before you open your mouth. Take care, or you might live to seriously regret those words.'

'No, I bloody won't!' he roared. 'You've deliberately set out to ruin me, *and* my family, by adopting this workhouse child. Father would turn in his grave. And as for Mother, I shudder to think what she would say. Lucy believes that it is sheer desperation which has driven you and Amelia to such lengths, but we'll not let you get away with it. We'll not have some snotty-nosed bastard deprive our own children of their rightful inheritance. I'll fight you through every court in the land, if I have to.'

'You don't seem to have understood a word I've said. The company is *not your children's rightful inheritance*.'

Charles wasn't listening. He was roaring at the top of his voice. 'I'm damned if I'll apologise for awarding myself a greater share of what should have been mine in the first place.' At which point he stormed out of the office, leaving the door swinging open.

Aunt Vera, Aunt Cissie and all the uncles and cousins stood in the hall watching open-mouthed as he departed the building in a lather of temper. After a small, telling silence, Vera said, in her calmest tones. 'He always was an impetuous boy with a penchant for tantrums. Now Eliot, I do hope you are ready to begin this meeting. I have two more before the day is out, one for the Church fête and the other for the repairs to the vicarage roof. Can we get along now, please?'

Chapter Eleven

The day Callum was up and dressed, happily playing with his bricks on the nursery rug, was the day Amelia made it clear to Kate that if she was to keep her position, then in future she must obey orders to the letter.

'We've had a close shave. We might easily have lost him, and all because you took a foolish risk. You must have known that your friend would take him into her home, and you, Kate, above all people, know well enough what that home is like. It was a very dangerous, thoughtless thing to do.'

'Yes, ma'am.' There was no point in arguing, or defending her reasons, since Kate agreed wholeheartedly. She was ashamed, stricken to the heart by her own folly. It had been a stupid thing to do, and all for nothing.

Kate's fears over Dermot having been drowned proved to be entirely unfounded. Someone must have been alerted by her enquiries, because before the week was out a note had been handed in at the kitchen door. It was written by Clem in his fine, sloping hand, stating Dolly had turned up to explain that Dermot was working in Liverpool. He was sorry for not having written to tell Kate where he was, but that he'd been working all summer as a deckhand on board one of the ships on the Mersey. The note went on, 'Dolly says that he's now settled back in

Ireland where he hopes to start his own business, once he has a bit put by. She intends to join him there by the New Year.'

'And good riddance to bad rubbish,' was Kate's furious reaction to the news. 'Making me worry me head off all this time. Dolly is welcome to you. She'll have her work cut out trying to make something of you, if'n ye ever manage to save more than a penny piece.' No doubt he was at this very moment swilling back the whiskeys in Donegal, so there was fat chance in Kate's unblinkered view. Oh, but she'd miss the daft eejit, so she would. Who knows when she'd ever see him again? Her own brother, the only family she had left. Wouldn't it be grand to go back to Ireland with him? But how could she? Not without Callum. Kate felt so alone, so dependent upon the Tysons that at times it filled her with fear. If they ever tired of her, or she did something foolish which offended them, they'd turn her out. Oh, but that didn't bear thinking about. She must never make such a mistake again, for the prospect of losing her position, of being sent away and banished from this house, never to see her lovely Callum again, was more terrible than she dared contemplate.

And if that put her in daily contact with temptation in the shape of Amelia's husband, then she'd just have to go more regularly to mass and say a few extra Hail Marys for the sake of her soul.

–

It took Charles almost two whole weeks before he finally plucked up the courage to tell Lucy what had occurred, continuing to go out every morning and returning at odd hours to throw her off the scent. Then one day she confronted him about a rumour she'd heard at Mrs Hetherington's tea table, and that had been it. He'd been forced to own up to the truth. She went white to the gills, picked up a vase and threw it at his head. Admittedly, it was not one of her favourites but even so, she burst into noisy tears, blaming him for the loss of it, screaming that he shouldn't have ducked but caught it, and now look what he'd made her do.

'How *dare* you come home and tell me you have been *sacked* like some common factory hand!' Reaching behind her, her hands closed around a rather nice French ormolu clock and she threw that too, followed by a Royal Worcester figurine and a cut glass decanter. All Charles could do was duck and dive to avoid being decapitated, but if he didn't stop her soon it was going to cost him a small fortune to replace all the broken items.

'Lucy, Lucy darling. Don't shout at me, Beloved. *It's not my fault!*'

Something in the plaintive note of his voice, broke through her fury and touched her heart. 'Oh my darling, of course it isn't. How dreadful of me to take it out on you. How could I be so cruel?'

And then she was on him like a bitch on heat, fastening her mouth to his, ripping the buttons on his trousers with frantic fingers in her urgency to get them undone, tugging at her own clothes as she did so. The nice silk waistcoat she'd recently bought for him made an ominous tearing sound as she yanked him on top of her, sending the rest of the china smashing to the ground. 'Don't worry about it, darling. It can be replaced,' Lucy gasped. 'Put your fingers here. Ooh, that's lovely. No harder. Push, push, *push*!' The next instant he was panting like a dog and taking her there and then on the dining room table, amongst the scattered remains of their dinner.

Later, as they lay in bed, sated after repeating the procedure a time or two more, Charles realised that engaging as the evening had been and a great relief to divert Lucy with sex rather than have her berate him over the loss of the Sevres tureen, now he'd only added to his worries. As sure as eggs make fat little chickens, this evening's work would cost him another mouth to feed, not to mention a fortune replacing broken china. He cleared his throat and tried again to explain their situation.

'A little belt-tightening is all that is required, my love, but not for long, I do assure you. Just until we are on our feet again, out on the straight, as you might say.'

'I'm afraid I don't understand what you mean by "belt-tightening", or "out on the straight". I never use such common expressions.'

'Something will have to go, dearest. Cuts must be made. Perhaps you could let your French maid go for a start?'

'Let her go where?'

'Sack her, my darling.'

Lucy looked utterly shocked. 'I couldn't possibly. Celeste is essential. Who would do my hair?'

'I'm afraid I must insist, dear heart. And at least two of the housemaids must go too, and the renovations on the Lake House will have to wait a while longer.' All too aware that her face was growing purple with the effort of self-restraint, he wagged a playful finger and rushed on before she had time to draw breath. 'Once this difficult patch is over, you shall not only have a French maid but a butler too. How about that, my precious? Only the very best for my little duck, eh?'

'A butler?' Now this was something even the Cowpers didn't have. 'Oh, Charles, you are so good to me.'

'Don't I always do what is best for you, my sweetheart? I only want to make you happy. You aren't going to punish little Charlie boy for being naughty and dipping his fingers in the family coffers and mucking things up for us, are you, dearest? You aren't going to smack him too hard, are you, my love?'

And since he looked so very contrite, his soft eyes so full of pleading, plump jowls quivering with such fear, Lucy sternly informed him that she most certainly was. Slipping from between the sheets, she went to the blanket box which stood at its foot, aware of him watching the soft bounce of her breast, the sway of her hip, every movement of her naked body as she pulled out the cane which lay buried beneath the soft blankets. 'Charlie has been a *very* naughty boy, and he must be a brave little soldier and bend over for the teacher.'

-

The following morning Lucy sat and glared at herself in her dressing mirror, hating the tired, bedraggled woman she saw framed in it. Although she adored the old rascal, he was still not entirely forgiven. How could he be so stupid as to get himself dismissed from the company? At least he should have made absolutely certain that whatever he'd done, couldn't be traced back to him. Let Swainson be dismissed, not her darling Charles. She had come closer to meaning the smacks she'd given him last night, than ever before. Only her very real love for this pompous, overambitious, opinionated, fascinating man, and her belief that it was Eliot who was really to blame, had checked her.

Lathering her face with cream, she began to smooth the fine lines of disappointment from the corners of her eyes, privately mourning how her once pretty mouth seemed to be forever turned down in a perpetual sulk these days, already showing signs of bitterness.

And no wonder. This was not how life was meant to be.

When she'd first married Charles Tyson, she'd been promised wealth and comfort, fine gowns and servants to wait upon her every need; a town house, naturally, and one in the country in which to entertain their many friends in style. Now, not only had Charles cut down on servants so that nothing was quite as clean or as warm as it should be, but he'd absolutely refused to allow her to refurbish or refurnish, even to have any new curtains at all, let alone Chinese silk.

Once having taken possession of this drab Lakeland mansion, Lucy had dreamed of furnishing it in the French style, with elegant little couches, low tables and desks, a central chandelier perhaps in the drawing room, shaded in a soft pink, and a huge French window opening out on to a regal terrace which would overlook the lake. She'd planned to build a conservatory with marble busts, huge ferns and jardinières; plus establishing a library with bookshelves lining every wall and padded window seats for quiet contemplation. Instead, the rooms must remain dull and dark and dreary.

And then there was the humiliation over the motor. Hadn't she told all her friends and new neighbours how

Charles was about to purchase a Renault or perhaps even a Daimler which would have put her in the very glass of fashion along with some of the best of twentieth-century hostesses such as Lady Warwick and the Duchess of Sunderland. Lucy had even ordered an entire new wardrobe to accompany it, with all the essential dust protectors, furs, hats and veils in spotted net and fine silk. She would have looked quite splendid, a delightful *chauffeuse*.

And look at them now: up to their ears in debt, the bank pressing for repayment of a loan, the mortgage payments crippling, and instead of the hoped-for equal partnership, Charles had been turned out – *dismissed* – from his own company. The shame of it was appalling, degrading, utterly humiliating. Lucy fully intended, of course, to put it about that he'd left of his own free will, otherwise she might never be able to hold up her head again. But deep down, she wasn't certain that everybody would believe this fiction.

How she would ever manage to endure Christmas with that dreadful family, she shuddered to think. The whole thing would be a nightmare from start to finish. And she would certainly have a few words to say to that impossible brother of his.

–

Her first Tyson family Christmas was a delight so far as Kate was concerned. Everyone was so happy over Callum's full recovery that even the servants began to speak to her again. Mrs Petty herself invited Kate into her private quarters for a mince pie, piping hot, accompanied by a generous serving of cream and a large pot of tea.

A fire blazed in the cast iron fireplace and on a polished desk close by stood the household account books, a pen holder and a photograph of a stern-looking gentleman with one hand resting on his wife's shoulder as she sat before him, a baby on her lap. Kate wondered if they could be Mrs Petty's parents, finding it hard to imagine the stout housekeeper as that baby in the white broderie anglais gown.

As the housekeeper poured the tea she cleared her throat, then the words came out in a rush. 'That were a fine thing you did for Mrs Tyson, lass, sticking by her in her hour of need. I know you and me didn't see eye to eye over this issue of the bairn, but I'd like you to know that happen I were a bit hasty in me judgement.'

'Thank you, Mrs Petty. You don't know how it warms me heart to hear you say so. I'd never give me babby away, if I hadn't thought it was for his own good. It seems hard here, with all this plentiful food around, the Christmas goose and all those puddings ye've been making, to remember a time when I would gladly have eaten the shoes off me own feet, I was that hungry.'

The housekeeper had the grace to pause in the act of lifting a mince pie to her open mouth, and look suitably shame-faced. 'Aye well, I come to realise that like. It's easy to forget need, when yer not suffering from it theeself.' She took a large bite of the pie and chewed on this thought for a while. 'Truth to tell, I should understand more than most.' She set it down again, brushed away a few crumbs, and glanced back over her plump shoulder as if to check they were not overheard, although since the door of the housekeeper's room was firmly closed, it was unlikely. 'I'll trust thee not to let this go any further but I had a bairn of me own once. That were wrong side of t'blanket an' all. Cut me parents up summat shocking, that did.' And she gazed sadly upon the photograph of the solemn looking pair, and heaved a sigh. 'He were adopted too, my boy, by a fishmonger and his wife. Not so fancy or as well placed as the Tysons, but better off than me, a young lass. I were nobbut fifteen at the time, and taken advantage of, if ye get me meaning. Anyroad, I weren't so fortunate as you. I never saw my lad again.'

Kate was deeply moved by the older woman's willingness to share this secret with her, so decided not to correct the repeat of her misconception that Callum was illegitimate. 'Oh, Mrs Petty, I'm so sorry to hear that. 'Tis a terrible thing to lose a child. At least I still get to care for Callum, to be with him every day. God alone knows how I'd manage if I ever lost that.'

Having reached this amicable state of agreement between the two of them, Mrs Petty refilled their cups and offered Kate a second mince pie. 'I don't reckon you'll have any more difficulties with the other servants in future. They're all pleased as punch that the little chap is himself again. You'll be joining us for Christmas dinner in the evening?'

'If I'm invited.'

'Aye, course you are. You're one of us now, so put yer glad rags on. Happy Christmas, lass.'

'Happy Christmas, Mrs Petty.'

–

Christmas Day dawned clear and blue and bitterly cold, with a hoar frost sparkling on the grassy banks that sloped down to the River Kent. Breakfast was a jolly affair with bacon and kidneys, followed by church which gave Mrs Petty and her band of helpers in the kitchen an hour or two to rush around roasting, baking, stuffing the goose, making gravy and chestnut stuffing, and all manner of other festive tasks; a mixture of tears and hysterical giggling over unexpected disasters, such as when the trifle upturned in the larder, and the brandy sauce curdled. Fortunately, Mrs Petty always kept reserves of everything, and didn't turn a hair. But it wasn't surprising that the servants were beginning to flag with exhaustion. It had been all hands to the pump for weeks with all the shopping, cooking, baking and preparations to be made.

With several family members staying for the entire holiday period, Christmas Eve had been spent in a whirl of bed making, airing of rooms, dusting, sweeping and polishing, not forgetting the laying of half a dozen bedroom fires. Fanny had at last allowed Kate to help her, and Callum toddled around with them, helping to put soap in dishes and hang lavender bags in wardrobes.

The two aunts had arrived on Christmas Eve at four o'clock sharp, with their Gladstone bags and leather trunk, giving the impression they might be staying for a month rather than two weeks. Dressed in a black bombazine frock, leavened only by a cream fichu of lace at the throat, Aunt Vera looked even more stern than expected: short and square, with her straight dark hair clipped as neatly as the pruned privet hedge in her garden at home. Not that you could see much of it until after she had finished afternoon tea, which was the moment she removed her best black felt hat. She had at least agreed to take off the equally funereal overcoat which very nearly reached the toes of her button boots, handing it over to

Fanny with lengthy instructions on where it should be placed and how it should be brushed. She had worn black ever since her father had died some thirty years before, and not even the festive season would make her change the habit.

Cissie, younger by three years, was altogether more brightly attired in a ginger-brown tweed skirt and a rather baggy green sweater, somewhat moth-eaten, with cuffs which looked as if someone or something had chewed on them, as perhaps they had, the culprit undoubtedly being one of her dogs, upon whom she doted as if they were children. She kept several pointers and wherever they went they caused pandemonium, always wanting to chase something, and preferably eat it. Fortunately, on this occasion, they'd all been left at their somewhat untidy home in Heversham, with 'the girl', who had also been left strict instructions to give the place 'a good clean through'.

'Are you quite sure this is wise?' Vera said to Amelia as Callum was brought in for inspection.

'Yes, Aunt Vera, I've never been more certain of anything in my life.'

Cissie held out her arms in an ecstasy of longing. 'Oh, may I hold him?' But then seeing Vera's frozen expression, dropped them again. 'He looks such a dear.'

Amelia chuckled. 'He is indeed. An absolute darling who steals hearts wherever he goes, so do take him, Cissie, and I'm quite sure he'll capture your heart too.'

Cissie sat entranced with Callum on her knee while wreaths of holly and ivy were brought in from the garden and Amelia put swathes of it along the tops of pictures and wound about the banister rail. A large sprig of mistletoe was tied from the chandelier in the hall, ready to catch unwary visitors.

And so, on Christmas morning, as they all trooped back in from church, kicking snow from their boots, pulling off gloves and blowing on cold fingers, Callum, who'd been thought too young to attend, ran to greet Amelia and she swung him up in her arms to give him a resounding kiss under the mistletoe. 'Happy Christmas, darling boy.'

'Kiss for Nursey,' Callum said, and, laughing, Amelia gave Kate a peck on her cheek too. The next instant Eliot was looming over her too, smiling into her eyes.

Kate thought her heart might stop if he actually touched her. She'd never felt quite the same about him since that moment when he'd held her close on the stairs, and tenderly mopped up her tears. He'd comforted her with such sensitivity that he'd captured her heart utterly. Today she could smell his cologne, all tangy and clean, and she felt suddenly plain and dull in her crisp, uniform dress, forgetting how proud she'd been to put it on not so many months ago. Grasping her gently by the shoulders he kissed her firmly on each cheek.

Kate carried the imprint of that kiss with her for the rest of that day.

Just before lunch, everyone was ushered into the small parlour where the Christmas tree, adorned with tinsel and tiny candles, and with a fairy perched high on the topmost branch, kept stately vigil over a pile of presents. Everyone laughed as the little boy excitedly set about opening each gift with increasing wonderment and delight. Aunt Vera didn't even bother to preach about the greater good being found in giving rather than receiving. Cissie, who clearly adored him, got down on her hands and knees in her best tweed skirt so she could help him to rip the paper off. Callum's gifts included a farmyard complete with animals, a wooden ship and toy soldiers, a whistle, glossy pictures for his scrapbook, several books and puzzles, plus a money box from Mrs Petty and the servants. A very lucky boy indeed, as Aunt Vera kept reminding him. She'd bought him a copy of the New Testament in white leather, beautifully illustrated and inscribed. Amelia accepted the gift on his behalf, with grave reverence. Cissie gave him a woolly toy dog she'd crocheted herself, and promised him a real one as soon as he was old enough.

'One of my best pointers, don't you know, and I'll teach you how to hunt with it, child. We'll have such dashed good fun.'

It seemed that whatever reservations the maiden aunts might privately hold over this unusual adoption, they were giving no sign of it on this special day.

Charles and Lucy arrived in time for Christmas lunch with their own two children in tow: four-year-old Jack, and three-year-old Bunty, a precocious, blonde-haired pair who clearly had never been taught the importance of the maxim of being seen and not heard. And George, of course, the new addition to the family, who was placed in his pram in the hall, although later, Kate would take him upstairs to the nursery for his feed.

As a special treat, the children were to be allowed to eat with the family and as Kate placed Callum in his chair, tied him in with ribbons and fastened on his bib, she thought the atmosphere almost as frosty as the weather. Even though she was kept busy helping Fanny with the serving, she couldn't help noticing that whatever joy and laughter had been present earlier, had been flattened by a definite air of awkwardness and tension in the room.

Charles Tyson seemed particularly morose. It was the first time Kate had viewed him at close quarters and she didn't much care for the look of him at all. His face was florid, and she noted bloated cheeks and a slack jaw beneath the whiskers. He piled his plate with food in a most ill-mannered way, and then complained that the goose was cold, which was absolute nonsense. Mrs Petty would never allow such a thing. Eliot bluntly told him that if he spent less time grizzling and complaining, and more on eating the excellent food set before him, then it wouldn't be given the chance to go cold. 'You're running to fat, Charles. Take care. You've piled enough on your plate to feed an army.'

Lucy Tyson coldly remarked, 'Indeed, who knows when we might get another meal,' which Kate thought a very odd thing to say.

After that, Charles kept casting sidelong glances at his wife, who never spoke another word throughout the entire meal, although like her husband, she certainly ate plenty.

Amelia, as always, looked lovely in a crimson gown trimmed with silver lace, if a little wan and tired, revealing how much Callum's illness had taken out of her. Her husband was as attentive as ever, showing his concern over her lack of appetite.

'You're losing weight, my darling. You must eat more.'

'Don't fret, my love, my appetite is small. Not like our fine boy here. See how he is eating. Doesn't he look well?' But as Eliot turned to give more attention to his adopted son, he failed to notice how his wife laid a hand to her side and winced slightly. Kate saw, and hurried over to her only to be shushed and sent away with a whispered assurance that it was nothing more than the result of too little sleep and too much worry. Amelia was determined that this slight feeling of being off-colour, would not in any way mar their first Christmas together as a family. Her eyes shone, her smile never faltered and she devoted all her time and attention to feeding Callum, merely picking at her own food, despite all of Eliot's efforts to persuade her to eat more.

Chapter Twelve

While the gentlemen were enjoying their port, the ladies and the children withdrew to the drawing room. Jack had already broken his Noah's Ark within an hour of starting to play with it, thrown a tremendous tantrum and been in a sulk ever since, constantly pinching his sister's toys. This created friction between them and so Kate was invited to accompany them and supervise their play. Lucy looked not only quite worn out but thoroughly ill-tempered to boot. She'd barely been presented with her cup of coffee before she began to unleash her bad mood upon her hostess.

'Have you any idea, Amelia, what has possessed Eliot to behave in this outrageous fashion towards Charles? It really is quite appalling to dismiss him, his own brother, in such a peremptory fashion. And at Christmas time, too. What are we supposed to do? *Starve?*'

Amelia flushed bright pink. She hadn't the first idea what her sister-in-law was talking about, but realised instantly that Eliot had obviously attempted to shield her from some unpleasant business or other at the factory. He'd probably thought she had enough on her plate with their lovely son being so ill. She glanced helplessly across at Aunt Vera, who instantly came to her aid:

'It may have something to do with the fact that he no longer trusts him. Brothers are not always on the same side, don't you know. In fact, my own used to drive me potty, I seem to remember. A martyr to work was our Georgie, never content unless he was out on the road selling his precious shoes, if he wasn't criticising everything his workers did, that is. He was known to take the last out of their hands and do the job himself if he wasn't satisfied with the standard of workmanship. But then he was devoted to making the company profitable. Trouble is, unlike Charles, he rarely thought of anything else. Obsessed with the company you might say and certainly succeeded in what he set out to do, otherwise we wouldn't all be here, would we now?'

'Indeed we wouldn't,' Aunt Cissie agreed, nodding eagerly as she always did at her sister's words.

'Hard work is good for soul, don't you know. Charles should follow his father's example and go out on the road too, or serve his time as a shoemaker,' Vera continued in her most hectoring tone. 'Make Tyson's more of a priority, instead of simply trying to line his own pockets.'

Lucy gasped, all the colour draining from her face and then rushing back again so that twin spots of scarlet flagged each quivering cheek. 'I will not have him so maligned. Of course Tyson's has always been a priority for Charles, but really, he is not prepared to stand by and see everything destroyed and taken away from him. Why should he be deprived of what is rightfully his? That is too much to ask.'

Amelia looked at her blankly. 'In what way is everything being destroyed, or taken away from him? Has something dreadful happened to the company?'

There was a small embarrassed silence while everyone considered the open innocence in her face. It was clear that Amelia had given no thought to how the adoption of Callum might be viewed by the rest of the family. Cissie and Vera certainly entertained grave reservations on the subject themselves, though were too fond of dear Eliot and Amelia to own up to them. And it was certainly no fault of the child's. Even so, they exchanged a speaking glance while Lucy drew breath ready for the next attack.

'You know perfectly well to what I am referring,' and she looked furiously in the direction of Callum, who was happily struggling to make his top spin.

Kate took the full impact of the glare instead, and felt her blood run cold. There was pure hatred in it, an indescribable venom, and she felt a prickle of fear pierce her breast. Like Amelia, Kate had never for a moment considered the impact of the adoption upon the rest of the family. Now she saw the implications and felt a paralysing chill.

Lucy's voice was rising as she grew ever more frenzied and nobody seemed quite able to stop her. 'Some things are beyond endurance. To be ousted by a workhouse brat, one of Eliot's by-blows no doubt. Let's not mince words, a *whore's bastard*, who has robbed my precious darlings of their rightful inheritance. It's too much to bear. No wonder dear Charles was forced to take steps to protect himself. I dread to think what your late lamented brother would have to say on the matter, Vera, since, as you quite rightly say, he was so passionate about building up the business for the benefit of his *own family*, not snivelling interlopers. Grasping little offcomers. It's utterly disgraceful!'

Vera, for once in her life, was struck speechless and sat opening and closing her mouth like a stranded fish, while

Cissie fluttered her hands and kept murmuring, 'Oh dear – oh dear, dear, dear!'

Amelia had gone desperately pale. She felt as if someone had plunged a knife into her heart, robbing it of breath and leaving it throbbing with pain. She couldn't begin to take in the full import of these words yet it was as if she were trapped in a web of unspeakable horror. Was Lucy referring to Callum? How could she be, since he was not – not what she had accused him of being. Eliot had never looked at another woman. Indeed never would. Didn't they have a perfect marriage? Mistress and maid's eyes met and a message was exchanged. Perhaps it was this silent communication of understanding which gave her the courage to respond.

'I think you've said enough, Lucy. I – I'm not quite sure what it is, exactly, that you are implying but I won't stand for it. It simply isn't true to say...'

Bunty, who'd been given a Pollock's Toy Theatre for Christmas, chose precisely that moment to let out a piercing scream as her brother snatched one of the paper actors out of her hand. Having witnessed all of this dreadful scene with growing horror, Kate grasped at the opportunity of a diversion with heartfelt relief. Leaping to her feet, she announced in her briskest, nanny-like tones: 'Now Master Jack, I think we are getting a trifle out of sorts. Come along, children. Time for our naps, is it not? Let us tidy away our toys like good little boys and girls, and we'll all go up to the nursery for a little rest before tea time. Say good afternoon to the ladies nicely, and if you are very, very good, I shall read you a story from Callum's new book.'

She was only too delighted to escape this dreadful scene, longing to have her child to herself for a while, to give him the present she had bought him. It was a lovely book called *Little Stories for Little Folks*, and she looked forward to cuddling him on her lap while she read to him; to kiss the soft, pink curve of his plump cheek and breathe in the dear, sweet baby scent of him.

Gathering her charges, she led them quietly from the room. As she softly closed the door, Kate paused and waited for a moment, fearful that mayhem might again break out but after a long, painful silence she heard Cissie's voice pipe up.

'Got a new bitch the other day. I think she'll be a cracker. Good show dog potential. Bound to be a winner at the County Show in a year or two, mark my words.'

Kate heaved a sigh of relief and left them to it, hoping against hope that Lucy's vindictive outburst would not be repeated. She also prayed that these slurs against her own character would not affect the way Amelia felt about Callum, or result in her being dismissed. She paused again at the foot of the stairs. Glancing back at the closed door, she gathered the children safely about her ready for the ascent, anxiously wondering if Amelia had believed all that nonsense about Callum being Eliot's by-blow. Then the door opened and there stood her mistress. Calm and unruffled as ever, she looked the very picture of the perfect hostess dealing with a minor indiscretion on the part of a guest who had unnecessarily upset one of the servants.

'Ah Kate, I'm glad you haven't quite gone.' She hurried over, grasped the knob at the foot of the banister and peered earnestly up into her face. 'Don't let Lucy's words upset you. I shall make it perfectly clear to her about your married status and how Callum's father was tragically killed. As for my dear sister-in-law's other comments, I shall treat those with the contempt they deserve. I want you to understand that no matter what she might say, I don't believe a word of it. Eliot is true to me, and always has been.'

'I'm obliged, ma'am.' Kate wondered if she should curtsey or something, but Jack and Bunty had grown bored with waiting, and were starting to climb the stairs on their bottoms.

'As for the adoption... well, Callum is our son in every way that matters.' Amelia dropped her voice to a confidential whisper. 'And just between ourselves, Kate, whoever inherits the business is really none of her business. That is for Eliot to decide. As if I would dream of interfering, or think to intervene on her children's behalf. Tush, the very idea! Not women's business at all.'

Kate inwardly smiled at this complete and utter trust and dependence upon the male of the species. But then Amelia had never been compelled to earn her own living, or fend for herself in any way. 'I'm sure you know best how to deal with the matter, ma'am. I'd hate it if you and Mr Tyson were wounded by malicious gossip.'

'It won't happen. We won't allow it to happen. We – I – believe in you utterly.'

'Thank you, ma'am.' Kate felt a surge of gratitude and such a rush of loyalty and love for her mistress, she very nearly put her arms about Amelia and hugged her, but stopped herself just in time. Jack and Bunty had reached the first landing. 'I'd best take the children up now, hadn't I, ma'am?'

'Yes do, Kate. I just wanted you to know that you are not to worry. It has been such a lovely Christmas, with our little boy fit and well again. I refuse to allow one of Lucy's tantrums to spoil it for us.' Then she leaned over and kissed Callum on his soft, flushed cheek. 'He isn't too hot, is he?'

Kate smiled. 'No ma'am, just falling asleep in me arms, and what a weight he is to hold these days. Yer looking after him too well, I'm thinking,' and both women laughed, united in their love for the child and agreeing that Kate would bring all three children, and the new baby, down again later, after their rest.

As Kate reached the landing and captured Jack just as he was attempting to slide down the banister, she saw Amelia pause at the drawing room door before stiffening her spine and walking inside with a bright, 'Now where were we? Vera dear, do you think you could manage a small sherry, it being Christmas?'

Kate read the story, enjoying a precious half hour with her son. The little boy was as good as gold, as he always was for her, rubbing his sleepy head against her breast, as if he instinctively knew that here was where he truly belonged. The new baby had been fed, and changed, and gone off to sleep again without a murmur. Jack and Bunty were another matter entirely, as naughty as they could possibly be, refusing to get into the little beds prepared for them, pulling each other's hair and squabbling the whole time. Bunty kept screaming and stamping her little foot in a fury of temper and Jack peevishly pinched his sister's bottom. A fight ensued and Kate had to drag the pair apart and scold them firmly, leaving Bunty in tears and Jack in a scowling sulk. It took an age but she'd just got all the children settled down, and quiet had descended, allowing her a few moments peace at last, when there came a tap at the door. Oh no, not more trouble, she thought, putting down the magazine she'd been nodding over. Getting wearily to her feet she opened the door to find Eliot standing there with a parcel in his hands.

'I'm playing Santa Claus and delivering your present.'

Kate gasped. 'I wasn't expecting one.'

'The servants will be getting theirs later, of course, after supper, and there'll be a small one for you, nuts or a handkerchief or some such. But you are different, Kate, and deserve a little something extra. I know things haven't been easy for you below stairs, so thought it best if you opened it in private. We've said nothing about the problems you've been having with the other servants, because we weren't sure how we could help, but we want you to know that you are particularly special to us, Kate, for giving us Callum.'

Kate swallowed the hard lump which had sprung into her throat. How she wished they wouldn't keep reminding her of that fact. How she wished she hadn't felt compelled to hand him over to them in the first place, just as if he were a stray dog or cat. Couldn't they understand how very difficult it was for her? There were times, like now when she'd been reading him a story and putting him to bed, that she wondered why on earth she'd agreed to his crazy scheme. But then, would Callum have lived to see this Christmas if they'd stayed in Poor House lane? She very much doubted it. 'Mrs Petty and I had a lovely chat only this morning, sir. I'm sure things are going to improve in that department.'

'I'm glad to hear it.' He handed over the parcel, wrapped in plain brown paper and tied with a red ribbon. 'Open it.'

'Thank you, there was really no need.'

'There is every need.'

Kate took it from him, feeling the slightest touch of his cool fingers as she did so, then hurriedly set the parcel to one side. She could tell at once that it was a book, but she could feel her cheeks growing hot and flushed with the embarrassment of this oddly personal moment. 'I'd like to open it later, when I'm alone, if you don't mind.'

'No, no, I insist you open it now. I need to know if you approve.' He came in and made himself comfortable on the rocking chair she'd just vacated, briefly stroking Callum's sleeping head before looking up at her with a smile. The gesture, and the fact that he looked so very much the excited schoolboy, meant that she couldn't possibly disappoint him. Kate found that her hands were shaking as she removed the wrappings. The book was a compendium of flowers and trees, almost as if he were willing her to understand his own passion, and to share it. Her first reaction was to smile, but then Kate experienced a terrible longing to sit down and cry her eyes out.

'You like it?'

'I do indeed, sir. Thank you kindly.'

'I'm a dreadful garden bore, I'm afraid.' He was smiling too but made no move to go. After a moment the smile faded but still he kept on looking at her and, as before, she found herself mesmerised by that gaze. There it was again, that frisson between them, that yearning which seemed to paralyse her brain, leaving her utterly breathless and quite unable to move or drag her eyes from his.

'You won't ever leave, will you, Kate?'

'As if I would leave Callum.' Or you, she thought. 'Never. Anyway, how could you all manage without me?'

He chuckled. Once again he was struck by her vulnerability, her apparent fragility. Still too thin but bright of eye and steady as a rock in her resolve not to complain but to deal with whatever life flung at her. He admired that in her, enjoyed their little chats together, the fact she felt able to freely speak her mind. She'd certainly given him short shrift that time over his neglect of the business, and she'd been absolutely right. 'That's good. So long as I know you are here, I am content.'

'And why would you not be content, I'm thinking, with all of this?' Her hand lifted to encompass the house, the lovely view of the river. Callum. But inside, her heart was fluttering like a wild bird caught in a cage. Did he mean that he couldn't bear to be without her? That he loved to have her near him? Kate could still recall the magic of those kisses under the mistletoe, one on each cheek, and her knees almost buckled as she imagined him doing it again, with no one else around this time.

'Perhaps one has to suffer a little before one properly learns to appreciate what one has, otherwise I expect we would take it for granted.'

'I'm sure that is so.'

'But then I often fail in my duty, Kate, perhaps because I don't have your strength of character.'

'Tch! I don't believe that for a moment. Too soft-hearted for your own good, that's all that's wrong with you. But aren't you the boss of yer own empire, with the power almost of life and death over the poor souls who work for you?'

He was openly laughing now, leaning back in the rocking chair with one leg propped comfortably upon the other, revealing his contentment to be there with her, just talking. 'I reckon the unions would have a say in the matter if that were true, which fortunately it isn't. But I love to hear your frank views. Don't ever be afraid to express them.' They both turned their heads as they heard the sound of raised voices from below. Eliot got reluctantly to his feet, a rueful expression on his face. 'You know that I shouldn't even be here.' He sounded sad but not regretful, as if he'd be quite glad to stay, instead of returning to the fray of domestic disharmony downstairs.

'Indeed, I dare say you shouldn't.'

'The gift was simply an excuse. I just wanted to see you.'

Kate's heartbeat hammered in her chest. What did he mean by that? An excuse for what? Why would he want to see her?

He went on to explain that Amelia had meant to give her the book later that evening, when Kate brought the children back down. 'But I wanted to see you, just for a moment, to say how grateful I am that you agreed to the adoption, and stayed to look after Callum so well. His presence has made a world of a difference to Amelia. She is quite her old self again: relaxed and happy. I also wanted to say how very pretty you looked earlier, so pink-cheeked and shining that I simply couldn't resist leaving my guests and sneaking upstairs. I hope you don't think me very wicked?'

'I think you very foolish.' Kate chuckled. 'I also think you've drunk too much port and you had best go down now before you wake the children.'

He made as if to obey her but at the door turned back, his eyes shadowed, unfathomable, unreadable. 'It's very important to me that you are happy, Kate. I hope you understand that? We love having you here. Callum is now my son and I love him, but you are still his mother, in a manner of speaking, and I'm very fond of you too. We both are. How could we not be when you've given us such a fine boy? You are very much a part of this family. I hope you feel the same?'

She wasn't used to people being kind to her. They never had been before, not since Daddy had passed away. Dermot was, well – Dermot, and had gone off to Ireland to seek his fortune, forgetting all about her. Daddy had loved her uncritically, of course, and she him, but that had been different. Only right and natural. The love she felt for this man was of a kind which wasn't right at all. Finding a better life for her son had cost her dear, yet she couldn't help but love him, couldn't even find it in her heart to hate his wife. She should resent Amelia for having so much: wealth and comfort in this lovely home, a radiant beauty, and this wonderful man. Eliot Tyson had turned out to be much kinder than she'd been led to believe, good natured and so handsome with skin tanned from the long hours he spent in his garden. Dark brown hair falling in shining waves almost to his collar so that the urge to run her fingers through it was almost unbearable. His gentle brown eyes had lines fanning out from the corners, and they would narrow slightly when he was puzzling over something or shrewdly summing up his competitors. Even the fact that he was clean shaven, which was quite against the fashion, set him apart as his own man.

He was looking at her keenly, perhaps attempting to read these thoughts while he waited for her to speak. But Kate could say nothing, merely stand drinking in the sight of him, loving him with a pain that almost cleaved her heart in two. She found that she was trembling, and bit down hard on her lower lip in an effort to control her emotions, desperate to stop herself from doing what she most longed to do: melt into his arms. She could recall the feel of them around her only too clearly.

It was Eliot who broke the silence between them. 'I would never wish to cause Amelia the slightest concern. You understand that, don't you, Kate? No matter what the circumstances.'

'Of course.' Now what would he be meaning by that exactly? She wished she understood the enigmatic expression in those deeply mysterious eyes of his. Was he referring to Callum, saying that Kate mustn't be too proprietorial over him? Or something else entirely? Why was it that every word he uttered left her in two minds over its meaning?

'Nor would I ever risk hurting you, or driving you away. I want you to know, Kate, that you are quite safe here, living under my roof, and will ever remain so.'

He hesitated a moment longer, as if needing a response to this puzzling statement at least – expressions of gratitude perhaps. And still Kate could say nothing, feeling utterly bereft of words, could scarcely breathe, let alone think. Safe from what? Not from her own heart, certainly. Were it not for Callum, wouldn't she pack her bags and leave like a shot? Whatever she'd felt for her husband, and she'd loved him for sure, the sensations of longing running through her now were so tangible she felt certain Eliot must see them radiating from her like heat waves, not to mention the emotion which must be plain in her face.

Fond as she was of Amelia, if he'd made one move towards her then, Kate would not have been unwilling.

Chapter Thirteen

Over the weeks following, despite Kate's exemplary behaviour, the servants were given plenty to gossip about. In due course it found its way into neighbouring kitchens all along Kent Terrace, Thorny Hills and as far as Stramongate; from maids below stairs to their mistresses above, from workers at the factory to their wives at home, until the whole south end of the town was buzzing with rumours.

There was the quarrel between the two brothers for a start, which had resulted in Charles quitting the company and devoting his time exclusively to running Marshall and Stone, the leather currying firm. Word had it that this new business was already in difficulties as the days of vegetable-tanned leather were numbered and a new process, called chrome tanning, had appeared.

Old Askew the gardener was heard to constantly bemoan the fact that the master had lost interest in his garden and was now spending most of his days incarcerated in his office at the factory with his accountants and foreman, or closeted in meetings with his bank. This left far more digging, weeding and hedge trimming for the old man than he could rightly cope with, so he'd taken to hiding away in the shed to smoke his pipe, which meant that the gardens were running to rack and ruin.

More entertaining still was the tale of the two sisters-in-law who were said not to be speaking since their little contretemps at Christmas.

Ida, who'd been refilling the coal scuttle and able to slip in and out unnoticed, had heard at first hand how Lucy Tyson had demanded her husband be promptly reinstated, declaring that she didn't in the least mind swallowing her pride in order to make the request, as she had her babies to think of. A state of affairs which Amelia couldn't possibly understand since she'd been driven to adopting a Poor House brat to fill her cradle.

Apparently, tempers had become more and more frayed as the afternoon had gone on, with Aunt Cissie wailing about not disturbing the children, and Aunt Vera pontificating upon Christmas goodwill. By the time Eliot had arrived upon the scene, it had been too late to save the situation and Ida had also been able to describe how furious he'd been to discover that his wife had been accosted in her own drawing room. Goggle-eyed, she'd crept out to tell Fanny who in turn had told Dennis, who mentioned it in passing to Old Askew. Mrs Petty elicited juicy morsels from each and filled in the gaps after a little gentle interrogation of Kate herself, who'd witnessed the start of the quarrel.

Embarrassed by his wife's uncalled for defence of him, Charles had taken his family home forthwith, not even staying for the substantial tea of raised pork pie, cucumber sandwiches, Christmas cake and the delicious hot mince pies which Mrs Petty had so painstakingly prepared. Dennis had driven them home in the carriage, earning extra rations in the kitchen afterwards with his tale of how the couple had not spoken a word to each other throughout the entire journey. 'Even those noisy nippers kept their traps shut. You could've cut the atmosphere with a blunt knife, so help me.'

As a result, Lucy Tyson had been banned from the house save for family occasions when she was accompanied by her husband. 'Almost as if she were a naughty child being kept on a leading reign,' murmured the matrons of Thorny Hills, lapping up the gossip with glee. 'How very shocking!'

Fanny found it remarkable that the master was prepared to allow his brother to continue to visit at all, having caught him in the act of defrauding the company and given him the sack for it.

'The toffs think different to us, girl,' Mrs Petty assured her. 'Family is everything. Blood being thicker than water, and all that. Though how would you know, when you haven't a drop of decent blood in your veins?'

'No, it's pure milk stout,' Dennis agreed with a grin, and was given a slap for his trouble.

And all of this brought about by the fact that Amelia Tyson was unable to produce a son and heir, so that her husband had foisted one of his by-blows upon her, said the matrons as they sat in their church pews whispering behind their hymn books. And as if that wasn't bad enough, he'd forced her to take in the natural mother as well, a no-good piece of rubbish from the Kirkland workhouse on Poor House Lane.

It was a Sunday in early March, a gloriously bright spring day with the morning sun slanting rays of white gold over Gummer's How, lighting Rusland Heights and Furness Fells, burnishing the lake to a silvered blue. Beauty enough to take anyone's breath away. Anyone save Lucy, who was in a rage. Lucy neither noticed nor cared about the majesty of mountains, nor the crisp, sparkling air. She paid no heed to the shy crocuses and snowdrops peeping through the spears of new grass, nor the tightly furled buds bursting open in a pink flush on the horse chestnut trees. The snow-capped peaks of the Langdales did not captivate her, nor the lush green fringe of woodland that stretched down to the lakeside fascinate.

Lucy knew only that she was alone. Charles had swiftly devoured a substantial breakfast of scrambled eggs and bacon but instead of going off for a sail, as he had once used to do in the good old carefree days, or helping her to devise some picnic or trip out in their newly purchased steam yacht which stood to attention in the lapping water beside their very own jetty, he'd dropped a hasty kiss on her brow and said that he must return to the office at once, as he had business to attend to.

Lucy had been outraged. 'Not on a Sunday, Charles, surely?'

'I'm sorry sweetheart, but that's how it is. We're being dreadfully undercut by the chrome tanning people, and I have to find a solution. To make matters worse, Eliot has decided to dress his own leather in future. He's bought the patent rights of a process used by a company in Doncaster, and I was depending on Tyson's to really get us launched. He said that if he couldn't trust me to work for him within the company, why should he risk sending any Tyson business my way.'

Charles's face looked grave, lined with worry which she hated to see, but for once Lucy had little sympathy for him. She felt irritated at being left to endure yet another entire day alone; stuck here with the children and the servants right at the bottom of the lake in the middle of nowhere, with not even any house party arranged to divert her. Utterly unbearable.

'What nonsense! You must insist. Remind Eliot you are still family and deserve his support.' Details of the business bored her. Why didn't Charles simply insist on his rights?

'Yes dearest, though I doubt he'll listen.'

'You give in far too easily, that is your trouble. You must insist that he sees sense and allows you back into the company.'

'He won't have me back. He's made that perfectly clear. Besides, I don't need him. I prefer to be in control of my own destiny.' Charles spoke with courage but there was a desperate look in his eye which said the exact opposite. As he made a dash out of the door, he was still wearing his napkin tucked into his waistcoat front.

He'd even forgotten to kiss her goodbye but Lucy didn't run after him to remind him of that fact. She snapped at the maid who came to clear the table, then flounced off to the drawing room in a furious sulk and pretended to read the paper.

All of a sudden she hated this draughty house, hated the mud, the acres of woodland garden that had to be supervised, the packing and unpacking which transporting three children and a host of servants every weekend demanded. And she'd forgotten how very messy it was to live in the country. As a girl, her one dream had been to escape the bleak emptiness of woods and fields, so why had she allowed herself to be persuaded back? Because she had believed it would be different. She'd thought that this time it wouldn't be an insignificant farm house but a substantial country mansion, with huge fireplaces and stately rooms, as well as sufficient servants to keep the place clean and the fires blazing. That they would be courted by the country set. But it wasn't like that at all. Throughout the dark days of winter she'd felt trapped behind the glass of rain-streaked windows, and cold, always so cold. It had felt as if she were living in an ice box. Now that spring was at last here, she'd insisted they buy the steam yacht, even though Charles had moaned and groaned that he didn't have the money for it, not yet.

'Poppycock! How am I ever to go anywhere without transport, or get to know any of our neighbours without the proper means to entertain them?' Lucy had kicked her heels and thrown a tantrum until the deal had been struck. Days later the steam yacht had been delivered, a handsome vessel done out in crimson and gold, its brass and copper gleaming to perfection. Since when, she'd spent a small fortune fitting it out, and had been looking forward to their first Sunday afternoon picnic of the season; a practice run as it were, before sending out invitations for their socially elite neighbours to join them on an outing. And now, despite the sunshine, and all of her effort, Charles had decided he must work instead.

'Will somebody come and see to this dratted fire?' Lucy screamed, although the coal scuttle stood yards from where she sat.

When nobody came in answer to her shout, she jumped up and furiously rang the bell which hung by the mantelshelf. It echoed somewhere for several long moments in the depths of the house. Above her head were the children, no doubt playing and jumping about with their nurse, or whatever they did when not at lessons. Occasionally she went up to see how they were getting along. But whatever went on in the bowels of the kitchens and servant quarters, Lucy did not know and had no wish to know, except that if someone didn't come soon, she'd dismiss the entire staff and start afresh.

Fortunately, at that moment the door opened and a maid hurried in, pink-cheeked and out of breath from rushing up many flights of stairs. 'Were you wanting summat, ma'am?'

Really, these common little people. '*Something*, were you wanting *something*. And tidy your hair, for goodness' sake. Where is your cap?'

The maid's round face became transfixed with horror. 'Ooh heck, it must have blown off when I were fetching in the kindling.'

'*Bringing* in the kindling. Oh never mind, go and find it, this instant. No, not *quite* this instant,' as the girl turned on her heel to rush off at once. 'What do you think I wanted? Why do you think I rang?' Lucy then looked pointedly at the dimly burning coals in the fire grate and managed to indicate her displeasure without saying another word. The maid ran for the coal scuttle and set about her duties.

'When you've found your cap and refilled the scuttle, you can bring my coffee and also a selection of homemade biscuits, if you please.'

'Cook hasn't had time to make any this morning, it being Sunday like and having to make the dinner, and it being her afternoon off.'

'Then we'd best cancel her afternoon off, hadn't we? If she's slacking in her duties, she doesn't deserve one, nor anyone else for that matter.'

The little maid looked stunned. 'Cancelled? Nay, she'll not like that. She were going to see her sister over in Grange-over-Sands, said how nice and convenient it were, us being so close.'

'Well, it isn't convenient for me.'

'Begging yer pardon, ma'am, but does that mean that I can't go and see me mam in Arnside? We were going over in the governess cart after t'dinner were cleared away.'

'It certainly does. No one is going anywhere.' If she couldn't go out, why should they? 'And it's *lunch*, not dinner.'

'Oh ma'am, she'll be that cut up.' The girl gave a great hiccupping sob and then continued, greatly daring. 'Cook won't be happy to lose her afternoon off. She'll be handing in her notice, if yer not careful.'

'Go away, you silly girl, and do as you are bid. You could all be without a job before the winter is out, if you don't buck your ideas up.' And having reduced her most biddable servant to tears, Lucy watched with some satisfaction as the girl fled, coal scuttle clattering as she attempted to do a proper curtsey and close the door as quickly as possible so as not to let in any draughts.

Lucy screamed with fury and stamped her foot, then flopped down on to a sofa, picked up a magazine only to fling it down again. How she loathed the loneliness without Charles, the emptiness and endlessness of her days. And their games above stairs seemed to have come to a halt. Whenever she suggested one, he would complain that he was too tired, but she knew he was nervous of having another child before they could afford one. Money was his overriding obsession these days and he never seemed to have any time for her at all, always making excuses about some business matter or other which required his immediate attention. It had been this way ever since that dreadful weekend when he'd confessed to being dismissed by the company.

Oh, but someone must be made to suffer the full weight of her wrath. It wasn't poor Charles's fault at all. Was he supposed to sit by and do nothing while that bastard child took everything, stole the bread from the mouths of his own children?

Lucy got through the rest of the day as best she could, toying with her luncheon which was worse than usual, probably due to Cook's annoyance at having her afternoon off stopped. Serve the woman right, whatever her name was, she'd be dismissed next week and a new one found. Cooks were two a penny.

After lunch, the afternoon stretched before her, like an empty desert, or rather a freezing landscape. To add insult to injury, the fickle sun had gone and it started to rain, so there wasn't even the possibility of a walk in the gardens. Oh, how she hated winter here. It seemed to go on forever. Why couldn't they go to Italy, or the South of France for a while, as they had used to do? Where was the point in Charles having his own business and being his own boss, if he couldn't take time off whenever he wished to? She longed to go straight home but no one of any significance returned to town until Monday.

Finally, bored and disgruntled, Lucy went to bed alone, rather the worse for wear from the several glasses of Madeira she had consumed with her lonely dinner. She would absolutely insist on having a house party next weekend, economy drive or no, and whether Charles had to work or not. There was absolutely no reason why she should endure such unnatural, enforced poverty and utter misery. It was too much.

Her plans did not quite work out as the following weekend Charles insisted upon a display of family unity by inviting Eliot, Amelia and that dratted bastard child over for the day. It proved to be a complete failure as the rain poured down yet again, Eliot refused absolutely to take Charles back into the business, or discuss the matter further. Amelia had not brought the nursemaid with her because she believed the silly girl needed a day off, and so the pair of them were forced to mind their own children for once.

Raging inwardly, Lucy found an opportunity over luncheon to stick a pin into that dreadful bastard child, making him scream out loud, though not a soul guessed why, despite Amelia flustering and fussing over him. The episode, small as it was, brought her enormous satisfaction. And she'd do it again, without question. She'd do worse than stick pins into the little monster if she got half a chance. Oh, yes indeed, she'd get her revenge one day. She just had to bide her time. Nobody treated her precious Charles in this cavalier fashion, least of all his own brother.

–

Much to everyone's disappointment, conditions and pay for outworkers had not improved in the slightest with the departure of Charles Tyson from the firm, and Kendal folk began to worry that perhaps the firm itself was in difficulties. None of the workers at Tyson's factory were particularly sorry to see the back of Charles, but they did regret that Swainson had stayed on as foreman. Many were convinced that he too was involved in the fraud, though no proof could be found, perhaps because Master Eliot was too trusting to look for it. As a result, the man still held sway where the handing out of work was concerned. Millie, for one, wished with all her heart for the man to vanish in a puff of smoke.

Soon after Kate had left, Millie decided she might as well put her friend's departure to her own advantage, and went along to see if Swainson would take her on instead. If Kate could stitch uppers, then so could she.

Millie hadn't much cared for the way he'd leered at her even then, or how he'd let his hands linger on her shoulder as he'd given her a kindly pat but he'd agreed to give her some work and for that she was grateful, Clem still having no luck in finding employment. In no time at all, though, she regretted this decision with all her heart, realising that she was to pay a high price to keep her babies from starving. She'd already known that the pay wasn't good, that being an outworker brought yet more dirt and disease into the home, and that Swainson had his own set of rules, which must be kept if you were to see any money at all.

One of these rules was that two hours of work must be completed before breakfast. Most shoe manufacturers had stopped this practice, on the insistence and advice of the National Union of Boot & Shoe Operatives. When Clem tackled Swainson on this very point, accusing him of exploitation, he'd callously laughed and shrugged his shoulders with contempt. 'Let NUBSO catch me at it, first. Your wife isn't going to tell, is she? Not if she wants work from me in future.' By way of punishment he'd left her without work for two whole weeks, during which time one of their youngest fell sick and very nearly died. Millie wisely urged Clem not to complain again.

Another rule was that an outworker was only allowed to call at the workshop to deliver the finished work and collect new material once a week, but that he was permitted to call upon the outworker at any time, to check she was doing the job right. The first time he'd appeared at her door, Millie had been surprised and flustered, worried that he might find fault with her work and not give her any more. She'd thought nothing of it when he'd brusquely told Ma Parkin to go for a little stroll while they discussed their 'bit of business'.

'And wait outside on the steps till I say you can come in,' he'd instructed the old woman.

Only after she'd gone did Millie learn exactly what the bit of business amounted to, what working for Swainson actually entailed. Almost before the door had closed, he'd curtly ordered her, 'Take off that filthy frock, don't complain and do as yer told, if you don't want your children to go hungry. And look sharp about it. I haven't all day.'

When she'd resisted, loudly protesting that he'd no right to touch her, her being a married woman, he'd given a nasty snort of amusement and pushed her down on to the ramshackle bed where two of her youngest children happened to be sleeping. He'd ripped the dress off her, followed by the equally grubby shift. Millie had whimpered and begged, desperately trying to cover herself with her hands, pleading for mercy but he'd paid no attention.

'What yer going to do, set yer one-armed husband on to me? Nay, I'm shivering in me shoes. Just remember what happened to young Dermot. Folk who cross me live to regret it. If they live at all. Young Dermot were lucky, getting off with a few broken ribs and a black eye, but it could have been so different. Remember that, girl.'

He held down Millie's stick-like limbs and scrawny, malnourished body with easy indifference while he pawed her breasts, licking and sucking till he was panting with excitement. Then with no further ado, opened up his trousers, pulled out his cock and plunged into her, jerking and pushing with all his might. Millie bit down hard on her lip so that she didn't cry out and startle her babies. So fiercely, blood trickled down her chin. Despite being bruised and ruthlessly used, she made not a sound.

'That wasn't so bad, was it?' he sneered as he buttoned his flies and buckled the belt at his waist. 'All you have to do, girl, is keep me happy and the wages will keep on coming. I'd not mention it to that crippled husband of yours, if I were you, not if you want to keep him safe. Mind you...' and here he leaned down close to where she lay curled up in pain, desperately trying to stifle her whimpering. Millie could smell the stink of his genitals, see the hairs in his broad nostrils as he breathed heavily upon her '...if'n you don't come up to scratch, then you're out. You have to please me with the standard of your work in every respect, do you see?'

Millie saw very well the trap that had opened up before her and could manage nothing more than a nod of agreement. A great wedge of fear had lodged in her chest as she realised with terrifying clarity that Kate had been right all along. This man was evil and pitiless in his demands, and there was no possible escape. Her children were better fed, but at what cost?

Over the following weeks and months, Ma Parkin would quietly withdraw, without being told, whenever the foreman appeared on the doorstep. She said nothing, kept her own counsel but fussed quietly over Millie on her return. Millie accepted the old woman's ministrations without comment, just as she learned to endure and obey Swainson's commands with silent contempt. He never showed a scrap of kindness to her, or any degree of gratitude. He took what he wanted, making more and more demands as time went by, devising all manner of titillating tricks to amuse himself at Millie's expense. 'Suck it love. Go on, get on with it. Don't be shy.' And all she could do was obey. Swainson held the power of life and death over Millie, and her children, in his vicious hands.

Chapter Fourteen

With the coming of summer, Amelia and Kate began to go out and about around town once more, perhaps calling in at Robert's bookshop for something to entertain the children, or to John Brunskill's woollen and linen draper in the Moot Hall. Unfortunately, these were not always such happy outings as evil tongues still wagged. The gossip had reached that state of fantasy and make-believe which all malicious talk achieves in the end. Now, not only was Eliot an unfaithful husband who had foisted his mistress and bastard on to his poor wife, but she was actually complicit in the outrage.

'Who knows what goes on behind closed doors?' said the gossip-mongers with great glee.

Old friends and acquaintances appeared embarrassed to see Amelia, and would cross the road rather than speak to her, or walk past with their noses in the air. Never once did Amelia remark upon this, though it must have hurt her greatly. Perhaps she realised how utterly pointless it would be; like trying to hold back the tide. The busybodies of Kendal knew a scandal when they saw one, and this was one of enormous proportions.

Worst of all, her friends had stopped calling. Day after day Amelia would sit in the window of her small parlour and stare out at what seemed suddenly to be a bleak and empty landscape. The room in which she sat with its fine display of glass display cabinets, pretty porcelain and pictures became like a prison to her. She wanted to show off her lovely boy, to proudly boast to her friends about how he had learned to recite 'Mary had a Little Lamb', how he could manage his own little fork and pusher with very little assistance, and looked such a fine little man in his new tartan jacket. But nobody came. Nobody saw. Nobody listened.

She would sometimes sit in the summer house, staring gloomily at the slow passage of the River Kent, not showing any interest in helping Eliot to plant dahlia bulbs for the autumn. Or she'd saunter down to Nether Bridge, so that Callum could watch the cows wading in the water and the workmen clearing the heap of rubble where the Malt Kiln cottages used to stand. But depression was taking a firm grip and even her shopping expeditions were gradually curtailed.

Kate became deeply concerned and, unable to bear the sight of her poor mistress so sunk in gloom, made a suggestion. 'Forget the shopping trips, why don't you start your calls again? I expect that's what all your friends are waiting for. Why wait for them to call on you?'

Amelia's eyes lit up. 'Oh, do you think I should?'

'I do. What harm can it do? You lost the habit from staying home to look after Callum, and somehow never got back into it when the wee boy got better. Time you did. At least you can leave your card.'

'Oh, you are right. Sitting here moping does no good at all. We won't let Lucy's ill manners spoil everything for us, will we, my little man? We'll beard them in their dens. What should he wear?' And in great excitement she began to get ready. Not for one moment could Kate imagine Amelia being turned from anyone's door. She was too lovely, too kind, had too much class and had always received complete respect from everyone, neighbours and servants alike. She was far too nice a person ever to be treated with contempt. Kate was disastrously wrong.

She had to go too, of course, to wheel the big pram, and so that she could mind Callum while the ladies took tea and chatted. Unfortunately, the afternoon did not go according to plan. Neither Mrs Gilpin nor Mrs Hetherington were at home, although it was quite obvious that the latter certainly was, as chattering voices could be heard quite plainly coming from the drawing room. The Greaves' maid accepted the card but made no offer to relay it to her mistress, simply setting it on the tray in the hall. This happened at the next two houses they called upon as well. At the Whiteheads, the moment Amelia and Kate began to walk up the path, they saw a curtain twitch in the parlour, but no one came to the door, despite their rattling the brass knocker for some moments.

'At least we have given Callum a nice walk,' Amelia said, determined not to be downcast by their failure. 'And I've left my card in several households. Perhaps that will help. But I think we'll take tea at home after all, Kate, don't you?'

By the end of the year, the Gilpins, Hetheringtons, Whiteheads, Greaves et al were further rewarded with yet more fascinating news from the Tyson household. Poor dear Amelia Tyson who had foolishly allowed her husband to use her in that appalling way, and suffered so much as a result, was said to have practically faded away to nothing. She was, apparently, most dreadfully unhappy, which they did not wonder at. Moreover, that girl was still living there, resident in the house complete with *that child*. Quite shocking! And poor Lucy Tyson, Amelia's own dear sister-in-law, was still not allowed to so much as set foot in the place.

The matrons blamed Eliot entirely for Amelia's sorry state, not recognising the possible impact of their own malicious tittle-tattle, or thinking to offer any degree of support to their erstwhile friend. And then just as they thought they had heard everything, and could never be shocked again in their morbid fascination with the Tyson marriage, they were startled to learn that poor dear Amelia had discovered that she was not ill at all, but *enceinte*.

Eliot and Amelia were naturally both delighted and if their Christmas that year was quiet with no family at all present, not even the aunts, at least it was a happy one. Only Kate worried that perhaps with a child of their own they might then reject Callum, and how would that make him feel? She ventured to mention this fear one afternoon to Amelia, as the pair of them sat with their knitting.

'As if we would, Kate. What do you think we are? Callum is our son now, and always will be. Another child would be a bonus, not a replacement.'

Eliot showed little of his concern in front of his wife, yet he was troubled, and fearful for her well-being. She did not have a good history where childbearing was concerned and he was anxious that she be properly looked after. He urged her to call in the doctor at an early stage, but Amelia only laughed at his fears.

'See how well I am! Now that I have Callum to love, and Kate to look after me. I'm perfectly fine, Eliot, don't fuss. This is women's business, leave it all to us.'

And so he did just that. Eliot had his hands full in any case, now that he had to carry out Charles's duties as well as his own. The business had suffered a serious blow as a result of the fraud and it was less healthy than before. The accountants and bankers were concerned by Tyson's heavy losses, and anxious for these to be replaced. He still took no pleasure in acting as a travelling salesman and this was not the moment to start, not with Amelia pregnant. He hated to leave her for any length of time but he was impatient to set matters back on a proper footing.

Perhaps, he thought, the problem lay in the vast number of workers they employed. Not only at the factory but the outworkers as well. Although outworkers were still used for some tasks, some time ago Eliot had decided that hand stitching each individual shoe was too expensive and had brought in machines to do the task at a fraction of the cost, employing girls to operate them as they were much cheaper than men. This move had very nearly caused a strike but the latest sewing machines were much better, and he'd met with no opposition at all when installing them. So the lesson surely was to stick to his guns, to do what he thought best for the company and to hell with anyone else.

Looking at the figures, Eliot decided that the cost of manufacture and employing all those people to carry it out, was still far too high. They needed to expand and bring in more profit. The solution, he decided, may be to buy in shoes ready-made. What's more, he would employ a salesman dedicated to the task of selling them. If this worked and earned him a fair profit, then costs could be further reduced by trimming down the work force. Not that he would allow this fact to be widely known. Not at this stage.

–

By April 1907, five months after Amelia's excited announcement of her 'delicate condition', Kate finally persuaded her to call in the doctor. He came with some reluctance, since he found pregnant ladies something of a trial. They were always full of fears and questions over what was, after all, a perfectly natural process in his opinion. Generally, he thought it best to leave them in the very capable hands of Mother Nature until it became necessary to call in the midwife. On this occasion, however, he had stretched a point since this particular patient had suffered more than her fair share of losses in the past. It had come as a great surprise to learn she'd fallen with child again, which didn't bode well for the poor woman.

Now he put his stethoscope to Amelia's swollen abdomen and gave one of his non-committal grunts. He gave her a full examination, embarrassingly thorough so far as Amelia was concerned. Kate was, of course, obliged to remain present throughout, watching with anxious eyes.

When the doctor had washed his hands and asked a few questions about whether Amelia was sleeping well, if she was eating properly and so on, he begged leave to withdraw and have a word with Mr Tyson.

'There's nothing wrong with the baby, is there?' Amelia begged the doctor as Kate plumped pillows and smoothed down sheets. She'd done nothing but worry ever since her monthly courses had stopped, despite her excitement over this unexpected development.

'Of course not, dear lady. Do not fret yourself. We don't want one of your attacks of nerves, now do we? It is vitally important that you remain calm.'

'For the baby's sake?'

'Of course.' Again the doctor glowered reproachfully. 'For the baby's sake.'

'I do get most dreadfully tired, but it's all so exciting. It would be so wonderful to give Callum a little brother or sister.'

'Indeed, indeed.' Doctor Mitchell glanced at the young child leaning against his nurse's knee and sniffed loudly, not quite masking his disapproval of this unconventional situation. So this must be the child from the poor house. 'You must stay in bed and rest, dear lady. Keep up your strength. Perhaps with some beef tea,' he suggested, glaring at Kate from beneath bushy eyebrows.

'Oh, don't say that. Kate is always nagging me to eat,' Amelia laughed. 'Now she'll be offering me beef tea every single day.'

'Then see that you drink it.'

The doctor left Kate to her ministrations and went straight to Eliot whom he found in his study. The doctor felt a nudge of pity as the young man rose to meet him with a smile of welcome on his good-natured face. Doctor Mitchell was sorry that he must be the one to cause that smile to fade.

–

'I don't think I quite understand? What exactly are you implying, doctor?'

'I am implying nothing. Rather, I am *stating* a fact Mr Tyson. There is no baby, no child, nor will there ever be one. Your wife is not pregnant, she has a growth, which should have been removed months ago. It's a pity I was not called in sooner since now I fear it is too late.'

'Too late? No child?' Eliot was staring in disbelief at the doctor. He'd been equally stunned when his wife had told him of her suspicion that she was pregnant in the first place, but, as her stomach had swelled, giving every impression of a growing baby within, he had naturally come to believe her. Now he was being told not only that Amelia had been mistaken, but that something was terribly wrong with her.

'You're saying that my wife is ill?'

'I'm saying that your wife is dying.'

–

'She will get better, Kate, won't she? I truly cannot imagine a world without my darling Amelia.'

Kate couldn't think what to say. Despite all the care the poor lady had taken to keep Callum safe, she couldn't hold back the inevitable so far as her own health was concerned. It had been all too clear for some time that Amelia was fading, but the pair had been so wrapped up in their hopes and dreams for her to have a child of their own they'd refused to see it. As her abdomen had swelled, so the weight had fallen away from the rest of her body.

'I'm sure she will, sir. Don't we just have to keep faith in the Good Lord's mercy?'

Their conversation was being carried out in whispers as they stood together in the dimly lit bedroom, looking down upon the sleeping patient, each loving and grieving for her in their different ways, and both devastated by the terrible news.

'Are we being punished, Kate, for wanting a family? Is that the reason Amelia is ill, because we weren't satisfied with Callum?'

'Don't talk like an eejit,' was Kate's immediate response, as brusque as ever. 'Of course she was satisfied with Callum. Who wouldn't be? The poor lady tragically mistook nature's signals, that's all. 'Tis a terrible shame, but no fault of hers or yours.' Kate blamed this abiding obsession of her mistress to have a child of her own, almost entirely on the gossip-mongers. Amelia had been perfectly content over the adoption until they had started brewing their malicious rumours and spreading spiteful lies, making the poor woman feel inadequate.

And to be fair, Amelia had never for a moment believed a word of the evil which Lucy had concocted about Eliot and Kate, and which had spread with the speed of a forest fire. She'd maintained a firm conviction that her beloved husband had been completely faithful to her, and that Callum was indeed who Kate said he was, the child of her own legal marriage. But the hurtful comments had cut deep and the battle had taken its toll.

'Oh, Kate, what would I do without you?' Eliot murmured.

'I'm sure you'd manage well enough, though thankfully ye don't have to try.' Kate's love for this man was such that she could even wish his wife would stay well, for his sake, just to keep him happy.

Yet gazing upon the desperately sick woman, breathing so shallowly in the bed before them, they each knew only too well they would soon be obliged to manage without Amelia. Dear Lord but she would be missed, Kate thought. Her kindness, her sweet smile, the joy she'd found in playing with Callum and reading him stirring tales of adventure which he loved, for all he didn't under-stand the half of them. Her unobtrusive skills at ordering her household, and the thoughtfulness which so endeared her to the servants. The way she would be adamant that Sunday lunch be served promptly at twelve so they could enjoy as much of their afternoon off as possible. How she would insist that the horses not be kept waiting should the family be going out in the carriage, when really it was Dennis she was concerned about, fearful he might catch cold. And never once did she complain to Askew about the piles of leaves he never quite got around to sweeping up. Without exception, they all adored her.

So how would they ever get by without her? Callum was three and a half now and all of Kate's fears and regrets at letting him be adopted had long since evaporated in the face of her mistress's goodwill. This was where he belonged, where they both belonged. Amelia had given them both a new life, made them welcome, a part of the family and been so anxious to share this lovely wee boy that it had been quite impossible to bear any resentment towards her.

Kate and Eliot exchanged a speaking glance, and, looking into her eyes, he saw that their liquid sheen this morning had nothing at all to do with their lovely misty grey colour, and everything to do with the unshed tears which trembled on the golden lashes. He'd wanted so much to believe all was well that he'd shut his mind to any other possibility. Now, as he looked into Kate's troubled gaze, he was compelled to face the truth.

The workers at the factory were growing restless, fearful that new machinery and bought-in footwear were beginning to affect the manufacturing output and would ultimately lose them their jobs. Already there were murmurs of disapproval because during the last months Tyson's hadn't replaced workers who'd left through illness, retirement or death. Eliot attempted to allay these fears but since there was indeed some truth in them, his efforts weren't entirely effective. He was depending upon an increase in sales to justify his actions, which so far hadn't happened, so he urged the young man he'd taken on to be responsible for winning orders, to work harder, travel further and stay on the road longer.

One morning he arrived at the factory to find the men standing about in the yard, refusing to work. Afraid of eventually losing their jobs, they were out on strike.

'Where is the point in this?' Eliot demanded, standing on the front steps to address the men as a fine drizzle started, coating his head and shoulders with beads of moisture in seconds. It was a dismal morning, with a grey mist enveloping the town, blotting out the famous view of the castle and lending another meaning entirely to the title of Auld Grey Town, which generally referred to the limestone architecture. It seemed, in that moment, as if the whole world, even God, had turned against him. The weather certainly did nothing to lighten Eliot's mood as he gazed upon their set faces. This was the last thing he needed with a beloved wife at death's door.

'You know that trade isn't good, profits are down with the extra competition we're up against, and that I'm trying to pull the company back from the brink after one or two recent problems.' He wasn't entirely certain how much the men knew about Charles's attempt to purloin funds from the company and transfer it to his own business, so he glossed over that part and hurried on. 'Orders are slack and I'm doing my best to cut costs, and to encourage more business. What else can I do? What more do you want from me? Why aren't we getting the orders we should? Tell me that.'

'Happen because the quality isn't there any more. Have you checked the leather recently?'

Eliot, who dealt with paperwork and was not a man to understand the finer details of different grades of leather, which of course his father had been, looked confused. 'What are you saying? That the company is going downhill because I don't know my stuff?'

'If the company's going downhill then we'll all be in the mire,' roared one man, and Eliot wished he'd kept quiet.

'Stick with quality,' shouted old Harry Crabtree. 'That's what we allus used to produce here at Tyson's in yer father's day. Quality.'

If there was one thing Eliot hated, it was to be compared with his father who'd spent his entire life criticising him. 'I believe we still do produce quality, Tom, but it is expensive and our shoes are not selling in sufficient quantity so we must do something else as well. Market other lines. We can't risk putting all our eggs into one basket.'

Swainson took a step forward from where he'd been lurking in the doorway of the factory listening to all of this, and confronted the crowd, a mixture of angry men and troubled looking women. He didn't like all these awkward questions about quality. Before you knew it, someone would be asking to see the manifests, chits and dockets; wanting to check the bends of leather ordered and how much was actually paid for them, as opposed to what was written in the book.

So far, Eliot had not linked Swainson with his brother's swindles. Lady Fortune continued to smile on him, and he was still an innocent man in his boss's eyes. Long may it remain so – long enough for him to finish feathering his nest before disappearing over the horizon with his pockets heavy with brass. The Tysons weren't the only ones with gentlemanly aspirations. Now the foreman squared his shoulders and took another step forward into the mêlée. 'Happen you're suggesting *I'm* the one not doing me job properly, Crabtree, is that it?'

'If the cap fits.'

'And you can do better I suppose?'

Another voice piped up, 'What happens if this bought-in stock is all the customers want in future? What are we supposed to manufacture then with all these fancy new sewing machines?'

Eliot answered swiftly. 'Tyson's will always be involved in manufacturing, but it's true there may need to be a slight reduction in the work force. I'll do my best to keep it to an absolute minimum, I promise.'

'And what job could we hope to get here in Kendal if we do get the sack? At the sock factory, happen? Well, I can't bloody knit!'

Eliot lost patience. 'No, Ted, I don't suppose you can, so you'll just have to trust me, won't you? And if it's all a bit slow in coming right, then I'm sorry about that. I can't stand about here all day discussing how this company ought to be run. I'm cold, and wet, and damn' well fed up. I've enough on my plate at the moment, as it happens, not to mention a deal of work waiting to be done. As have you. Why not get back to it and leave me to sort these matters out as I think fit. When have I ever let you down before?'

There were a few shamed faces, boots were shuffled on the cobbles and murmurs of agreement voiced, the discomfort of the crowd palpable. There wasn't a man or woman present who didn't know that the mistress was ailing, and without exception they all liked her. She'd always been kind and cheerful, had a reputation for helping those in need without making them feel beholden or being in any way patronising.

A few women began to rail at the men, reminding them how hard it had been for the poor lady losing her bairns, and weren't they only making matters worse for the master? With set faces they began to drift away towards the factory, and one by one the men followed. The heat had gone out of their argument, the danger passed, but Eliot had felt the draught of their anger, and would not forget it.

Chapter Fifteen

The doctor was sympathetic but recommended Amelia not be told. Eliot at first protested. 'But won't she realise when no baby emerges at the end of nine months? Surely that is most dreadfully cruel? She has lost too many babies already, how can I allow her to go on excitedly believing that all is well?'

The doctor tweaked his moustache and said nothing, but the expression in his eyes said everything, silently informing Eliot that his wife would not survive long enough to feel the loss of another child. 'You have your adopted son. Let her spend as much time with him as possible. It may bring her some joy in her final days.'

And so as spring changed into summer, Callum would be taken to visit with his mama each and every morning and afternoon, long enough to entertain and cheer her, but not so long as to tire her.

Eliot kept up his strength by working – a form of denial, admittedly, as if by pretending that everything was normal, then by some miracle it would be.

Deep down he knew that he could never have coped during this endless, dreadful summer without Kate, who nursed her mistress uncomplainingly throughout a long and painful illness. She didn't seem like his Amelia now.

Her lovely face had grown skeletal, there was a brittleness to her emaciated limbs, a yellow pallor to her skin.

But not once did she suspect there was anything wrong. She submitted to their fussing, and to the enforced bed rest, for the sake of the child she believed she was carrying. Fortunately, in her confused state, she lost track of time and had no notion that the time for her confinement, had there actually been a child, was long past. And both Eliot and Kate kept up a front of robust cheerfulness, as if they too were looking forward to the new arrival.

Even the servants, who of course had to be put in the picture, were firmly instructed not to weep but always to smile when in her presence. Mrs Petty spent hours searching through her receipt books for new delicacies to tempt a failing appetite. Dennis took to helping old Askew pick vegetables and soft fruit to keep the kitchen well supplied, and Fanny was being unusually agreeable by helping to mind Callum whenever Kate was otherwise occupied, which seemed to be most of the time, as she rarely left Amelia's bedside. She, poor lady, tossed and turned in the August heat. Once or twice Kate helped her outside so that she could sit in the sun for a while, but by September even this small treat was too much for her as she soon tired and asked to be brought back in again.

'You must be so bored, sitting here with me all day, Kate.'

'Not at all. Aren't I practising me knitting? We can't have his or her majesty, when the babby deigns to arrive, having nothing fit to wear, now can we?' Amelia herself had instructed her in the skill and insisted that a layette be prepared. Kate had continued with the task ever since, even though it was not needed. Privately, she'd made up her mind to take the garments to her friend Millie at some appropriate juncture. Millie always had use for baby clothes. In the meantime, it kept her hands occupied and provided Amelia with a giggle as she dropped and hunted for stitches.

'Oh, but it seems so long drawn out. How much longer, dear Kate, before my child is born?'

'Not long, I'm sure,' Kate said, hoping the stiffness of her lips didn't reveal itself in her smile.

'You do know that a child of my own will make no difference to my feelings for Callum. He will still be my beloved son, that I'll love him every bit as much.'

Emotion held Kate silent for a moment before she was able to go on. 'Don't I know that already, ma'am. And doesn't he love you an' all? His dearest mama.'

Amelia's eyelids were fluttering closed again, the short conversation already tiring her, but yet she seemed content. 'And isn't he the luckiest of boys to have two mothers?'

Kate did not pause in her knitting, in the hope that keeping her fingers working would stop the tears from falling. She sat on for another hour while Amelia slept. The afternoon waned and as dusk began to fall Kate heard the front door open and the familiar sound of Eliot's voice, his footsteps striding across the hall and up the stairs, bringing the usual beat of anticipation to her heart. She glanced again at Amelia, saw the eyelids flutter and her voice whisper, '*Eliot?*' followed by that infinite, unfathomable silence which takes place when the anticipated next breath never comes. By the time Eliot breezed into the room, still wearing his overcoat in his anxiety to reach his wife, he was too late. She had gone.

Despite the long drawn out end, Amelia's death still came as a shock to the entire household. It seemed to Eliot that one minute he had a beautiful, lively wife revelling in her adopted son, the next he was a widower, bereft and alone. He shut himself in his room and conducted his grieving in complete privacy, making it clear he had no wish to be disturbed, not for any reason whatsoever. Fanny would creep up the back stairs, tap on his door and when there was no response, set the dinner tray down beside it and creep away again. The next time she came, the tray would still be there, untouched.

The servants went about their daily duties in doleful silence, mourning a much loved mistress. Kate did not have time for such an indulgence, nor even to think. There didn't seem to be a minute of the day when she wasn't busy with something or other, not least looking after Callum, who kept asking when he could go and see Mama. Kate it was who washed her mistress's emaciated body, dressed her in a pretty nightgown and laid her out in the satin-lined coffin provided by the local undertakers, in the front parlour. Old Mr Askew brought flowers in from the garden to set at its foot, and Mrs Petty carefully covered all the mirrors so that the devil couldn't capture her soul. Young Ida insisted on keeping a small fire in the grate, because madam was so cold. Not one quite had the heart to stop her.

Kate tapped on Eliot's door and said that the under-takers wished to know if he had any particular instructions regarding the funeral. Should she call in the vicar to say a prayer over Amelia? Had he notified all of Amelia's family and friends, or did he want Dennis to take round a note?

'If so, have ye any black edged cards in yer study that we could use? Shall I fetch them to you sir, so you can write them, or would you be wanting Dennis to give the message personally, from his own lips as it were?'

His only response was to tell her to go away and not to bother him with such trifles. 'I can't make any decisions right now, Kate. I can't even bear to see her like that. You deal with it.'

And so, grieving for the man she loved as much as for her lost mistress, Kate walked sadly away and found she had no choice but to take complete control. She chose the time and place for the funeral, even the hymns she thought Amelia would have approved of. She'd no idea who to inform, or where they might live but Mrs Petty listed the most important members of the family and Kate wrote out the cards, in her best hand writing taught to her by her father, for Dennis to deliver. And she personally delivered the notification to put in the Westmorland Gazette. If it weren't so tragic she would have gained a sadistic sort of pleasure from the pain this would cause to all her old friends who had so callously and cruelly deserted her.

It was shortly after she returned from this errand that the front door burst open and Lucy stormed in without bothering to ring the bell or wait for Fanny to show her card.

She roared through the house like a tornado, ransacking the drawing room with an all-encompassing glance, then rushing up the stairs to the nursery and when she found nobody there either, running back down again, only then thinking to look in the front parlour where she found Kate seated by the coffin in silent vigil. 'My God, it's true then? I couldn't believe it when I read the card.'

Kate genuflected and, getting quietly to her feet, respectfully indicated with a slight frown and finger to the lips, that perhaps Lucy should lower her voice somewhat in the presence of her newly departed sister-in-law.

Ignoring her completely, Lucy marched over to the coffin and looked calmly in upon Amelia's lovely face, no longer lined with pain and suffering but almost as sweet and beautiful as it had been in life.

'It does not surprise me in the slightest that she's gone in this way. She was never a strong woman. Eliot shouldn't have allowed her to try for another child. A very dangerous thing to do, and look where it's got her? Though how he'll react to her death I cannot imagine. He'll be a lost soul, poor man. No doubt he'll give up the ghost, and the business, after this; hide himself away among his trees and flowers and paintings. Charles will naturally have to return to the company and take up the reins again. Who else is there?'

Kate felt herself growing hot around the collar, an anger growing inside as she became increasingly enraged by the arrogance of this woman. How dare she march in and start dividing up the spoils while standing over Amelia's coffin? The poor woman had barely gone cold and already she was pensioning off her grieving husband, itching to get her grasping hands on the company. Kate smoothed down her starched apron and clenched her mouth tight shut, to stop it from saying what was on her mind, though she tried to indicate with a frown how inappropriate was this behaviour. Lucy, however, was oblivious to the expressions and opinions of a mere maid.

'Is Eliot in his study or his bedroom?' I'll just go up and tell him not to worry. Charles will deal with everything from now on.'

'The master has made it clear that he is not to be disturbed.'

'I'm quite sure that rule does not apply to family.'

'To be sure it does. It's more than me life's worth to allow anyone to go up unannounced.'

'Oh, very well then. Pray tell him that his sister-in-law is below and wishes to speak to him.'

Kate reluctantly went upstairs, tapped on his door and, unsurprisingly, received the usual response. As she withdrew, to make her way quietly back down stairs again, she found Lucy had followed her up.

'I wanted to make sure that you delivered my message correctly. Is he in?' Whereupon, to Kate's utter horror, the woman began to knock loudly upon the panelled door with one neat, black gloved knuckle. 'Eliot! I know you are in there and not quite yourself, but there's no need for you to worry about a thing. Charles will take charge.'

'*No!*' The voice that bellowed from within was so loud and forceful that Lucy actually took a hasty step back from the door, startled by the power of it.

The door burst open and there he stood, hair awry as if he'd been tearing it out with his own hands, shirt collarless and open at the neck where the stud should be. His waistcoat hung open and his trousers looked as if he'd slept in them, which he probably had. 'Charles will do no such thing. You can tell him to leave me alone. Everything is in hand.'

Lucy was flabbergasted. Kate hid a small smile, gaining both reassurance and a deep sense of pride from his instinctive and violent objection to Lucy and Charles taking control. But then why would they imagine Eliot to be a weak man, simply because he had a heart? Something the rest of his family clearly did not possess.

'Someone in authority should be here to oversee matters. There are matters which need to be arranged.'

'Go home, Lucy. Mind your own business. Kate will see to everything.'

The look of horror on her face was a picture, and Kate suffered a fit of coughing which served to cover a most disrespectful and inappropriate spurt of laughter.

'I never heard of such a thing. Never in my entire life! A nursemaid dealing with a family funeral? Utterly preposterous! And you have no right to speak to me like that. No right at all. I know you are grieving, Eliot, but I think you have quite lost your mind. If you imagine we will stand by and say nothing while this doxy here...'

'Go home *now* Lucy. This minute, if you please, before I personally despatch you down those stairs.'

'Well, really!' And turning to Kate, 'Don't think you have won, miss,' she hissed, inches from Kate's face. 'You haven't heard the last of this.' Casting her a final and furiously withering glare, Lucy marched down the stairs in a huff, clearly intent upon summoning reinforcements.

Later that night, as Kate was on her way to bed, she heard unmistakeable sounds of weeping coming from the master bedroom. She hovered, undecided for some long moments, wondering whether she should intervene, longing to offer him comfort but fearful of being seen to intrude. Men so hated to be caught out in these private moments, and nothing could be more so than grieving for a much loved wife. At length, she proceeded to her own room but found it impossible to sleep. Kate kept thinking about Eliot enduring his grief alone, but what could she do? She was, as Lucy had quite rightly pointed out, only the nursemaid and shouldn't really be dealing with such matters as organising a funeral for the mistress, let alone offering comfort to the master.

And then she heard his footsteps on the landing, and was out of bed like a shot. 'Were you wanting something, sir?'

He was standing at the top of the stairs as if he'd set off with some purpose in mind and had quite forgotten what it was. Kate had quickly pulled a robe over her nightgown though the September night was warm. Now she asked if he would perhaps like her to bring him a glass of milk, or a small nightcap of his favourite Irish whisky.

He shook his head in a dazed sort of way, showing no real indication of having understood or even heard the question, and still seemed undecided about where he was going, or why. Kate went to his side and took hold of his arm. 'Sure now, 'tis no time to be wandering around the house. Let me see ye back to yer room, sir, shall I?'

Once back inside the bedroom he slumped into a chair while Kate quickly tidied the bed, which revealed all too clearly what a restless night he'd suffered. The candle on the nightstand guttered and died, and she had to hunt about for a new one, and the matches to light it. When the pillows were plumped, the sheets smoothed and turned back, she went and took him by the arm, giving him a little shake to encourage him back to bed. Eliot made no protest as she led him across the room and sat him down on the feather mattress while she attempted to pull off his boots. He was still fully clothed in his shirt and trousers, although he'd removed the waistcoat. Kate considered it too immodest for her to suggest that he undress properly and get into his night attire, confining her attention to the boots. Kneeling, she struggled with the hooks and buttons in the dark and it was as she got to her feet that he seemed to become aware of her presence for the first time.

'Kate? Is it you?'

'It is so. Now just you lie down and try not to think of anything. Don't ye need yer sleep, with all you have to face over the next few days?'

'Ah Kate, thank God you didn't leave me too. What would I do without you?' He pulled her close, drawing her between his knees and laying his head against the flat of her stomach while his arms encircled her. Kate was stunned but didn't like to protest, the poor man surely being beside himself with grief. Filled with pity she stroked the dark curls, gently patted his broad shoulders and as she felt them shudder, held him tight as if he were a child. She could feel the power of his thighs pressing at either side of her hips, his hands at her back, smoothing gently up and down in a rhythm that was producing a most odd effect upon her, weakening her already tired limbs and making her heartbeat do odd little stops and starts.

She was never sure afterwards how it came about but somehow she was sinking on to the bed beside him and he was kissing her: her throat, her eyes, her mouth, with an urgency that was growing more fevered by the second. There was an impatience in both of them, and nothing could possibly have prevented what followed, nor allow them time to consider the rightness or otherwise of their actions. Their need and agony was too great to allow pause for thought, too hectic and flushed with the raw necessity to prove that life would prevail and beat back the shadows of death. The cotton robe and nightgown were discarded in seconds and Kate groaned with pleasure as his hands slid over her bare skin, cupped and fondled her breasts. Hadn't she longed for this? Hadn't she ached for him to love her?

Kate was no virgin and not unused to a man's attentions but this was a coupling the like of which she had never known before. Perhaps because she wanted him so much, he brought her to a pitch of desire she could not have imagined possible. As he entered her, she wrapped her legs about his waist, instinctively rocking with the rhythm of his body, discovering a new intensity of joy so that by the time he slumped upon her, sticky with sweat and passion, she was there before him. But then hadn't she loved him for what seemed like a lifetime already?

It was the first streaks of dawn peeping in through the curtains which woke her. His arm was still around her, cradling and protecting her, or so it seemed, and yet his head was turned away, sunk into the pillow. In that instance Kate felt such a rush of love and warmth for him it almost overwhelmed her. She longed to reach out and wake him, to bring him to her again but sanity slowly surfaced. What had she done? She shouldn't be here at all, not in the master's bed. But then if she'd helped to ease that pain a little where was the harm? Kate looked tenderly down upon the sleeping figure beside her. So long as she had the good sense not to read too much into this. Hadn't he only made love to her because he was out of his mind from grief over losing his beloved wife? Not for a minute must she imagine that it meant anything else.

Kate slid hastily, almost guiltily from his bed, fumbled about the floor till she found her nightclothes and snatching them up in her arms, fled from the room, not even pausing to put them on. She was across the landing and into her own room in a trice, quite certain no one had seen her.

–

On her way down from the attic to commence her morning duties, Fanny paused when she heard footsteps on the first landing, not wishing to meet the master if he was going to the bathroom to relieve himself. Leaning over the banister she caught a fleeting glimpse of Kate's fleeing, naked figure, and watched, open-mouthed, as she disappeared from view.

Reinforcements arrived later that same morning in the shape of the two maiden aunts who moved in lock, stock and barrel, ready and willing to take charge, indeed positively relishing the challenge. There was nothing they thrived on better than bad news. And Vera's customary funereal black for once was entirely appropriate. Cissie too looked uncharacteristically tidy in an ankle-length black coat and large feathered hat. Both ladies were also swathed in fox fur wraps, despite the heat of an Indian summer.

'Good thing they're here,' Fanny said to Dennis, as they enjoyed a quick cuddle in the glasshouse while she collected a few tomatoes for lunch. She'd told him what she'd seen earlier, and he'd been as startled as she, though had warned her to keep mum and say nothing to anyone else.

'We'll keep this under our hats, girl. 'Oo knows when a bit of useful information like that might come in handy.'

Fanny, itching to spread this titillating tidbit and announce Kate's immorality to the world by putting a notice in the *Westmorland Gazette*, did her best to smother her disappointment. 'I wouldn't put it past that little madam to think she can get her feet under the master's table, as well as in his bed. If that's the case, the aunts will soon put her right. Selling her child were bad enough, worming her way into becoming the next Mrs Tyson before the mistress is even decently buried, is even worse to my mind. Nasty piece of baggage she's turned out to be. And if she thinks she can smarm her way round me, she's another think coming.'

Gossip flared again among Amelia's fickle devotees in the tea rooms and shopping halls of Kendal who whole-heartedly agreed that it was far better Vera and Cissie supervise the delicate matter of the funeral and poor dear Amelia's affairs, rather than that dreadful little guttersnipe from the Kirkland Poor House. 'Vera will soon lick them all into shape.'

It was certainly true that as the two maiden ladies swept into the hall, and Dennis staggered after them with their trunks, Gladstone bag, several small brown leather suitcases, and innumerable hat boxes, Mrs Petty was heard to remark: 'May the saints preserve us. The aunts have come to stay.'

Chapter Sixteen

The funeral took place on a typically dismal, wet Lakeland day, with gloomy black clouds and rain hammering on the black umbrellas of the bereaved gathered in the graveyard, and on the shiny roofs of the many carriages. A service, held in the Parish Church, had been planned by the aunts down to the last detail. They discarded most of the hymns Kate had chosen and selected different ones, half of which Amelia had probably never liked, or even known. They permitted only white flowers in tasteful wreaths, and printed a special Order of Service filled with prayers and psalms and lengthy readings. Mrs Petty said that if the service finished before midnight, it would be a miracle.

Afterwards they partook of ham and a cold collation, laid on by Mrs Petty and her trusty staff, using Amelia's best Royal Worcester porcelain and her finest lace tablecloth. Nobody, Mrs Petty declared with pride in her voice, and a challenging glint in her eye, could say that the mistress hadn't been laid to rest with proper dignity.

Dozens of Amelia's friends and family, far more than she'd possessed in life, or at least since that fateful Christmas, turned up to remember her in death. Everyone remarked upon how splendid a funeral it was, how suitable was the hymn, *O Perfect Love* and such a pity nobody had known the words to the other hymns. What a memorable sermon the vicar had given and how appropriate of him to recall the dear departed's sweet generosity and many acts of charity, and her simple and honest desire to help the weak and unfortunate.

It seemed that Amelia had ceased even to have a name now, and no one wished to recall her most generous act of all, that of taking a Poor House child into her home to offer him a new life, and then generously taking the mother as well.

There was one person missing from this solemn occasion. Kate herself. She'd never expected to go since Callum was far too young to attend his mama's funeral, and naturally she must remain behind with him, in the nursery. When Eliot had called her to his study shortly after breakfast, Kate assumed that was what he was about to say.

'Ah Kate. Do come in.' She entered with some small degree of embarrassment, unwilling to meet his eye in view of what had taken place between them just a few nights previously. He didn't offer her a chair but seemed equally reticent to meet her gaze and stood with his back to her at the window while he addressed the rain filled sky. 'I've been thinking about Callum. He's far too young to...'

'I know, don't worry. I've arranged with Mrs Petty that he and I will stay and keep an eye on things in the kitchen while you're all at the funeral. We reckon that'll be for the best.' And prevent all those busybodies from gawping at him, she thought, and gossiping behind their hands.

'Ah, good, good.' He seemed to breathe a sigh of relief, followed by a long drawn-out silence. So long, in fact, that

Kate wondered if he'd forgotten she was still in the room, or if she should quietly go now that this matter had been settled. But then he suddenly turned around and made for the door. With his hand on the knob, he again addressed Kate with his back turned to her. 'About the other night. I'm not sure how... I mean I never meant... I really cannot think what came over me. I've no wish for you to take all the blame upon yourself. It was quite outrageous behaviour on my part, and after all my promises that you would be safe under my roof. I humbly apologise.'

He was apologising for making love to her. That somehow seemed the most shaming part of it. He said he didn't know what had come over him. He half turned towards her and she willed him to look directly at her but he kept his gaze fixed somewhere above her left ear.

Kate felt as if her heart were sinking to her boots, even as she longed to run to him on a flush of warm sympathy to ease his private torment, to hold him tight in her arms and tell him that it didn't matter, that she loved him and had wanted him to make love to her. She'd known all along, of course she'd known, that it was all a mistake. How could it have been otherwise? His words cut deep, but what else could he say?

"'Tisn't anything to be ashamed of. We were both at fault, so we were, so there's nothing to apologise for. I understand perfectly. It was the pain of – of everything. Of losing your lovely wife.'

'That's it. That's it exactly. A momentary lapse. And I swear it won't happen again.'

It was Amelia he wanted, Amelia he'd longed to hold in his arms and make love to, but Amelia was dead. And so he'd used Kate instead.

Oh, but she really didn't mind. Loving him as she did, Kate had thought of little else since. She would like him to make love to her every day of her life. And she couldn't help but hope that he might come to feel the same way one day. For all the inappropriateness of the timing, and the acres of differences that lay between them, it had been lovely to have him hold her and love her like that. Blissful, and she'd do it all again, so she would. She didn't care what anyone thought. She just wanted him, in any way he was prepared to accept her.

She gave a bleak little nod, unwilling to trust her own voice. After another achingly long pause Kate became aware that he was at last looking at her properly and wished with all her heart that he wouldn't, not now there were tears threading their way down her face. He pulled open the door, a brisk tone coming into his voice. 'Thank you for being so understanding. Whatever there is between us Kate, *was* between us, it can't be allowed to flourish. It wouldn't be right.'

She cleared her throat. 'No sir.'

'I dare say I should ask you to leave, and, in different circumstances, that probably would be for the best. But since the fault was not entirely yours, and because Callum needs you, I hope you'll stay.'

'Leave?' Nothing had been said to her about leaving. Such a thing had never crossed her mind. Why would he send her away because of something neither of them had been able to help? She looked into his face, startled, and it was then that their eyes finally met and she saw in them no warmth at all, rather a coldness that shocked her. The chestnut eyes had grown hard, like a pair of polished pebbles, and there was a cynical twist to the wide mouth.

'The last thing we must do is add fuel to the gossip's fire, eh Kate?'

She could think of nothing to say to this. 'I'd best go and see to Callum, if you'll excuse me, sir.'

'Yes, Kate, do that.' And she practically ran from his presence, wincing as she heard the study door crash to behind her.

—

If Eliot was sorry, Kate was even sorrier. She stood at the window with tears in her eyes and watched the carriages draw away, so that the picture wobbled and spun giddily, as if washed away by the rain. The tears continued to run unchecked down her face till she was sobbing uncontrollably into her sodden handkerchief. Oh, but she would miss Amelia, she surely would. No one could have asked for a better mistress, nor a kinder lady with a sweeter nature.

And yet the night before Amelia had properly been laid to rest, Kate had made love to her grieving husband. How could she have been so heartless, so cruel? What had she been thinking of? That was the trouble, of course. She hadn't been thinking at all, she'd been acting purely on her senses. As had he. Now they must both live with their guilt.

Kate knew she'd been dazzled and astonished by his sudden need for her, wanting only to please him, to show him how much she cared. She'd felt unworthy of his love, grateful almost that he even noticed she existed. But of course it hadn't been her that he was loving at all, only his dead wife.

And if, because of a silly family squabble, the wagging tongues of Kendal could so destroy a lovely, innocent lady who had done no wrong, save to take a wee boy to her heart and believe in a good and faithful husband, what would they say if they discovered what had taken place that night? In a way, Kate had justified their maliciousness by making the gossip come true. Their cruelty, lack of charity, and holier-than-thou attitude towards the sanctity of marriage would be as nothing compared to how they would react if they learned that a servant, a girl from Poor House Lane, had pretensions to become the mistress, or even, in her secret dreams, the wife, of Eliot Tyson.

He was right. She should leave. Were it not for Callum belonging here, in this home, with the man who had adopted him, Kate would pack their bags and go before ever the family returned from the funeral. As it was, she was trapped, by her love for him, and by the shamefulness of her behaviour.

—

It was a relief when the day was finally over and all visitors and mourners, save for the two aunts, had finally left. Kate kept her mind firmly away from her troubled thoughts by working extra hard. In the days following, as well as minding Callum, she helped Fanny clean and tidy and restore order to the house. The housemaid had withdrawn into one of her sulks again, for no reason Kate could think of; barely uttering a word despite their working together changing bed linen and laying bedroom fires, dusting and polishing, not to mention acres of carpet needing to be beaten and swept after all the food that had been trodden in. Kate assumed she too was grieving for the mistress, and made no comment.

Fortunately, there was little time to be morbid, as operations were directed by Aunt Vera with the precision of a military operation.

'Don't you gels imagine for one minute that you can start slacking, simply because your poor dear mistress has sadly departed this life. Standards must still be maintained.'

'Yes, Miss Vera,' said Fanny, bobbing a curtsey.

'Miss Tyson to you. Though you can address my sister as Miss Cissie, to avoid confusion.'

'Thank you Miss, er – um Miss Tyson, ma'am.'

The two maiden ladies swooped upon the task of clearing Amelia's room with relish, urging Fanny and Kate to help sort her gowns, day clothes, footwear, even her nightgowns and underthings into different piles. Those which could be distributed amongst the cousins and other family members; those which might be used by carefully selected, needy individuals. The remainder were gathered into an indiscriminate heap to be taken along to the Union Workhouse. Kate grimaced at the thought but selected a few useful items for Millie, and secreted these away in her room. She meant to go and see her friend soon. She hadn't seen her in months, not since Amelia had fallen ill. She would take these few items, and the knitted baby clothes.

Lucy arrived one morning with her three children and nanny in tow with the prime purpose of picking over the primary items of Amelia's wardrobe. She gathered together large Hessian sacks full of garments, shoes and pretty stoles and purses, even a selection of Amelia's favourite books and jewellery, calling for Dennis to bring the carriage to take her home.

The greedy madam, thought Kate, but prudently kept these thoughts to herself.

Later, in the kitchen, the servants were agog over the visit. 'I doubt there's anything left worth the pinching,' Mrs Petty muttered. 'You'd have thought they'd've given us first refusal, being part of the household like and after all the years of service I gave the mistress.'

'I always fancied that long blue velvet skirt meself,' said Fanny. 'Ooh, and I would've loved that taupe costume for me going-away outfit,' casting a coy glance in Dennis's direction. No date had yet been fixed for their wedding and Fanny was getting anxious.

Kate said nothing, thinking it was all somewhat unsavoury to be sieving through a person's belongings before they were cold in their grave, though who was she to talk? Hadn't she helped herself already to Amelia's most valuable possession?

'Dennis says that Madam Lucy looked like the proverbial cat who'd swallowed a pint of cream. Relishing the fact that she'd seen off her rival good and proper, and picked over the spoils.'

'They say as how Mr Charles isn't doing too well at that new job of his,' said Askew, unexpectedly taking the pipe from his mouth to join in with this conversation. 'No one expects it to last.'

They all looked at him in surprise, as if they'd quite forgotten that he could talk, let alone have an opinion worth noting. 'Bless my soul,' said Mrs Petty, if that's the way the land lies, I'd say that Master Charles will be back in harness at Tyson's afore the month is out, mark my words. The master won't stand by and see his own brother go under.'

She was proved to be absolutely correct in her surmise, as was Askew. By the end of October, Charles paid a visit to his brother and a new deal was struck behind the closed doors of his study. Tyson's Shoe Manufactory bought out Charles Tyson's leather dressing business, complete with its considerable debts.

'We'll just have to hope we don't all live to regret the master's kind generosity,' Askew said again, excelling himself in his chatter on yet another evening of below-stairs gossip. No one responded, but there were a good many thoughtful expressions.

–

Millie didn't seem to be at all herself when Kate finally got around to calling, but oddly withdrawn and sullen. She kept Kate standing at the door for so long, barring the entrance with arms folded about herself, that Kate had to ask if she was ever going to be let in. 'I feel a bit of a lemon standing here. Don't I even get a cuppa?'

They sat in the all-too-familiar, overcrowded little room that seemed to smell of stale urine and mice more strongly than ever. There was the usual gaggle of emaci-ated, lethargic children scattered upon the bed with its odd assortment of ragged covers and old coats, as well as on the clippy rugs on the earth floor. How many more children had Millie produced in the last eighteen months or so, she wondered? There was also a heap of leather pieces by the chair, as if she'd interrupted her in the middle of her work, which Kate made a mental note to ask about later. Best not to charge in with questions, she decided, but come to it gently. Kate felt like an alien being, or worse, like a lady-bountiful come to visit 'the poor'. Millie confirmed this impression with her first words.

'I'm surprised you'd sink so low as to call in here now you've got so high-and-mighty.'

'What a thing to say! Course I haven't gone all high-and-mighty, and you're still me friend, I hope.'

'You've not brought Master Callum, I notice.'

'No, he's out with El… with his papa, fishing.'

Millie rolled her eyes. 'Papa is it now, not Dad? And fishing, at three?'

'He's four, actually.'

'Oh, *actually*, is he indeed? My word, isn't he going to be the little toff? Still, what would I know of such goings-on?' She gave a half shrug and, looking at the skinny shoulders, Kate thought she'd shrunk even more.

'I was wondering how things were with you, that's all.' When Millie didn't respond, Kate tried again, keeping her voice resolutely bright and cheerful. 'So, how are things then? I see ye've added to yer family since I was last here.'

'I had the twins last year, aye,' Millie said, with no inflection of joy in her tone.

'And ye've another on the way I see, so isn't it a blessing that I called? Look what I've fetched for you and the babbies.' Holding out the parcel of clothes she'd so painstakingly knitted for the baby that never was, as well as a few items which Callum had grown out of, which she thought might be suitable for Millie's brood. Neither the Tyrolean jacket, nor the tartan kilt, were amongst them.

Millie didn't even bother to unwrap the parcel. She just sat pleating the hem of her grubby blouse with her stumpy fingers. It was Kate who, with a click of impatience, pulled back the paper. 'See, some warm little jackets, and knitted trousers. Won't they be fine come the winter?'

'It's very generous of you, I'm sure.' The voice remained cold, distant. Abandoning the blouse, she began to chew on her fingernails instead.

''Tis not at all generous. This is me, your old friend, Kate, remember? When have I ever had anything worth the giving? I didn't when I lived here with you, and I still don't. The only thing I ever gave away that was of value, was our Callum, and I wish to God I'd never had to do that. Aren't these from the mistress, who recently passed away, much to our sorrow, and in case you didn't notice.' There was a defensive note in her tone now, a brittleness to her response, clearly adding herself to the list of those who mourned Amelia's passing.

'I – I'm sorry. I didn't realise.' Millie went back to pleating the shabby blouse, every now and then combing her fingers through greasy strands of hair and glancing across at the door every five seconds, as if she half expected it to open and reveal yet another unexpected visitor.

'She was a fine woman, so she was. I'll not find a better mistress in a long day's march.' Kate suddenly realised that these weren't just words or false sentiment, that she truly meant what she said, and her throat tightened with emotion. Oh, but she would miss her, she surely would.

And suddenly it was as if Amelia were there beside her, a voice whispering in her ear, what are you doing here, Kate? Didn't I warn you to stay away? I don't belong here any more, in this place which I once thought of as home, Kate thought.

It seemed that her life had changed so radically since those days, not only in physical comforts but in attitudes too. Once she would have hated the ruling classes, no matter what. She'd never have thought to take their part or defend them, and now here she was not only speaking up for her late mistress and mourning her, but sleeping with the master. At least, she'd slept with him once and would again, given half a chance. Now there was something she'd never dare tell Millie. Kate found she was blushing, simply at the memory of that night, let alone the hopes and dreams she'd foolishly entertained of repeating it, at least until they'd been so firmly dashed by his apology.

She considered her friend with shrewd speculation, brow furrowed in thought. 'So, are ye going to tell me how y'are, or what's eating into you to make you look so much like a wet fortnight, or shall I go?' Kate suddenly glanced about her, at the familiar muddle, the muck and the mess that she'd used to spend her entire day cleaning up. Something was wrong. Something missing. And then it came to her what it was. 'Where's Ma? Oh no!'

'Aye, she died last back end. Took away by a racking cough.'

'Oh Millie, I'm so sorry. You'll miss her sorely.'

'I will, Kate. I do.' And Millie stopped plaiting the hem of her blouse, stopped chewing on her fingernails to look pleadingly up at her old friend as if seeing her for the first time and marvelling at the sight of her, eyes filling with tears. 'By, but it's good to see you love, I – I…' She couldn't finish the sentence before emotion choked her, and then the two friends were holding each other tight, both weeping and sobbing on to each other's shoulders, Millie for her lost mother-in-law who had cared for her as if she were her own, and Kate for her own sense of loss and tortured emotions.

The tears had been mopped up, a pot of tea brewed and Millie had even consented to accept a slice of the cherry cake which Mrs Petty had kindly sent; largely because the children's eyes had nearly popped out of their heads at sight of it, and it would have been far too cruel to deny them this pleasure despite Millie's objection to charity.

They'd chatted about Clem, about the hope they still entertained for him to get a decent job, or of them finding a better place to live. Now, Kate was asking more pertinent questions about the pieces of half-stitched leather she'd seen on the mat. 'You're working for Swainson, right?'

Millie's face seemed to fold in upon itself, the eyes becoming dark hollows of livid fury. 'I do it because I must. Our Clem gets nowt, not with his missing arm, even though he lost it at a decent job, working in a factory. No boss gives a damn about workers' accidents. Why should they? All that matters is their profit, and Swainson is another such.'

'I did warn you, Millie, but I can see that you've really no choice, not with all these babbies. But watch Swainson doesn't ask for more. I don't trust the bastard as far as I can throw a ball of cotton wool.'

It was as if she'd unlocked a sluice gate. Millie opened her mouth, still full of cherry cake, and began to howl. The whole sorry tale came pouring forth. How he'd forced himself upon her, used and abused her, and how she was forced to submit or else starve for want of work. And the worst of it was that she didn't have the first idea whether the twins were really Clem's bairns or Swainson's, let alone this one she was carrying now. Millie sobbed as if her heart would break, so upset that she started vomiting and it took some time to calm her down. More tea had to be made as Kate sat with her arm cuddled about her friend, holding her tight until the storm of weeping was spent and, exhausted, she finally subsided into hiccupping sobs. Seeing that their mother had stopped crying at last, the watching children crept closer, a couple of them climbing on to her knee, hollow-eyed with fear.

'There, there, love, I'm fine. Don't fret our Susie, yer mam's just a mite poorly today. It's helped a bit just talking about it all and getting it off me chest like. It'd all built up inside, now ma isn't here to help any more. She knew what he were up to but never said nowt, not to Clem, nor even to me, never chastised me once. She'd just clean me up, mend whatever he'd ripped or broken and make tea till I'd stopped shivering and got a hold of meself again. Oh, but it's terrible hard without her. He's gone worse now he knows there's no one here at all during t'day. He comes at all times and stays for hours, making me do all sorts o' mucky things to him.'

'Oh Millie, you must tell him to stay away. There must be other ways you can earn a living.'

'Oh aye, there is, and you know what they'd be. And happen I will go on t'streets, in the end. At least I'd get paid for what I do then.'

'Don't say such terrible things. I can't bear to hear you talk like that. So help me, I'll see his head on a platter afore he touches you again.'

Millie looked suddenly panic-stricken. 'Nay, don't you get involved, Kate love. You've escaped. I'm that jealous of you but at t'same time, I don't want you back here, suffering same as we do. Tha's got away and Ma were right to tell you to stay away. Say nowt. I'll sort it, one way or another.'

'There must be something I can do, and Jaysus, I'll find it, so I will. And before you say it, don't ye fret yerself, I'll make sure that whatever it is I decide to do, it won't reflect back on you and yours in any way.'

Promises that were easily made, but Kate hadn't the first idea how she was going to keep them.

Chapter Seventeen

Aunt Vera and Aunt Cissie made it their task that winter to stay and support Eliot in what they judged to be his 'hour of need'. Their first task each day was to speak to Mrs Petty and ensure that something suitable was to be served for dear Eliot when he returned home from business (they never referred to it as the factory – far too common). The next was to ensure that the maids were properly aware of their duties for the day, and woe betide them if the linen closet should become untidy, or the brass fender tarnished.

Much of their day was spent in sewing for the needy. When they were not thus engaged, Vera kept herself busy with her innumerable committees, at the church, the hospital, or various charitable institutions within the town, and Cissie would often go off fishing or walking her pointers. Fortunately she'd brought only two with her, known as Napoleon and Josephine, although the pair created mayhem enough, digging up Askew's newly planted leeks, and leaving dog hairs all over the drawing room sofas, not to mention unsightly scratch marks on the kitchen door in their efforts to beg food off an obstinately unhelpful Mrs Petty.

Following a frugal lunch, the aunts would permit themselves a short nap, generally taken in the drawing room, ensconced in matching wing chairs with their heads thrown back or nodding in time to their accompanying snores.

After this short respite, they would wake refreshed and set about the main business of the day: paying calls. They kept a diary of the ladies they had called upon most recently, those amongst their near neighbours who merited more frequent attention, and invitations which must be issued, counting out the cards they would need for that particular afternoon with punctilious care before ever they set off. They prided themselves on not being in the least judgemental, although anyone who had not attended poor dear Amelia's funeral were likely to find themselves cold-shouldered, even if those who had cut her so cruelly at the end of her life, were not.

Nevertheless, they were careful to confine their conversation on these occasions to more general matters, such as their charity work and the church, and avoid any mention of the 'domestic situation' at Tyson Lodge.

Kate found that with the aunts in residence, her own duties multiplied threefold, and the work she did to help Fanny was no longer voluntary but an expected part of her day. Maintaining a proper nursery routine for Callum who, as a lively four-year-old was much more demanding, appeared to be very by-the-way, given no priority at all. The aunts did not approve of him trailing after her while she carried out her duties of sweeping, bed making, cleaning windows or brasses, which meant that he must remain in the nursery unattended for short periods alone, which greatly troubled Kate.

'What possible harm can he come to?' Vera would stoutly remark when once Kate expressed her reservations on this practice.

'He gets upset when he's on his own, and what if he should wander about looking for me and fall down the stairs, or have an accident of some sort? I should be there to watch over him.'

The aunts, in particular Vera, were privately of the opinion that delightful as the little boy might be, actually adopting him had been one step too far. They naturally blamed Amelia and her obsessive need for a child for this decision. Nor did they wish to consider too closely the unpleasant rumours about dear Eliot, which were rife. Who the father of the Kirkland Poor House child might be was certainly none of their business. Men were a law unto themselves, after all, and they didn't consider it their place to act as judge and jury on the subject.

The mother, however, was another matter entirely, and showed every sign of getting above herself. Writing and sending out Announcement of Death notices, giving orders to undertakers and attempting to organise poor dear Amelia's funeral without any discussion with the family, was quite beyond the pale. Quite shocking! As for imagining she could plan the entire day exclusively around this child of hers, and at their expense, was sheer impertinence on her part.

'Stuff and nonsense, girl. I can't be doing with molly-coddling infants,' Vera declared in stentorian tones, just as if she were an expert on the subject. 'You have your duties to attend to. We can't have you lolling about all day in the nursery, playing with your child.'

'Will he be going to school soon, when he turns five, do you think?' Kate dared to ask.

'I'm sure I wouldn't know. That is entirely up to Eliot. He may well decide to send him away to school. Indeed I would advise it. Certainly something must be done if the child is not to turn into a savage.' And having issued this dreadful indictment of Kate's son, her small, solid figure marched briskly away, not a hair on her neatly clipped head moving an inch as she did so.

–

Charles was in deep trouble. His currying business had been under-financed from the start and having been hit by a new process which left vegetable tanning outdated and expensive, which he hadn't even seen coming, it was a miracle it had lasted as long as it had. The fact that Eliot had agreed to buy him out and take over the failing business should have been the answer to all his problems. Hadn't he wanted to return to the fold, to have his old job back in Tyson's? And he'd got it, admittedly with strict limits curtailing his power. He no longer had access to the accounts of course, and all orders he made had to be double checked with the firm who had made them, plus any decisions he made must be discussed with Eliot first. It made him feel all the more inadequate, unwanted and useless.

'Don't you trust me?' he would demand of Eliot.

'No, why should I? The last time I did that, you robbed me. A person has to earn trust, Charles, not assume it by right.'

'I'm your brother, for God's sake.'

'Exactly. That's why I thought I could trust you in the first place. I was wrong. Have you done nothing to curb Lucy's spending habits, or your own for that matter?'

Keeping two fine houses going was proving to be a considerable drain on his purse, alarmingly so, and yet didn't seem to make Lucy happy. It was certainly true that he'd managed to restrain her spending for a while, but the moment the takeover had gone through, she'd reverted to her old ways.

'Thank goodness for that,' she'd declared. 'Now we can get on with enjoying life again. We shall have the Cowpers over for dinner on Sunday.'

Charles attempted to explain that money was still tight, that in fact none had actually changed hands. Eliot had simply agreed to take the debts of the currying business off his hands, which was a great relief, but did nothing to solve the problem of their other substantial debts, which seemed to be growing at an alarming rate, nor pay off the mortgage.

Lucy either didn't listen or wasn't interested. She set about furnishing and equipping the Lake house to the highest of standards. He had the latest bill in his hand at this moment: two hundred guineas for a fine mahogany dining table, not even counting the set of twelve chairs. He couldn't imagine how one piece of furniture could cost so much, and why on earth they would ever need to seat twelve people in any case.

And that wasn't the only expense. He flicked through several more bills that he kept stuffed in a box at the back of his desk which were equally frightening. Fifty pounds for a Persian rug. Seventy-five each for some gilt chairs she'd had specially made in the French style. And then there were any number of pieces of Chinese porcelain, tapestries on the walls, screens, mirrors and pretty little tables which had happened to catch her eye. The house looked more like a French chateau than a Westmorland country home. She'd even started looking at masterpieces and talked of buying a Gainsborough or a Reynolds, a prospect which made his blood run cold.

Charles felt close to despair. He also possessed a letter from his bank manager. He read it through one more time then tore it to shreds and dropped it in the waste paper basket. Where was the point in going to see the man simply to receive another lecture, particularly when there was nothing to be done.

Perhaps he should try one more time with Lucy. He began to rehearse what he might say, pouring himself a large whisky to help the process along. It certainly wasn't going to be easy but he must find some way of imparting to her the severity of their situation.

–

It was almost as if Eliot was avoiding her. Kate hadn't set eyes on him for months, following their painful discussion in his study on the morning of the funeral. A part of her wanted to avoid him too, and yet another part ached to be with him, to have him hold her as he had done that night; to have him need *her* and not confuse her with the memory of a much loved wife. If only she could catch Eliot alone to speak to him about these fears. But he seemed to have forgotten all about Callum in his grief, and was making no provision at all for his welfare.

Fortunately, Callum was a good little boy and Kate would set him small tasks of reading or writing, or small sums for him to try, hoping that Eliot would find him a school soon, though one in Kendal. She couldn't bear the thought of him going away. And what would happen to her then? She would no longer be needed, no longer have access to her son. The thought filled her with fear.

Besides concerns about Callum's education and her own future, in order to keep her promise to help Millie, she must somehow confront Eliot with what was going on behind his back where his outworkers were concerned. He couldn't be allowed to remain in ignorance, and who else would have the courage to tell him, but herself? Kate had been twice more to console her friend, reaffirming her promise to help but explaining it might take longer than she'd hoped. Millie seemed oblivious, expecting nothing.

Eliot always seemed to be fully occupied at the factory and she didn't like to trouble him too much. Kate went there once but had been refused entry by a sour-faced woman who told her the master was too busy for visitors and wasn't taking on any more operatives. Kate had objected, saying she wasn't seeking employment, that she was his son's nursemaid. When Eliot had appeared looking fraught and bad tempered, waving her away with a dismissive hand, she'd seen at once that it was a waste of time.

'Not now, Kate, not now. Can't you see I'm busy.' And he'd walked away. Swainson had given his supercilious smirk as he'd turned and followed his master back inside.

Kate had tried twice more, to no avail. Now she was hovering about in the passage, hoping she might catch sight of him on his way home from the factory when Aunt Vera hove into view.

'And what do you think you are doing here, girl? You should be upstairs in the nursery, with Master Callum.'

'I was hoping to have a word with himself, so I was.' Kate winced, knowing her Irish brogue came out all the stronger when she was anxious.

'Haven't I told you a dozen times, there is a correct and an incorrect way of going about such things. Lurking in the passage, hoping to waylay the master and waste his time with a lot of foolish girlish nonsense, is not the proper way at all. If you have any problems, you must address them to me directly, each morning after breakfast. Should I deem it necessary for you to see the master, an interview will be arranged at his convenience, not yours. Is that clear?' Not waiting for a reply, she briskly continued, 'Now be off with you and about your business. You are not paid to stand around doing nothing.'

Aunt Vera and Aunt Cissie firmly believed that domestic routine must be shaped to suit masculine needs and requirements. The fact that during Amelia's lifetime Eliot would always defer to her on most things which were not directly connected with business was quite by the way. His wishes were now paramount, or whatever they imagined his wishes should be.

The aunts themselves had never done paid work, spinsters or no, as this would have reflected badly upon their father for not having properly provided for them, and latterly upon Eliot, their favourite nephew, who ran the family business in which they held shares. If this meant at times that they must deprive themselves of small treats and excursions, they looked upon this as a way of instilling fresh fortitude in themselves against life's adversities. They had never expected, nor called for equality, and yet were formidable adversaries whom few men would have had the temerity to cross. Kate certainly didn't attempt it now. She hastily apologised, bobbed a curtsey and beat a hasty retreat, aware of Miss Tyson's stern glare watching her every step of the way. When she returned to the nursery, it was a relief to find that Callum was still sleeping soundly. She should have asked Fanny to sit with him while she went downstairs but the maid was being particularly contrary these days, never quite agreeing to anything Kate suggested.

Yet somehow, despite the two old aunts' interference, she must find a way to speak to Eliot alone. How to achieve it, that was the question.

-

Lake Windermere was at its most magnificent, the woodlands thick and lush and green. The summer days endless and golden. Charles sat watching the public steamers chug back and forth the length of the lake with the last of the season's cargo of trippers and felt deeply depressed, almost as if he were spinning downwards into a dark pit from which there could be no return. There was an actual pain in his chest, as if he were about to succumb to a heart attack. And was it any wonder? In his hand he held the bill for the completed conservatory, yet another expensive monstrosity Lucy had insisted on having built at vast cost, and for which the builders were harassing him for payment, threatening court action if there were any further delay. But how could he pay, if he had no money?

In his heart, Charles knew that the evil day could be put off not longer. He must speak to his wife.

He found her among the ferns and the lilies. She looked enchanting, of course, as always. Soft red lips that he so loved to kiss, shining ebony hair curled and teased about her brow, rising into a delightful coiffure that could only have been achieved by the new French maid. And her breasts, so full and round and comely. He almost reached out and fondled her there and then before he thought better of it, reminding himself that he had come to play the role of scolding husband and he must stand by his decision not to give in to her charms.

'Sweetheart, there you are.'

Just looking at her lovely face should make it all worthwhile but somehow, even though she turned to him with the smile she'd used to give in the early days of their marriage, when he was in funds, her radiance didn't excite him the way it had then. Perhaps he was too concerned with what lay behind the smile, that she might be about to ask for some other treat essential to her happiness.

Before he had the chance to speak, to say a word of his carefully rehearsed speech, or broach the subject which had become a nightmare for him, she flung her arms about his neck and, squealing with delight, said, 'What do you think I've found?'

His spirits plummeted. Dear Lord, let it not be another picture. He'd been thinking of sneaking the Constable back to the gallery to get a refund until he realised he hadn't yet paid for that either. How she charmed these people into giving her so much credit was quite beyond him, yet she never failed to do so. Presumably brandishing the name *Tyson* about as if it meant he was some sort of walking bank vault. 'Not another work of art, sweetheart, I trust? We don't have the wall space.'

Lucy giggled girlishly. 'What a darling you are! No, no, this is much more fun. Come and see.'

She pointed through the arched, conservatory windows, and there it was, standing on the drive. A motor car. Not any old motor, but a brand new Daimler. 'Didn't you say that you liked those best, darling? Well,

I've bought you one, for your birthday. Isn't it wonderful? Aren't you excited?'

Charles thought he might very well pass out on the spot. Lights were spinning in his head, rose coloured, green, purple, yellow and blue, all colours of the rainbow that had nothing to do with the glory of the woodlands, pounding and beating behind his eyes, their only benefit being that they blotted out all sign of the expensive motor which was completely hogging his drive.

Lucy was still talking. 'I've engaged a chauffeur, of course, to go with it. Can't have my sweet darling tiring himself out by driving. Didn't Eliot always say that a gentleman never drives his own carriage? I'm sure it is even more true of the internal combustion engine. There, aren't I clever to have learned such words? And I picked all of it up from my *Woman At Home* magazine, would you believe? Well, what do you think? Are you thrilled?'

Charles managed to discover his voice at last. 'You really shouldn't have, beloved,' he said weakly, as if she'd bought him a new puppy and not this – this most expensive, unasked for, unexpected, *disastrous* piece of merchandise. 'But, dear heart, when you say you bought it for me, how did you do that exactly? I mean, how much did it cost?' Charles could hear his own voice rising hysterically and valiantly attempted to curb it, finishing more quietly, 'Where on earth did you get the funds?'

She kissed him lightly on the cheek. 'Now you aren't going to start getting all grumpy about money again, are you, pudding? Well, of course I didn't actually have the money on me. I never carry cash, silly boy. I gave them your name, of course, at the garage, and instructed them to deliver it today, for your birthday. You don't mind paying for your own pressie, Charlie Boy, do you? I mean, it's the thought that counts.'

Later, when Lucy went into the study to check why Charlie Boy hadn't come down in answer to the dinner gong for his birthday repast with at least twenty invited guests, she found him sitting looking out of the window, a great smile on his face. Except that when she got closer, she found that he was holding his hunting rifle between his knees, and it wasn't a smile at all.

–

Charles's funeral was nothing like so grand as Amelia's. Besides, following on so swiftly upon that previous sad event, no one quite had the stomach for it. Nor could it take place at the Parish Church, since he had tragically taken his own life. A few stalwart members of the family stood around while the body was disposed of as quickly and discreetly as possible, and then returned to their respective homes without another word. Charles would probably never be spoken of again, certainly not in polite circles.

Lucy was too numb to react. She showed no sign of hysterics, shed not a single tear. Whether she grieved for her husband in private, nobody quite liked to enquire. She didn't seem to hear even if anyone offered their condolences, mumbling odd remarks about a motor car having been sent back, and how it was such a pity that Charles would never get to drive it now. The only spark of life came when she was brusquely informed, by Eliot, that the house by the lake must be sold and she would have to make do with the one in Stramongate; that she could very well lose that one too, if Charles's debts proved too heavy.

She did not take this threat lightly. Embarrassed members of the household tip-toed past the door of Eliot's study, pretending not to hear the shrillness of her voice within, only thankful that they were not the one suffering the blast of her temper. 'You wouldn't *dare* to deprive my children of their only home as well as their heritage? You do realise, Eliot, that he wouldn't be dead at all, if it weren't for *you*!' And she'd stormed away giving him no further opportunity to defend himself, managing to look both brave and forlorn all at the same time.

In the weeks following, life itself seemed to be taken on tiptoe with everyone, servants and family alike, speaking in low, hushed tones, not quite knowing whether it would be proper to smile. It was the aunts who put a stop to this nonsense and came to the fore yet again, privately remarking how wise had been their decision to stay on. They certainly had no intention of leaving.

'Dear Eliot will need us more than ever now,' Vera stoutly declared.

'Oh, indeed yes. To lose a wife, and a brother. Dear, dear, dear. Poor man,' Cissie most heartily agreed.

'Charles was always a loose cannon, a wild boy who grew into an unstable man,' Vera stated in a tone which would not brook contradiction. 'It does not surprise me in the slightest that he chose the coward's way out.'

'Nor I,' agreed Aunt Cissie.

'All we can do is pray for his soul. Meanwhile there is work to be done, and a life to be lived.'

'Of course there is. So true, so true.'

And having made their point most firmly, they got on with the task of living, expecting the rest of the household to do the same.

—

The death of Charles, the trauma of disposing of his Lakeland home and effects, settling his debts and so forth, had deprived Kate of any opportunity to carry out her promise to Millie, for surely Eliot had far more important matters on his mind. But she had not her forgotten her pledge and visited her old friend regularly, growing increasingly concerned by her condition. One morning Kate managed to snatch a moment with Eliot before he set off for the factory. He looked surprised to find her patiently waiting for him on the landing, and not particularly pleased.

'What is this, an ambush?'

'I need to talk to you about Swainson. Didn't I say what a dreadful man he was, well now he's…'

'Kate, enough! I'm well aware of your dislike for this man but he is my foreman. So far as I am concerned, he does his job well and I'm not prepared to stand here and listen to tittle-tattle.' He made to walk on past her down the stairs but Kate grabbed at his sleeve.

''Tis not tittle-tattle, 'tis the gospel truth. He's after the women, so he is.'

Eliot drew in a long weary breath but the expression on his face was one of disbelief. 'And who told you that, I wonder, one of your women friends from Poor House Lane?'

Kate's cheeks flushed a guilty crimson and she saw by the way his eyes narrowed to ice cold slits that she'd made a bad mistake mentioning her old yard.

'You've been there again, haven't you? I understood my late wife had put that dreadful place out of bounds to you. Are you saying you've risked Callum's health yet again by venturing down there? Have you?'

All Kate could do was hang her head in shame.

'I'm of a mind to dismiss you on the spot.'

'Oh, please, don't, sir! I'm that sorry, so I am. It's just that my...'

'Have done Kate, and get back to your duties. And leave my blasted foreman in peace.'

Chapter Eighteen

September arrived and with it that mellow softness in the air so often found in a Lakeland autumn before the bite of winter takes hold, with the smell of leaf mould, sunshine and garden bonfires in the air. Life at Tyson Lodge slipped back into its familiar routine, the servants going about their daily chores, Kate minding Callum, still worrying about what would happen when he turned five, as he soon would do. Would he then have no need of a nursemaid? Would she be dismissed and a governess engaged, as Eliot had once implied might happen? She daren't risk pushing the subject of Swainson too hard, in case it backfired on her. The result of her last effort and Eliot's threat to dismiss her on the spot had chilled Kate to her very soul.

And the two spinsters showed no sign of leaving.

Their favourite occupation was to call upon 'unfortunates', wearing a suitably caring expression and carrying their parcel of charitable offerings before them like a flag of honour. The recipients were carefully selected women who had fallen upon hard times, and deemed to be in need of their time and attention. The aunts would offer a modicum of sympathy, larded with a great deal of worthy advice, largely of the 'converting them to come to church' variety, as the sisters firmly believed that poverty was somehow only inflicted upon the unchristian.

Occasionally they might agree to provide a small amount of cash to buy coal, a much needed overcoat or pair of boots but mostly they preferred to make their offerings in kind as they didn't quite trust 'these people' to spend the money wisely. And souls, they declared, were of far greater importance than bodies.

All of this put Kate in mind of her own time in Poor House Lane and when once they directed her to accompany them in order to carry the parcels, she absolutely, and steadfastly, refused.

'Wouldn't they all think I was lording it over them?' Kate explained.

'Utter tosh!' Vera retorted, quite unable to see the problem. 'Are you questioning my judgement, gel?'

'Indeed no, Miss Tyson, but I wouldn't feel comfortable. It wouldn't be right.'

Cissie saw her point at once. 'You'd be embarrassed, dear, is that it, as if you were making yourself out to be better than these poor people?'

'I would so. Sure and they'd think I was playing the Lady Bountiful.'

Vera took off her spectacles and polished them furiously, seeing that she had lost that particular battle, though she wasn't prepared to let it go without a fight. 'It is my firm opinion, that the poor are an unavoidable section of the system, one we are no more likely to be able to eradicate than we could change the laws of gravity.'

'A decent job, or mebbe a bit more book learning might help,' Kate said, unable to keep quiet in the face of such pig-headedness. 'Isn't that what I want – a decent education and upbringing for me own son.'

Both maiden ladies looked taken aback by this effron-tery on her part to speak out. They quite took their own more privileged position for granted, as if they were immune to such disasters as poverty. And didn't they do all they could to help? Indeed, they attended lectures on a regular basis which fully explained the rules of philan-thropy versus economics; how it was fine to nurture and champion the inadequate and the weak, so long as this didn't interfere with the capacity of business to make a profit. Surely everyone knew this simple fact, otherwise how would Tyson's Shoe Manufactory, for instance, ever survive? Clearly, this chit understood nothing.

'My dear girl, education is for those who are worthy of it, not for every Tom, Dick and Harry.'

But there was no stopping Kate now. 'I don't see why not. And a clean, healthy home where a woman can bring up her babbies safe and well, and people don't piss in the yard, wouldn't come amiss either.'

Vera looked as if she might very well faint, this informa-tion being far too much for her, as if she never needed to relieve herself at all, let alone in a place where insufficient lavatories were provided.

'I fully intend,' Vera explained later to her sister. 'To make it my duty to see that Miss Kate O'Connor learns her place and stays below stairs, where she belongs.'

'Whatever you think best, Vera dear.'

'Unless, of course, we can think of some fool-proof plan to rid ourselves of her entirely.'

Some time later, Aunt Vera confronted Eliot at breakfast with what Cissie could only be described as her implacable look. 'Cissie and I have found an excellent, sensible school for the boy.' Sensible in that it didn't cost a fortune, and its main advantage being that it was many miles from Kendal. 'It was recommended to us by the vicar,' as if that settled the matter, 'and the boy can start after Christmas which will mean that he'll no longer be in need of a nursemaid.'

Eliot sensed the onset of panic. He felt confused, as if he were being swept along by some tide over which he had no control. A tide of his own making, of desire and need, a lust which filled him with bitter shame. But it was Callum who troubled him the most. He was the most important factor in all of this. Whatever Eliot decided to do about this undeniable and soul-weakening physical attraction he felt for the boy's mother, he'd really no wish to lose his son to some school, however excellent, quite so soon.

'He's too young to leave home, at just turned five. Eight is surely early enough to send him away. Perhaps we're rushing matters somewhat.'

'Nonsense! This particular school has a kindergarten department, making it part of their policy to begin educating children as soon as possible. He will come to no harm at all. Far better he be in professional hands, rather than the uncertain care of a naïve young girl. Remember, we no longer have the benefit of poor dear Amelia to be a mother to the child.'

Eliot stared at the congealed bacon on his plate and considered saying that the child did still have a mother, but thought better of it. How could Kate be so described when she'd given up all rights to Callum once he'd adopted the boy? It was no longer proper to think that way. He'd been evading the issue long enough, unable to give the child the proper attention he deserved because of his grief, not to mention the problems resulting from

Charles's suicide. Eliot sighed and set his knife and fork to one side. He really couldn't go on vacillating. It would be much better if she did leave, thereby removing temptation from his sight.

'Perhaps you are right.' He stood up. 'I promise that I'll give the matter serious consideration. We'll discuss it later, or at some point during the next few days. We still have a week or two's grace, I am sure, before we must decide.'

The two aunts exchanged a speaking glance which Eliot did not intercept as he was already striding from the breakfast room. Aunt Vera hurried after him out into the hall. Cissie, her ever-permanent shadow, not far behind.

'You mustn't delay making a decision for too long.'

'No, no, not too long. Dear me, no,' said Cissie.

'Places are at a premium.'

'Yes indeed, at a premium,' agreed her echo.

Eliot snatched up his hat, bid them both good morning and fled from the house.

–

Kate was sitting on the nursery sofa one evening in October when the tap came upon the door. She set down her work with a sigh, fully expecting it to be one of the aunts come to complain about some unfulfilled task or other. They were rarely satisfied with her work and took every opportunity to point out her inadequacies which generally resulted in Kate having to do every job twice over.

'Yes,' she said with weary resignation as she swung open the door. But it was not Aunt Vera standing there.

'May I come in,' Eliot politely asked, 'or is it too late?'

Kate glanced back over her shoulder at the sleeping child in the adjoining bedroom and, putting a finger to her lips, answered carefully, with proper respect. 'Come into the day nursery. He's asleep.' She closed the door between the two rooms and returning to the sofa, picked up her mending again. Keeping her fingers busy might stop them from shaking, she thought, as Eliot drew near. To her alarm and discomfort, he chose not to sit on the rocking chair opposite but on the sofa beside her. She could hear her own heart hammering and was certain he must hear it too.

Kate cast him a sideways glance, watching as he sank back against the sofa cushions, intensely aware of his nearness. Oh, but he was a handsome man. Just the sight of him turned her insides to water, the way his dark curls tumbled over his brow, the mere scent of his cologne set her senses jangling. He chanced to look up as she was surreptitiously studying him and their glances held. Try as she might, she could not tear her gaze away. Something flared between them, an undeniable spark of attraction that brought a crimson flag of colour to each cheek. Only when he smiled, breaking the power of the moment, did she manage to drop her gaze and turn her attention back to the sock she was darning, except that her hand was shaking after all, and Kate was forced to set the needle down.

'Are you content?' he asked. 'Do you find your quarters comfortable? Are you managing all right – on your own?' He meant without Amelia, but couldn't bring himself to say her name.

Kate swallowed her nervousness and managed a weak smile. 'Yes, thank you. I'm very well.'

'That's good. More than anything, I want you to be happy, Kate.'

Oh, how she wanted him. How she needed him. It would be so easy to simply turn towards him, to let his hands caress her bare skin, let him have her and be done with it.

Which, of course, he knew.

She again addressed herself to the sock, compelling her fingers to work properly. She was puzzled and alarmed by this late visit, wondering what, exactly, was on his mind. The conversation felt stilted and studiously polite. But then was it any wonder? This man had turned her life upside down on two separate occasions: when he'd taken her son as his own, and the night following Amelia's death when he'd taken her to his bed. What could he want of her now?

Kate might secretly adore him, find him the most exciting man alive, but yet she remained wary of him. He kept her here, at Tyson Lodge, because it suited him to do so. Was he now about to tell her that her services were no longer required, that Aunt Vera had persuaded him to send the boy away?

Of all things, Kate hated insincerity and hypocrisy. He didn't love her, so why pretend? Why act as if he cared whether she was content or not? Why make comments about wanting her to be happy? How could she be, loving him as she did, and knowing that love not to be returned.

His first words confirmed her worst fears. 'Aunt Vera tells me she's found Callum a good school.'

'You aren't going to send him away?' She looked at him in dismay, her gaze silently adding, And me too?

His response was a sad smile. 'You know this is all quite impossible. Having you here – after what happened between us. Don't you think that it would be the wisest thing, for us both?'

He saw the small shake of her head, the light from the fire catch a blaze of colour in her hair, how the translucent skin suddenly drained of its normally rosy, apple-fresh colour. Yet the clear grey eyes were as defiant as ever, challenging him even now to brook her defences, if he dare. She didn't want to go, nor would she beg to stay. And then on the tips of her lower lashes he saw a tear. It hovered for a second before it spilled over and ran slowly down her cheek. Without giving it a second's thought, Eliot leaned closer and licked it away with his tongue. The eyelids flickered closed. He heard her soft moan, felt her body tremble, yielding instinctively to his touch. And as he reached for her, he quite forgot that he'd come to ask her to leave.

–

The next morning when she woke, they were still on the sofa, their limbs entwined, the weight of his body heavy and warm against her, the smell of the sun on his skin intoxicating, making her want him all over again. Kate lay beside him not daring to move, keeping her breathing slow and even, in an effort to pretend she was still asleep. She feared that when he woke, he'd be ashamed, and his sense of guilt would cause him to turn from her again.

But what else could she expect?

Wouldn't the aunts be appalled if they knew how their darling nephew had spent last night? No, no, they'd turn a blind eye, of course they would. It was all too common for a master to take his pleasure of a maid. Not for a moment would they consider it a sign of love. Why should they? There was no question of Kate stepping into Amelia's shoes and becoming the next Mrs Tyson. Quite unthinkable. Such a scandal would be the ruin of him. If Amelia's so-called friends could cut her off so brutally at the end of her life on the basis of a false rumour, when the poor woman had done nothing wrong and was entirely innocent, what hope could Kate have of them accepting her? She would forever be looked down upon as a servant, a pauper. The girl from Poor House Lane. Because that's exactly what she was.

And wouldn't they take out their spite on Eliot, if she even tried? They'd destroy him, and the business, just as they had Amelia. And she could never allow that to happen.

Kate smiled softly as he slept on beside her, his face as innocent as a boy's in repose. She stroked back a dark curl, dropped a tender kiss on his brow. Oh, but she'd never meant it to happen, not again. As he'd kissed her that first time last night, she'd kept her spine rigid with the resolve not to crumble. But it had proved every bit as difficult to deny him then as it had that first time. He'd cupped her face with a gentle hand, lifted up her loose flowing curls and placed his mouth against the beat of a pulse deep in the tiny hollows of her throat, threatening to shatter the last of her control. She'd tried. Oh, but hadn't she fought against her desire, pressed her hands against his chest to push him away, despite an ache inside her belly almost too painful to bear.

'You should go. I – I'm tired,' she'd told him, in the way recalcitrant wives had done for generations. But she wasn't his wife, nor even his mistress. She was only a nursemaid.

He'd remained silent for so long, looking into her face as if the very sight of her troubled him, that she'd thought for a moment he was about to do as she asked, and leave. But then he'd closed his eyes, very briefly, almost in a gesture of despair and pulled her close, warm and safe in his arms and he'd kissed her again, very softly on the lips. 'What is destroying me, what is tearing the heart out of me, is wanting you so much. I've been meaning to ask you to leave for weeks now, but I only have to come near you, to pass you on the stair and all my resolve weakens, my resistance melts.'

'And haven't men wanted women since the beginning of time? What makes you think you are any different?' she'd quipped, determined to challenge him and to keep her wits about her.

'Don't you think I'm different, Kate? Don't you see any sense of decency in me at all? Any honour?'

She'd tried to sit up, to restore some sort of order to the hair that was falling down all about her face and shoulders, aware of him watching every move she made. 'And why would I? You're a man, so you're used to having your own way, are ye not? Isn't a woman powerless when a man has that need on him, and can only do as she's bid?'

He'd given a soft chuckle at that, his eyes merry with unexpressed laughter. 'You've never struck me as the obedient type, Kate O'Connor.'

'Have I not?'

'No. Never.' He kissed her then till her mouth was rosy from his kisses, exploring it more fully with his persuasive tongue. And in that moment she had known that she was lost.

Nursing these sweet memories in her heart, Kate must have drifted off to sleep again, because when she woke a second time she was alone on the sofa. He had gone.

'Top of the morning to ye.' But no, there he was, standing in the bedroom doorway with Callum in his arms. 'Isn't that what you Irish say?'

Kate laughed. 'If we're feeling skittish, we do to be sure. Give him to me, I'll get him washed and dressed.' She suddenly felt shy to be here, half naked, with the master and her son. She reached for her robe, pulling it on quickly.

'He was bored, all on his own. Let him play. Do you want your wooden train, son?'

'Yes please, Papa.'

Eliot settled the child on the rug with his toys then went back over to the sofa to sit beside her, hands hanging loosely on his knees, his gaze never leaving Callum. 'I want it to be right for him. For Tyson's to be a good, strong business. For his future to be secure.'

'Sure and it will be.' Kate curled her feet under her and listened enraptured as he began to talk, to speak of his plans for the business, explaining how he hoped to save it from the current depression it seemed to be in by buying a new warehouse.

'We'll keep certain classic lines always in stock, so that our customers won't have to wait quite so long for fresh supplies. We need to keep their loyalty, and if they feel we have stock ready and waiting, we're more likely to get it.'

Kate was touched by his willingness to share these thoughts and dreams with her. Could he possibly be taking her seriously at last? 'You should consider designing footwear yourself. Aren't you the clever one with your pencil and eye for colour?'

He gave a disbelieving chuckle. 'Maybe I will one day. Who knows? For now, I shall stick to the tried and true lines, for safety.' The smile faded, to be replaced by a frown. 'You know there are murmurs of war in the Balkans, that Europe is in crisis. We've had the assassination of the King and Crown Prince of Portugal, and the arms race continues to gather momentum on all sides, one can only assume for good reason. Do you understand something of this, Kate?'

She looked at him with blank incomprehension. 'Not much, but I hear talk in the kitchen.'

'As if that isn't bad enough, Tyson's has been badly hit by Charles's overspending, by my having to bail him out of the near bankruptcy of his new firm, and now by his untimely death. Somehow, we have to claw our way back from all of that and strengthen our position before whatever is about to happen in Europe, eventually erupts. It isn't going to be easy.'

Kate was silent for a long time, striving to understand what he'd said, to appreciate his confiding in her and to comprehend the implications. 'It won't help the business having that evil monster as foreman.'

Eliot gave a low groan. 'Don't spoil this moment with that old chestnut. Not again, Kate.'

'Old chestnut is it? I can see why it pays you to turn a blind eye, making a fat profit out of the outworkers in order to rescue the company, but what about my friend Millie? She's trapped by that nasty little toad.'

She was on her feet now, needing to get this worry off her chest once and for all; to let her anger explode instead of having it fester inside her head as it had done for so long. She wanted to see that nasty, no-good Swainson who'd robbed and pawed her, beaten up Dermot, and was now practising his wickedness on Millie, get his comeuppance at last. 'You think not? You think he isn't an evil little shite, do you? Then listen to this. I'll tell you about Ned Swainson, so I will, and you can decide for yourself if he is or not.

'The fact of the matter is that Millie, that's her name, me friend. She's in dead trouble. I doubt ye've ever met her but she took over my outwork after I came here, and Swainson is up to his old tricks again. Worse, he's making her pay for the privilege of working for Tyson's in ways he shouldn't; ways I wouldn't care to describe to a gentleman such as yeself. But 'tisn't right, and the man should be punished for abusing a woman in that terrible way.'

For once he let her speak without interruption. She told him bluntly all about Millie, what she'd been forced to do in order to earn a crust to feed her babies, and still he said nothing. 'So what the bleedin' hell are ye going to do about it, eh?' Kate challenged him.

Chapter Nineteen

Swainson had believed himself to be safe. With Charles gone, there was no one now to point the finger and cast any blame in his direction. He'd got clean away with his part in the fraud, which made him chuckle with pleasure. Admittedly the factory was struggling, going through some hard times, and Charlie Boy topping himself hadn't helped one bit. He'd been ready to object if he'd been asked to take a cut in wages, although he wouldn't have protested too much had men been laid off, so long as his own job was safe. So Eliot Tyson telling him, with polite but cool detachment in his tone, that perhaps it would be best if he were to find alternative employment elsewhere, was like a bolt from the blue.

'I shall give you an excellent reference, do my utmost to assist you to find something which suits. And you can have more than the usual week's notice, a month if you need it, but I think it best if you go.'

Swainson could sense that his employer was not relishing this unpleasant task, was clearly anxious to get it over and done with as speedily as possible. Yet what were the grounds for dismissal? What could Tyson have on him? It riled Swainson to think somebody might have been telling tales about him, whether they were true or not, he'd like to know who it was. He made up his mind to be as difficult as possible. He'd certainly no intention of going quietly.

'And might I ask what offence I've caused, to be so summarily dismissed?'

Eliot had no wish to discuss so delicate a matter. He knew the man would simply deny it. There was no proof, after all. It would be Millie's word against his. 'Let's say I'm making a few changes. If Tyson's is to move forward in this new century, then we must dispose of old-fashioned systems from the past. Allowing dust and dirt and disease, which naturally comes from working with leather, to be taken into people's homes is counter-productive to that end. We must modernise.'

Swainson could feel a heat rising beneath his collar, spreading up his neck and jaw; a stink of sweat starting from under his armpits. Admittedly, he had no wife to go home to with excuses or explanations, no children who would suffer from his fall from grace, but *he* would suffer. He would lose face, and he couldn't tolerate the thought of that. The men would laugh at him, saying he'd had it coming, and he wouldn't be able to enjoy his little perks any more. Beaten by a mere girl from Poor House Lane. Oh aye, he could guess who had split on him. That little Irish whore with the big mouth. He'd seen her round the factory enough times lately, seeking the opportunity to spread her gossip. 'So what have I done exactly? You've never had no complaints before. If this is about that lass from Poor House Lane, she's had it in fer me ever since I chucked her. Had a fancy fer me once over, she did, but she's not my sort. Don't reckon she cared fer being cast off though, silly cow.'

'I really have no wish to hear details of your past love life.' It appalled him to think of Kate and this man together. What was he thinking of, letting himself be captivated by her? Yet he had to believe in her. He must. He thrust the picture from his mind as he got up from his desk to move to the window and look out over the factory buildings.

Swainson hated him for that proprietorial air alone. Most men of his class didn't show the least interest in business, being content to take the profit and leave the dirty work to the employees. Why couldn't Tyson be like that? Why couldn't he keep his interfering nose out of what didn't concern him?

Eliot cleared his throat before continuing, 'You'll be aware that I've endured more than my fair share of tragedies, but I still have my son to consider and, as I say, there are to be radical changes. I intend to build a warehouse for stock-holding which is the latest, most modern way of thinking, I believe. I shall extend the factory and, in the fullness of time, outwork will be stopped, and all manufacturing done within the factory itself.'

'For which you do not think me capable? Why is that?'

A short pause and then Eliot turned to him with a bland and distant smile. 'I think that perhaps we need new blood. Yes, that's it exactly. New blood. New ideas. A new beginning. Trade has not been good, as you know, what with the increase in the price of leather, competition from America, and rumblings of war which has added to the scarcity of raw materials, not forgetting our own personal difficulties. Losing my brother leaves me responsible for his family too, you understand. Money is tight, so we must do something fairly radical if Tyson's is to survive.'

The man was lecturing him as if he, the foreman of this dratted factory, didn't understand the first thing about the industry. 'I know all of this and you do realise I could go to one of your competitors, or start my own enterprise.'

'You must do as you think fit, whatever suits you best. Any future employer can come to me for the necessary character references. And of course you'll be provided with a handsome bonus for your long years of service.' There was a note of dismissal now in the tone, of wanting to draw the interview to a close, and nothing he had said gave Swainson one iota of reassurance. What kind of character reference would that be, he wondered.

'I feel I must object, most strongly.'

'I'm afraid there is no more to be said on the subject.'

'I could speak to my union. They'll have something to say.'

Tyson's frown deepened and his jaw set into a hard line. 'That is not an action I would recommend. Matters could get even more – unpleasant – were you to make a fuss. Go quietly, Swainson, if you've any sense.'

And that was it, the end of the line with Tyson's, cast off and dismissed like a pair of worn out shoes, to be replaced by *new blood*! Swainson was almost choking with rage, for he knew well enough who to blame for this decision, who to hold responsible. She'd had her revenge after all, the scheming little minx. Oh, but they'd find they couldn't cast him off quite so easily.

–

Fanny tied a sacking apron over her skirt, picked up the first candlestick and the bottle of silver cleaner with a weary sigh. The aunts were constantly finding her things to clean and her fingers were sore with all the scrubbing and polishing she had to do these days. The work seemed endless. She'd leave this place tomorrow if only she could persuade Dennis to go with her.

Mrs Petty sat opposite, comfortably ensconced in her housekeeper's chair with her skirt tucked up above her knees and her feet soaking like fat white fish in an enamel bowl of salt water. There was just the pair of them in the kitchen, Ida having gone off to see old Askew and bring in the vegetables for the evening meal. In theory, this was supposed to be Fanny's rest hour after lunch, but Aunt Vera had insisted the silver be polished now, without delay.

'Clean enough to see my face in it, Fanny,' she'd instructed.

'Silly old besom. Who'd want to see her vinegar face in owt, sour as an old pickle.'

'What was that, Fanny?' Mrs Petty opened her eyes, dragging her mind away from the blissful warmth of the water soothing her bunions.

Realising she'd spoken her thoughts out loud, Fanny quickly improvised, remembering a tidbit of information she'd heard from Dennis only that morning. 'I were thinking of what a pickle we'd all be in if the factory closed. We might all lose us jobs then, eh?'

'Don't be foolish, girl. The factory isn't going to close, and no one's going to lose their jobs.'

'Dennis told me only this morning how there'd been a threat of another strike. That Jack Milburn and his cronies, Bill Grigson and Tom Perry, weren't they the ringleaders responsible for the last one? Well, they've threatened to call another if Swainson isn't reinstated.'

Mrs Petty leaned forward, all ears. The last thing she wanted was to risk losing her position, not when she was so close to achieving that little house she'd set her heart on, on the Fylde coast. Trouble at the factory had a nasty habit of rebounding on them all. 'What's this about a strike? Don't garble, girl, draw breath and tell the story proper.'

Fanny set down the candlestick, glad of the distraction, and began to relate her tale. 'Dennis says that Jack Milburn were waiting fer t'master t'other morning, that pockmarked face of his hard as iron, demanding to know why the foreman had been dismissed. The master looked a bit flabbergasted like, Dennis said, but he didn't deny it and Milburn said he didn't recall the subject being mentioned or the union being consulted on the matter.'

'And why should he care?' Mrs Petty tartly enquired.

'Milburn says he might be the foreman but he's also one of them, one of the workers; "Swainson might have his faults but the men are used to him. Gives us a fair hearing when we need one." That's what Jack Milburn said.'

Fanny had adopted a masculine tone of voice, rather fancying herself as an actress. Mrs Petty put a stop to it. 'Get on with it, girl. Fair hearing indeed. Did Mr Tyson not tell him that there are some who would disagree?'

Fanny eagerly nodded, enjoying her performance. 'That's exactly what the master said. But Milburn puts on that snarl of his and says the men can't be held responsible for folk what don't like him.'

'Nasty piece of merchandise, that Milburn. Stoke up trouble in a barrel of herrings, he would.'

Fanny lowered her voice to a whisper. 'Dennis said that at this point there were a snort of laughter from someone at the back of the crowd. Then one chap, Billy Branthwaite, says, "And some women are mighty grateful for his care and attention." Can you believe it? What a thing to say?' Fanny's eyes grew round with excitement. 'Course, Dennis says that Jack and his mate Bill Grigson are probably in cahoots with Swainson over nice little sidelines they've got going for 'em, and other little jobs they do for him, like seeing to that Irish lad that time. You know, Kate O'Connor's brother. Gave him a right pasting, apparently.'

Mrs Petty had forgotten all about her sore feet as she listened with avid attention to Fanny's tale. 'Is this some yarn yer spinning me girl?'

'Nay, it's gospel truth. Jack Milburn doesn't bat an eyelid over these ribald comments about Swainson, says how the men were quite happy with him, that no one's bloody perfect.'

'Language, Fanny.'

'Sorry Mrs Petty, but that were Jack Milburn what said that, not me. Then he reminds the master how it wouldn't do the factory no good at all if there were to be another strike. "Happen you underestimate the strength of feeling among the men," he says. Then asks if he's had any complaints from the women outworkers, and t'boss says he hasn't. Course, who would listen if they did complain, Mrs P? Men never do listen, do they? My Dennis might as well be deaf, blind and dumb for all the notice he takes when I talk to him.'

'Get on with your story, girl. What happened next?'

'Well then Milburn smiles, if you can call it a smile. With them nasty yellow teeth he looks more like a ferret. Says he's heard of no complaints. Not one. "What about you lads?" he asks, turning to his mates, who of course all back him up.'

Fanny puts on a sneer in imitation of Milburn's expression. 'We'd advise you to let him keep his job then, Mr Tyson, for the sake of the company. All right? Best all round, wouldn't you say?'

'And is he going to?' Mrs Petty breathlessly enquired as she attempted to lift her feet, now gone quite cold, from the bowl and dry them off.

'Well he must, don't yer reckon, since he don't want the firm to go under, and seeing as how he's knocking off the nursemaid. So how can he blame Swainson for doing the self-same thing?'

Mrs Petty knocked the bowl flying as her feet crashed to the floor in shock, sending water splashing everywhere. 'He's *what*?' She really should put a stop to this impertinence forthwith, but hardly able to catch her breath or contain her curiosity, she could only warn, 'Mind what you say, lass. You'd best have proof for such an accusation.'

'Oh, I've proof all right. Saw her wi' me own eyes, didn't I? Coming from his room one morning, naked as the day she were born.'

–

It took no time at all for this delicious morsel to fly all around town and once more Eliot felt the cold shoulder of hostility. Whatever he had suffered previously was nothing by comparison. On that occasion the rumours had been entirely untrue, a complete fiction devised by Lucy's malicious tongue. This time he knew that he had no defence. He was guilty. He had indeed taken the girl to his bed. He could not deny it. Friends he had known for

269

years crossed the road rather than speak to him. Customers cancelled orders, Whineray asked if he might wish to consider resigning from the Town Council, which Eliot bluntly refused to do. Even his own servants either froze him with the ferocity of their disapproval or sniggered behind their hands.

Never having been the kind of man who took advantage of those in his employ, Eliot still couldn't believe how very stupidly he'd behaved, and deeply regretted his actions. The girl seemed to have bewitched him and he couldn't get her out of his head. Perhaps it was time that he at least get her out of his house.

It was a day or two later, a crisp autumn afternoon and the aunts were out, either 'going visiting' or 'paying calls'. Kate was playing hide and seek with Callum on the lawn. There weren't many places to hide and she didn't allow him to go anywhere near the outhouses but he was still of that age when, if he had his eyes covered and couldn't see you, he believed he couldn't be seen either. Kate would count to ten, pretend to hunt for him and then catch him, swing him up in her arms and kiss his plump, flushed cheeks. His floppy woollen beret which she had knitted herself and was meant to keep his head warm in the winter sunshine, would slide off and roll away, and then they'd both chase it, pop it back on and start all over again.

'Catch me again, Mammy. Catch me again.'

Ever since Amelia had died, she'd allowed him to start calling her by that name again, so long as they were alone. It was their secret.

The game came to an abrupt halt when she saw Eliot striding across the garden and, grabbing Callum up into her arms, she set off quickly in pursuit. There were matters

270

she still needed to discuss with him: not only whether or not Callum was to be sent away to school as the aunts had threatened, but also Millie's situation and whether he had done anything about that yet. This seemed as good a moment as any.

Kate caught up with him beneath the rose arbour. He used often to cut roses to bring into the house for Amelia during her long illness, and now he hovered uncertainly, clippers in hand, seemingly trying to decide whether to cut a few late blooms or not.

'They're beautiful, so they are. Wasn't the Dorothy Perkins one of the mistress's favourites? Such a heavenly scent. I'm glad to see ye home early from the factory for once, I was hoping ye might have a minute to spare. But then aren't I always pleased to see ye?' Kate couldn't prevent a smile twitching at the corners of her lips, and a stain of colour coming into her cheeks as she recalled the night they'd so recently spent together.

He gave not a flicker of a smile, merely frowned and spoke in brusque, clipped tones, and Kate felt herself shrink inside. How was it he blew so hot and cold with her? 'I'm afraid it is but a momentary escape. I felt the need for a breath of fresh air but I must return to work shortly.' As if to prove this fact, he began to walk away, clippers still in hand. Kate ran after him.

'Please don't go. I'd like to know what's happened about Swainson. It's important that I speak to you.'

Still he didn't pause but rather lengthened his stride, putting yet more distance between them. Once again Kate was forced to trot, the weight of Callum balanced on her hip slowing her down considerably.

'Mammy, let me walk. Put me down, Mammy.'

'Stop wriggling and keep still. It's quicker if I carry ye.' Kate began to feel hot and flustered, angry that Eliot could so mulishly ignore her, and quite out of breath with the effort of trying to keep up with him. 'Will you hold on a minute ye daft eejit.' She must have lost her head to address him like that, calling him names, and without even a 'sir', or an 'if you please' but still he ignored her. He pushed open the garden gate and set off towards the river as if he hadn't even heard a word. Kate really saw red.

'*Eliot*, fer God's sake will you stop fer a minute afore I drop him.'

He did stop then, but only to march back to her and snatch Callum from her arms. 'If you are not even capable of holding a child safely, then perhaps you're the wrong person to be taking care of him at all, and I should dismiss you.' The small boy, alarmed by their angry voices, opened his mouth wide and began to wail.

Kate told him to hush, instantly turning her attention back to Eliot. 'And what's that supposed to mean? What's got into you of a sudden?' She could feel her heart banging like a drum, since she believed she knew only too well. She'd become an embarrassment to him. He was out to find fault so that he could be rid of the problem of having her around, rid of the temptation. Couldn't she tell by the way he was glaring at her with such cold indifference, quite at odds to the looks she'd enjoyed from him the other night. She forced herself to be calm. 'Eliot, will ye speak to me properly, fer God's sake, and stop blowing so hot and cold? I don't know where the hell I am.'

'I think you've lost your manners, Kate O'Connor. It's *Mr Tyson* to you. Or sir.'

'Is it indeed?'

'Yes.'

'I didn't notice the need for such formality the other night.'

'It's needed now.'

'I see. And why is that, might I ask?'

'Because I am the master, dammit, that's why. And I'll not have you telling me what to do.'

Kate stood fuming in silent defiance but he was right, of course. Despite what they had shared beneath the sheets, he was still the master and she the maid. How could she deny it? He was as far removed from her as ever. Further, it seemed. She'd been wrong to succumb to her emotions so foolishly, although some would say he was more in the wrong for taking advantage of her. Yet, deep down, Kate knew it hadn't been like that at all. Neither of them had been able to help what happened, and she didn't blame him, not in the least. She just wanted it to mean as much to him as it did to her. Tears pricked the backs of her eyes which she blinked rapidly away, gritting her teeth in an effort to regain control. She must remember that her mission was for Millie, surely far more important than any tender sensitivities on her own account. She must concentrate on her friend's problems and stop daydreaming of what could never be, even if she had overstepped that fine line by instinctively using his Christian name, by asking, nay *telling* him to sack Swainson. But had he done so? Wasn't she itching to know what had happened to the old bastard?

Bored with the lack of attention, Callum was working himself up into a fine tantrum, yelling and tugging at her skirts, urging his mammy to play catch with him again.

'Will ye just wait awhile, me cushla. Mammy's busy. We'll play in a minute. Why don't ye sit on the grass and make Mammy a nice daisy chain. There ye are now. See how long ye can make it.' She gave him a kiss and plucked a few daisies to get him started, and as if by magic the tears abruptly dried. 'I'm sorry, *sir*. Don't I forget meself at times?'

'I think you forget yourself in more ways than one, Kate O'Connor. You are not this child's mammy. Not any more. Amelia was his mother, and will remain so in his memory for ever. See that you remember that simple fact in future, if you please.'

Kate felt her cheeks start to burn and the struggle for control grew harder; tears clogged her throat and her eyes began to smart in raw agony. She lifted a bleak face up to him. 'You're right. Course y'are. It won't happen again, only...' He started to walk away from her along the path, and Kate saw that through her own folly, she was losing him. She ran after him. 'It's just that I'm that upset over me friend Millie, d'you see?'

He didn't pause, not for a second, not seeming to hear her or want to listen, and Kate struggled to keep pace. 'Have ye done anything about poor Millie... have you? Answer me, ye miserable git? Or have you let that nasty piece of shite off yet again?'

He stopped at last, rounding on her with cold fury in his eyes. 'You really should watch your language, Kate O'Connor. Particularly in front of my son. As a matter of fact, no one seems to agree with your assessment of Swainson. There have been no other complaints about him. Not one. I've heard some vindictive nonsense from girls at the factory in my time, spreading malicious gossip over this, that and the other, but never any tale as fanciful as yours. And bearing in mind the grudge you already bear against that man, I've decided that your tale cannot be trusted.'

Kate gaped in shock. ''Tis the truth, I swear it. You need to sack him, get yourself a new foreman, so help me, before it's too late.'

'Oh come on, Kate, you've been out to get your own back on Swainson from the very first moment I set eyes on you, all because he refused to pay what you considered to be your due wages.'

'And he attacked our Dermot,' she burst out, biting her lip when she realised she'd only made matters worse by this interruption. 'And me.'

He gave her a wintry smile that froze her heart. 'So you once told me, not very convincingly, I seem to recall. And so, as the vendetta continues, you've decided to involve your friend, have you? Very clever. Except that it won't work. I'm not quite the fool you take me for. You're sadly mistaken if you think you can tell me how to run my own factory, as well as ruling every corner of my personal life, not to mention insinuating yourself into my bed.'

Kate jerked as if she'd been struck. 'El – Mr Tyson… sir… Sure and ye can't mean that. I don't believe ye do. Are you accusing me of forcing meself upon you?'

He had the grace to look a mite shame-faced and turn his gaze away. 'You understand my meaning well enough.'

'You think I lied, just to get me own back on that no-good piece of sh – dirt?'

He pushed his face down close to hers but there was no kindness in it, not a hint that he might change his mind and kiss her instead. It was almost as if those precious moments of intimacy had never taken place. 'I'm saying that you can push a man so far and no further, that I've reached the limit of my patience with you. The aunts are right, you are a very clever little manipulator, and know how to take advantage of a man, how to use your charm, your feminine wiles, but not quite clever enough. Now I suggest that you pack your bags and go.'

She taking advantage of *him*? Now there was a laugh! Wasn't she the victim here? Kate didn't understand exactly what being a clever little manipulator meant, though she could guess. Wasn't he just trying to run away from what he'd done, as all men did, particularly bosses, and had done so through generations of abuse upon women? And she'd been stupid enough to believe this one might be different. Hadn't he himself claimed to be different? She was deeply disappointed in him. Oh, but she'd never felt such rage in all her born days.

Kate stood her ground, arms akimbo, and shouted after him as he strode away. 'Ye've no right to speak to me like that. No right at all. Jaysus, Mary and Joseph, I'll make you take back every blethering word, so help me. Damn you to hell, Eliot Tyson. And will you stand still when I'm shouting after you, or do ye want all the neighbours to hear what ye've been up to, cause I've a mind to tell 'em.'

Not even this threat gave him pause. He strode away without glancing back, let alone returning to plead for her silence or to continue with an argument he considered closed.

Furious that she had failed on all counts: failed Millie, failed to keep control of her emotions, failed utterly to win his love, even failed Amelia, who had become her friend, and with all sight of him now blinded by tears, Kate stormed back across the lawn towards the house. Only when she reached the nursery did she realise that she'd left Callum behind. Drat the man! He'd got her into such a rage she couldn't even think straight. Dashing back out again, he was no longer on the lawn. Wouldn't she just strangle Eliot Tyson for this! He'd taken Callum with him. He'd rob her of her only son when she was at her most vulnerable. Well he'd see that she wasn't so easily disposed of.

Chapter Twenty

Kate made no attempt to leave. She didn't pack her bags. She made no mention to the aunts on their return that she'd been given the sack. She politely took their coats and hung them up, carefully sticking a hat pin into each discarded hat, then handed them the silver salver where a collection of cards waited for them from afternoon callers.

'Oh dear,' said Cissie. 'We missed Lucy again. She has called every day this week and found us out. We must pay her a return call tomorrow, sister dear.'

Vera did not respond but addressed Kate directly. 'Did you clean that closet, as instructed?'

'No. I mean, I've not quite finished it yet.' And, seeing the frozen stare, hurried back upstairs to get on with the job forthwith. Sure and wouldn't Eliot regret his harsh words the minute he calmed down? He'd not want her to leave, not at all. Hadn't they made a pact, for her to allow him to adopt her lovely boy, so long as she could stay on as Callum's nursemaid? Even if Callum was sent to a fine school, or Eliot employed a governess, surely to goodness he'd need her in the holidays, so how could he sack her, it would be breaking their agreement? It could never happen.

Deep inside, Kate was filled with uncertainties, but still she made no move to pack. She cleaned out the closet, as directed, and filled the rest of the time cleaning and tidying the nursery, carefully following all of Amelia's rules, using all the skills she'd learned from her lovely mistress.

Kate heard the front door bang around seven o'clock, and rubbing her hands clean on the back of her uniform dress, tidying her hair as she went, she set off down the stairs to face her employer. That afternoon while she'd worked, she'd given herself a thorough talking to, sternly reminding herself that Eliot Tyson was the master of this house, and of the factory, and she really should remember that. What had happened between them, on two separate occasions, had been a mistake: the result of grief after the loss of his lovely wife, or pure physical need, and not some deep attraction on his part. But that didn't make it a sin, no matter what the gossips might say. She loved him, even though he didn't love her. Though what she wouldn't give to see that smirk wiped off Fanny's face.

He was standing in the hall, taking off his coat, handing his scarf and hat to Fanny when Kate hurtled down the stairs, almost tripping over the last few steps in her eagerness.

She bobbed a curtsey and gave an awkward little laugh, wanting to show she bore him no ill will. After all, didn't they both know that he couldn't manage without her? And she, for one, was more than ready to apologise for her impudence, fully anticipating that he'd do the same, then wouldn't they be right as ninepence again? All well between them. After that, she'd collect Callum and enjoy a quiet half hour bathing him before putting him to bed. She had the water all ready and waiting, and his favourite currant biscuit to go with his cocoa.

'I'd like to say again how very sorry I am for me impudence this afternoon. It surely is none of my business who ye employ at the factory.' Kate desperately attempted to put proper sincerity in her voice. She certainly hadn't given up hope of getting rid of Swainson, but she'd obviously have to bide her time a bit longer. She really couldn't risk losing her place here, the chance to be with Callum.

He frowned down at her. 'You are absolutely correct in the assumption that it is none of your business, as I believe I've told you before.' Eliot gave her a sideways glance and saw that her smile, as always, was entrancing and he could feel his anger draining away, his resolve weakening. Yet he was determined not to show it, not wishing to be seen as easy meat. He'd lost his temper this afternoon, perhaps said things he shouldn't, but a part of him did wonder if what the aunts said was correct: that she was indeed a clever and manipulative liar, that she'd planned the whole thing from the start. The adoption, her being taken on here as nursemaid, and even their lovemaking. She was still talking and he hadn't heard a word.

'So, where is the little monster? Hasn't he been the lucky one, going to the factory, and being allowed to stay up so late? I'll never hear the last of this.'

'What are you talking about? What do you mean – staying up late? Hear the last of what?'

'Of Callum – of Master Callum I should say, being allowed to visit the factory with you. What else?'

'Callum? But he's not with me. He's with you, isn't he? I certainly left him with you this afternoon in the garden. Why in heaven's name did you imagine he was with me?'

Kate went very still. 'Dear God, then if he's not with you, where the hell is he?'

Lucy had never felt more pleased with herself. What marvellous luck that she had chosen that very moment to call. What an opportunity! She hadn't quite been able to believe her good fortune.

She'd tried for weeks to catch Eliot in, to demand to know why her allowance had been reduced to an almost penurious level. The man simply didn't seem to understand how very expensive children were to feed and clothe and educate. But then how could he, with only a workhouse bastard to care for, who'd be grateful for any scraps off his table? And then, as if by magic, the child himself had appeared before her, grinning in that inane way of his, and holding out some daisy chain or other. It had been the easiest thing in the world to pick him up and simply walk away.

She'd walked quickly, rapidly turning over possibilities in her mind. What could she do with him? The river was the obvious solution. Children were constantly wandering off. What would be more natural than that he should get too near the water and fall in. Yet there were too many people about, nannies walking their charges, maids cleaning the steps of the fine Georgian houses along Kent Terrace and Thorny Hills. Schoolgirls coming out of the High School building. People strolling on the wide sward of grass by the river on this pleasant autumn afternoon. Someone might easily spot one small boy struggling in the water. And how could she make good her escape quickly enough?

But she must do something. It was essential that she take full advantage of this piece of good fortune. There would be no question then but that her own darlings would inherit the company, as they should, as they deserved to do after what Eliot had done to Charles.

If it hadn't been for Charles being sacked, by his own brother for God's sake, her beloved husband would be alive today, and she wouldn't be reduced to begging for the small comforts of life she surely deserved. No tears welled in her eyes at this thought, no sense of bereavement. Lucy felt only a searing, burning anger, one which culminated in a powerful need for revenge.

And then it came to her, the perfect solution. She would take the child back where he belonged, to the workhouse. This time, to the big Union Workhouse up on Kendal Green where the Guardians would keep a better watch over him, or perhaps pack him off to some other, more distant, charitable establishment. She didn't have the time to search for such a place herself, but she was quite certain that once incarcerated in the workhouse, no one would think to look for him there.

And then her own children's future would be assured.

She would insist on positions in the firm for both Jack and Georgie, at an appropriate juncture. Hopefully, Eliot would not live to a ripe old age, or he would retire and ultimately hand it over to his two nephews. In the meantime, she would make certain that she at least squeezed a decent allowance out of him. The thought suddenly came to her that Eliot might marry again, arresting her galloping progress across Gooseholme and making her hide behind St George's Church to catch her breath while she considered this possibility.

The child was starting to whimper. 'Where's Mammy? I want Mammy.'

Paying no attention to his distress, Lucy's thoughts remained fixed on the problem of Eliot. What if he did marry again? Another, younger, more fertile bride would ruin everything. She dismissed the idea at once. By the time he'd got over grieving for Amelia, she would have thought of some way to put a stop on that too.

'I want Mammy.'

'Hush child. Stop your noise.' She gave him a little shake, which made him cry even louder. 'Oh, for goodness' sake, shut up!' she shouted.

Callum was so startled he jumped as if he'd been physically struck, then opened his mouth wide and began to howl. Lucy was furious, but felt obliged to pick him up in order to stop the terrible din he was making. She couldn't bring herself to actually cuddle the child but did jiggle him up and down for a bit, which, after a few minutes, seemed to do the trick. The sobs faded somewhat but he had a disgusting mess all over his face now, dripping from his nose. She put him quickly down again and set off at a cracking pace with a firm grip on his hand, dragging him behind her so that the small boy had to run to keep pace, his little plump legs going like pistons. Once or twice he almost tumbled over his own feet, and she had to jerk him upright, but the crying continued unabated.

Lucy took the precaution of finding a quiet corner of a back street, where she took off his smart little smock and shorts and removed his nice clean underwear. She then set about rubbing dirt and mud all over the sobbing infant, including his carefully washed hair till it stuck out in spikes all about his little head and his tears made tracks of dirt down his round cheeks. She couldn't do anything about the fact that he looked well nourished but she ruthlessly ripped and muddied his clothes before putting them back on him, minus the underwear, of course. That was much better. Now he looked as he should: a pauper in need of care.

'*Want Mammy!*' the small boy screamed, stamping his feet. '*Where's Mammy?*'

'Mammy has gone. You must come with me now.'

He resisted, dragging his feet as she tried to pull him along, then threw himself to the ground, screaming and kicking his heels in a frenzy of temper. For a moment Lucy panicked, looking frantically about to see if they'd been observed. Fortunately, there was no one around. And then she smacked him, very hard, on the backs of his legs and that quietened him beautifully. He was staring at her now with shocked and fearful eyes, small mouth pouted in deep distress as he gave great hiccupping sobs.

'Now be a good boy and do as you're told, or you'll get another smack,' she warned, and was gratified to see that he understood perfectly. Probably the only language bastards like him did understand.

At the back of her mind, Lucy had been planning what tale she would tell the guardians, turning over possible problems. Perhaps she should say that she'd found the boy wandering in the middle of the road, in dire danger of being run down by a carriage or motor. She felt wary of exposing herself too openly by crossing over the river and walking through the busy part of town.

Also, it occurred to her that the Poor Law Guardians might ask his name and he was perfectly capable, at five, of remembering it. They might even ask her own name, or insist she fill in a form or something, which would never do. Not that they knew her at the workhouse since, fortunately enough, she'd never been one to go in for charitable good works, as Amelia had done. Even so, she must take care to get it right. This operation was proving to be far more problematic than she'd first thought.

Undaunted, she readjusted her plans. She wrote, 'My name is Allan' on a luggage label she bought in a shop and tied it to his wrist. No one would have any reason to doubt that, and the name was near enough to the sound of his own to cause the child confusion in his present, distressed state. No doubt he was young enough to forget his real name, if they called him by the new one often enough. And looking so messy and dirty, they'd simply assume that his mother was dead, or couldn't care for him any more.

Lucy was perfectly certain that despite the workhouse being only a short walking distance from Thorny Hills, it might as well be a million miles away for all the good it would do one small boy. Once incarcerated within those solid stone walls, he'd never see his mother, or his adopted father, ever again.

She went the long way, taking a detour behind Sandes Avenue and up through the woods and back streets to Kendal Green. It was with great thankfulness that she finally spotted the limestone walls and high windows of the workhouse. She sat him on the step, the child's head now nodding with exhaustion, and ordered him sternly not to move. Lucy clanged the bell using the attached rope and rushed back across the street to hide round a corner, where she could safely watch proceedings. She saw the door open, light spill out and a woman appear. She noticed the child at once and didn't seem in the least surprised, merely took his hand, spoke a few quiet words to him then brought him to her side. Pausing only to glance up and down the length of the street, she led him inside and closed the door.

Lucy smiled to herself. Good heavens, if she'd know it was as easy as this, she'd have done it long since.

–

At first they weren't too concerned, thinking he might have become locked in one of the many garden sheds or outhouses as Askew had gone about his work during the course of the afternoon. When there was no sign of him there, nor anywhere in the house or conservatory, Kate gradually began to lose control. Where could he have gone? She found his soft wool beret lying discarded on the lawn, not far from where they'd been playing. Kate snatched it up and sank her face into it, breathing in the scent of him.

She felt numb with fear, convinced that he must have wandered off while she and Eliot were quarrelling, that he'd fallen into the river. Eliot's reaction too was to turn and run down to the slow moving river. It wasn't too deep in this part, but after a desperate search it seemed that this had not been his fate.

'How far could he have got though, in the time? As far as the weir?'

They both looked upriver to where the water slid over a shallow ridge below which it became fast moving, dark and deep. Standing on the bank, soaking wet, they considered this dreadful possibility in silence for some minutes. 'I hope to God, not that far,' Eliot murmured at last.

Kate was haunted by visions of him running away, after being frightened by their raised voices. Perhaps he'd even got as far as the town and who knew what might have befallen him there? Been knocked under the hooves of a runaway horse, run over by a motor. Or maybe he was still playing hide and seek and it had gone wrong and he was trapped somewhere: in an outhouse, or stuck under one of the bridges. Kate was frantic to know where to start searching, which might be the most likely place, there being far too many possibilities for a small boy to hide. And while she shivered and wept and dithered, Eliot took charge.

'Askew, go round the neighbours. Look in their carriage houses, their garden sheds and outhouses. They all know you, so you'll meet with no objections.'

Dennis was dispatched to alert the local constabulary, and Fanny and Ida ordered to search every corner of the house, though they'd done it twice already. 'He might be hiding in the attic, playing some silly game. Search every cupboard, every chest, every corner.'

It was Mrs Petty who put forward the possibility of abduction. 'He could have been taken by gypsies. They're often about at this time of year, heading north with their horses. Maybe one of them has pinched the li'le lad. He'd fetch a good price, being so bonny and red haired, if'n they sold him on to some childless family.' And then seeing the master's stricken face, flushed bright crimson as she realised what she'd said. Her warning was dismissed as another of her silly superstitions, something she was prone to.

Everyone searched for the rest of that day and all night, and for days afterwards; the servants, Eliot and Kate, the local police, friends and neighbours, even the two aunts grudgingly did their bit to help, but they found no sign of him. Kate refused to rest, couldn't eat, could no nothing but walk about in a daze of exhaustion, calling his name. Endlessly and restlessly searching the same places over and over again.

'We'll find him in the end. I know we will. I feel it in my heart. He isn't dead. I would know it if he were dead.'

In the days following, the entire district was alerted to keep a look out for the missing child. Sadly, it was over a week before a description of him appeared in the Westmorland Gazette, and then it was to describe him as wearing a smart blue smock and shorts, and polished patent shoes. A small, fuzzy picture was reproduced, taken the year before which didn't look like Callum at all.

'He's grown so big since then,' Kate groaned, still clutching his floppy beret to her breast, carrying it round with her like a talisman, as if to prove that he would soon be found, alive and well, and would be in need of it again. 'Oh, why didn't we have his picture taken again?'

'We'd need to take one every single month to keep a check on his progress,' Eliot sharply responded, not a jot of kindness in his tone.

Had anyone up at the Union Workhouse read the paper with more than their usual cursory glance, they would not necessarily have made any connection with that pretty little toddler seated on his mama's lap with any one of the half dozen or so pauper children who'd turned up on their doorstep in the last few weeks.

Another week went by, and then another, and still there was no sight of him. Deep down, everyone was beginning to lose hope, yet couldn't quite bring themselves to admit it, or to stop looking. Eliot was sorely neglecting his business, and Kate could think of nothing but her son, filled with guilt that it must all be her fault.

If only she'd not let him loose to play on the lawn. Why hadn't she kept a proper eye on him? How could he simply disappear in a matter of moments?

–

It was late in the evening and they were sitting in the parlour sipping a hot toddy, exhausted after several more fruitless hours of searching and, for the first time, the two of them talked as they never had before. Mostly they shared their feelings about losing Callum, their fears over what might have happened to him. Eliot even took her in his arms and Kate clung to him as she wept, united in their grief. His kindness brought a sort of comfort, and at the same time an increase in her pain, for Kate could tell by the way he sorrowfully patted her shoulder, that he still saw her as nothing more than a young, naïve maid towards whom he felt a considerable sense of guilt. She so longed to tell him that she didn't care about what had happened between them, she didn't blame him in the least, not deep down in her heart. Didn't she love the bones of him, so wasn't it the most natural thing in the world that she would give herself to him?

Instead, thinking of the loss of her lovely boy, the words came out all wrong. 'If only you'd listened to me about Swainson, instead of arguing and shouting, Callum would never have run away.'

Eliot looked at her and sighed. 'Oh Kate, is that all you can think of, Swainson? He is the least of our worries right now. If you hadn't been so obsessed with your petty vengeance against him, I agree, we might well have paid more attention to Callum.'

'And if you hadn't started shouting and frightened him,' Kate grumbled.

The brown eyes narrowed, taking on their familiar cool, distant expression, all too clearly reminding her that he was the clever, arrogant male, and she a mere woman. 'I quite understand that as hope has begun to fade, fear has turned to despair but we mustn't let it turn into anger and blame. Where is the point in that?'

'Where is the point? I'll tell you where is the point. Because he's my child. My *son*. That's the bloody point.'

'*My* son, Kate,' he softly reminded her.

She bit back the denial which sprang to her lips, swallowed the bitter taste of it. 'So what if we don't get him back? Ever?'

Eliot had lost a beloved wife, and now the child he'd come to think of as his own. He too could taste the bitter aloes of defeat and was irritated and annoyed by her obstinate determination to place all the blame on to him. 'Why can't you accept that not everyone has the same way of going about things as you? Swainson may well be a harsh taskmaster, a foolish man perhaps, but not necessarily an evil one. Otherwise why would the men at the factory support him?'

'No doubt because it's in their interests to,' Kate shrewdly surmised.

'Oh, Kate, you are growing paranoid.'

'Don't use your fancy long words on me.' And she burst into tears.

She rather hoped he would draw her into his arms once more but he leapt to his feet, chestnut eyes blazing with a blistering fury. His jaw tightened, mouth twisted with shock and disgust. 'How can you stand there arguing about Swainson when your child is missing? Have you no heart, woman? How can I believe in your innocence when you are so utterly callous?'

Kate gasped, realising with disbelief and horror that it was not with the foreman that he was angry, but with her. He didn't see himself as responsible at all. He laid the blame for Callum being lost entirely upon her. 'You d-don't understand. It all springs from that – from our argument about Swainson – and your stubborn refusal to listen. You're an obstinate, arrogant bastard, that's what you are, Eliot Tyson.'

'Am I indeed? And had you not been so set against my foreman from the beginning, I might have taken what you had to say more seriously. As it is, I don't believe a word. You're making it all up so that you can throw the blame for Callum's disappearance on to someone else. Well, it won't work, Kate O'Connor. Don't think you can wriggle out of your responsibility so easily. Had you been a decent mother to him in the first place, none of this would have happened. You were utterly feckless and irresponsible from the start.'

'I was not!' She wanted to leap at him, to claw that damning expression from his face, or fall into his arms and have him tell her he didn't mean any of it, that all would be well and her darling Callum would be found at any moment.

But he wasn't even looking at her. He was pacing the parlour in a lather of temper, pausing only to brandish a fist or wag an accusing finger in her face as he raged at her, their moment of rare intimacy gone. 'First you almost get the child run over by wandering in front of my carriage, then you take him back to Poor House Lane where he picked up a sickness that was almost the death of him, and *now* you've lost him altogether. *What kind of mother are you?*'

Kate felt as if she'd been slapped. She stared at him in stunned disbelief, the snarl of contempt on his face, in his voice, seeming to vibrate through every jangled nerve in her body. She couldn't quite believe that his kindness had evaporated so swiftly, and so completely. She took a steadying breath, desperately striving to calm herself. 'Is that what you really think?'

He snorted his contempt. 'Don't tell me you're going to pretend that you didn't benefit from the adoption. You were far more concerned with getting yourself a fine job, not to mention eagerly climbing into my bed at any conceivable opportunity, to pay proper attention to your own child. But then, what else would one expect in a girl from Poor House Lane?'

It was as if he'd stuck a knife into her heart, and then twisted it. Only when he saw the shock in her eyes did Eliot see that perhaps he'd gone too far. But it was too late. The words couldn't be taken back so he continued to glare at her in cold fury, stubbornly refusing to retract a word, or to allow a morsel of pity to creep into his heart.

Kate turned on her heel and walked calmly away. Up in the nursery she slipped out of the uniform dress and pulled on the only other frock she possessed, a plain brown fustian which had been provided in place of the one burnt on the garden bonfire. Then she wrapped her shawl about her head and left the house, all too aware of Fanny trailing after her, standing at the door and silently watching as she walked away.

Within a short half hour, Kate was back in Poor House Lane, back where she had started, back where she belonged; only this time with no hope of escape, and knowing her child was lost for good.

Chapter Twenty-One

It was worse than before. This time she not only had no work but also no hope of getting any. Bad enough to be without references, and live in the hovels of Poor House Lane but she couldn't even go to Swainson and ask for outwork, not now, not after all that had happened. And somehow she'd lost the stomach for living here; for the stench of sharing her bed with a gaggle of urine-soaked children while Clem and Millie made low grunting noises of love in some shadowy corner; for the overflowing privy and the groaning pain in an empty belly. She found herself thinking with longing of clean sheets, of her lovely nursery and lost privacy, of crisp clean uniforms and Mrs Petty's roast lamb dinners.

And all the time, Kate was haunted by the loss of her child.

She got through each day in a daze, spending much of it endlessly searching the back streets and yards of Kendal, just in case Callum had got himself lost and someone had taken him in, like a stray dog or cat. She would see his small, beaming face everywhere, recognise the bright copper of his hair and run to grab some child who proved to be a perfect stranger. There were no tears now, just a terrible choking pain clamped like an iron band about her chest. But then she didn't have time for tears. She was too busy searching. He must be somewhere. How far could one small boy travel on his own? And if he was in Kendal, she would find him, she was sure of it. If only she looked hard enough.

Every evening she would wend her weary way back to Poor House Lane and Millie would fold her arms about her friend, and the pair would weep silently together, grieving for this golden child they had both loved.

And then there were the nightmares: an awareness of some dark presence lurking in the shadows waiting for him, of a great weight pressing down upon her, stopping her from breathing, from running to save him from some unseen evil. She would hear the sound of tiny feet running away from her, she knew not where, nor with whom. Sometimes these images were so powerful that she could smell Callum's fear, see the river, the dark woods or the fellside, sense a terror greater than she had ever experienced and knew that some dreadful disaster was about to fall upon him. She would wake in a sweat, jerking upright, calling out his name at the top of her voice. Then she would get up from the bed in the middle of the night, pull on her shawl and go in search of the place of which she had dreamed.

Every night as she lay down to sleep, Callum was the last thought in her mind. Every morning when she woke, he was the first thought to come into her head, and her heart would plunge afresh with grief. But then, unexpectedly, she woke one day with an idea in her head, filling her with new hope. She pulled on her clothes and ran to Millie who was already working on the leather in the dim light of dawn that streaked in through the single filthy window. Without fail she got in her two hours before stopping long enough to make breakfast for her family. Not that Clem would be bothering much with that this morning. He was still fast asleep in a drunken stupor which was becoming all too common, snoring like a pig under the heap of tatty bedclothes.

Kate grabbed Millie's arm, stopping her in mid-stitch, to get her attention. 'I've thought where he might be. If he got lost, he could have been taken to the Union Workhouse. Someone might have found him wandering about and taken him up there. Why ever didn't I think of that before? I'm going now, this minute. I'm going to find out.'

'Be careful,' Millie warned. 'If they take one look at you in your present state, they'll lock you up too.'

'Don't talk daft, it isn't a prison.'

'Could've fooled me.'

Secretly alarmed by this warning, Kate hesitated for two more precious days but, in the end, couldn't get the idea out of her head and so decided to take the risk and go. She spruced herself up as best she could, aware Millie's concern was valid. She didn't look anything like as smart as she had in her nursemaid's uniform, particularly after a few weeks back in Poor House Lane. But she was prepared to lie if necessary, should anyone ask any awkward questions, by pretending she was still employed by Tyson's.

In the event they weren't in the least bit interested in her. They had more than sufficient inmates to cope with already, and nobody at the workhouse recognised the picture of a curly-haired two-year-old sitting on Amelia's knee in any case.

So although Kate was allowed to scrutinise every child, to her bitter disappointment, he was not there. Callum was not among them.

–

Lucy had grown nervous. She'd never seen Eliot in such a rage as he was now. And all because that stupid girl had left him. You would have thought he'd be pleased to be rid of her. Worst of all, he was still searching for that dratted child. She'd begun to fear that perhaps he might suddenly take it into his head to visit the Union Workhouse on Kendal Green, and would discover the boy among the other pauper brats. Lucy decided that drastic action was necessary.

She was not normally one to indulge in charitable good works but this was different. Fortunately, she had always been a regular churchgoer, as this was the expected thing for someone in her position and quite the best place to get noticed by the aristocracy. And she knew the vicar to be a crusader of good causes. It took no more than a few words after Sunday service, suggesting that perhaps something should be done to find new homes for the poor workhouse children, coupled with the promise of a generous donation, and her plan was swiftly put into effect.

'What a wonderful idea,' the vicar said. 'A truly kind thought. How very perceptive of you, Mrs Tyson, that you should understand how important it is for these children to find real homes, with proper families. And most generous of you to aid our efforts in this respect.'

Lucy didn't have any money, nor did she allow that to stop her. She would find it from somewhere, the bank, the sale of one of her last remaining pictures, or even from Eliot himself, which made her laugh out loud at the irony. How wonderful if her brother-in-law actually financed the removal of his adored adopted son from the neighbourhood.

'Of course I understand, Vicar. Haven't I lost my own beloved husband and am left to bring up my deprived children alone? My heart bleeds for these poor innocents, it truly does.' She even managed to shed a tear, which quite touched his heart.

The vicar helped draw up a list of suitable foster parents, travelled far and wide to visit colleagues in neighbouring parishes to see if they knew of other good people willing to offer a home to an orphaned pauper. And while he did that, Lucy found several farmers who were willing to offer bed and board, at least, in return for an extra hand with the labour. She made no effort to check out whether they were suitable for the task of providing a home for such a child.

When they had their lists, Lucy visited the Union Workhouse, wearing her smartest costume and her sweetest smile and found herself received with heartfelt gratitude. The place was apparently overrun with inmates: men, women and far too many children. Not that this surprised Lucy who had always known that the poor bred like rabbits; which was why they were such a drain upon the country's resources and needed to be kept very much in their place.

It took no time at all to choose the lucky recipients of her largesse and nobody noticed that among them was a copper-haired boy named Allan; nor that Lucy selected for him a remote farm high in the Langdales. Not even his own mother would think to look for him there.

-

The Union Workhouse had been Kate's last hope but she'd missed finding her son by a mere twenty-four hours. There seemed to be nothing left to live for now. She no longer showed any benefit from her time spent with the Tyson's, or from Mrs Petty's plain but wholesome fare. Her face was pale as parchment, her hair lank and lifeless, and the bonny plumpness gone from her body as weight fell from her. Millie would anxiously spoon porridge, or watery soup into her, save her the choicest bits of meat or bruised fruit, whenever Clem was fortunate enough to acquire any from the market; tempt her with home-made oat cakes, but her efforts were wasted. Whatever food she did manage to get down her, was as quickly vomited back up again.

One morning, just as Kate had finished heaving up her breakfast and was trying to settle her stomach with a mug of hot, milkless tea, there came a loud rap on the door.

Millie opened it and Kate saw her glance quickly back over her shoulder as if by way of warning, not needing to hear his voice to understand the silent message her friend shot her and know that he was here.

'May I come in?'

Millie stood confused, uncertain what to do. It seemed unthinkable that Eliot Tyson should want to come into their hovel, and yet he was already stepping over the threshold, ducking his head as he came into the gloomy, filthy room they optimistically called home. She saw how he reeled slightly at the smell but quickly recovered, and after a swift scan of the room's occupants, the huddle of children, Clem seated by the smoky fire, Millie with her arms full of babies, he fixed his eyes on Kate.

'I thought you would be here.'

'Where else?'

'There was really no need for you to leave.'

'There was every need.'

He fell silent, perhaps confused by the fact that she had not moved, not even got up from the table let alone come to him, and again allowed his gaze to rove about the room. Kate became acutely aware that he was staring at a mouse, quietly grooming itself in a corner after having evidently breakfasted on the contents of a nearby cupboard, watching as it scuttled beneath the floorboards to join its mates. She saw him take in the skein of cobwebs she hadn't bothered to remove, the cockroaches crawling over the dirty dishes in the brown stone sink. He cleared his throat and spoke in a hushed whisper. 'Could we – perhaps – speak outside?'

'Why? Does this place offend you?' For God's sake, said a voice in her head, it would offend anyone with a nose to smell, and eyes to see.

Millie moved over to her, gave her shoulder a little shake. 'Go outside with him, so's you can speak in private. Go on! The morning air, fresh or not, will do you good.'

They stood in the yard, on the slime of the cobbles with the rain drizzling down their necks and the smell of the pigs strong in their nostrils, not quite looking at each other. A boy trundled past, pulling a small hand cart in which were a few pieces of coal, several broken boxes, and a collection of indeterminate items he'd obviously picked up on the midden, the better pieces to be spruced up and sold, many no doubt destined for the fire, so that his family could keep warm and cook.

'Morning, Kate.' The boy nodded at her, then suddenly spotting a rat climbing the side of his cart, shouted, 'Gerroff, yer bugger,' and kicked it away. 'Bloody things!'

'Morning, Jonty. Quite a collection you've got today.'

'It'll do.'

Kate noted how Eliot's horrified gaze followed the boy as he went on his way. He looked as if he'd been found in a midden himself, dressed in rags, a tousle of filthy hair and sores on his face and hands. She heard the low exclamation of disgust in Eliot's throat when, on reaching the end of the yard, the lad paused, opened his trousers and peed in the gutter that ran down the length of it. Nodding again to her, he happily took off his cap before going indoors.

The look that Eliot turned upon her said everything.

Shame enveloped her. Kate felt degraded by her very presence in this place, as if it robbed her of pride in herself. She felt defiled by it, and bitterly ashamed. She had hoped for so much, and yet so little. A decent, clean home for her child. Where was the wrong in that? She'd so wanted Callum to be safe that, against her better judgement, she'd agreed to give up her rights as his mother. Yet look where her sacrifice had got her? He had no mother at all now, no mama, no mammy, no home nor father even. He was lost, probably imagining that she'd abandoned him altogether. 'I know I made mistakes,' she suddenly blurted out. 'I never meant to fall under your carriage, or for him to get sick. And I never meant him to get lost. I swear I thought he was with you.'

'I know. Things were said that shouldn't have been said. You must come back, Kate. You can't stay here.'

She shook her head. 'Where would be the use of that? You blame me, I know you do. You made that very clear. I just wanted Swainson to stop hurting Millie.'

She heard the small sigh of impatience. 'Oh Kate.'

'All right, don't believe me then. Just promise me you'll not give up; that you won't stop looking for our Callum.'

'Of course I won't stop looking, not ever. And I'm sure we'll find him, I swear I won't rest till we do. Aren't you going to come and help me?'

'I'll do it me own way, so I will. I can look in places you'd never think of, or set foot in.'

'I've set foot here, haven't I? Come home, Kate.'

She looked him straight in the eye. 'This is my home. Always was, and always will be.' Then she walked back up the steps, back into the awful, stinking room, closing the door softly behind her.

The very next day a note was delivered. It told her that he'd opened a bank account in her name, deposited a tidy sum of money in it. 'To help you build a new future. Let me do that at least for you, Kate. Get out of that place, for God's sake.'

'I'm not touching his dratted money,' Kate said, grey eyes clouding with misery at the thought he could so easily dispose of her with a few paltry pounds. Naïvely perhaps, she'd half hoped that he'd try again, that he wouldn't take no for an answer and come marching back up Poor House Lane, sling her over his shoulder and carry her off like some prince in a fairy tale. Girlish fancy. Stupid, romantic nonsense! And he didn't even see her in that light at all. Whenever he looked at her, she could see in his eyes the guilt he felt over betraying a much loved wife, and from losing the son he'd bought off her. 'Does he think he can pay me off too? Mebbe this is all some plot and really he has Callum tucked away safely, and this is just a way to rid himself of me for good.'

'Oh hush,' Millie said. 'Yer seeing plots everywhere.' Another rap came to the door and the two girls glanced at each other in sudden panic. 'It's him. It's Swainson.'

'Right, leave him to me.' And before Millie could stop her, Kate flung open the door and, lifting her chin high, met the foreman's startled gaze with a small smile. 'The work is going fine and will be delivered on time, but ye can't come in right now, so bugger off.'

'Well, well, well, I see you're back where you belong, among the pig swill. Step aside, girl, I've business to do.'

'Not here you haven't.'

'Who are you to deny me entrance?'

He made to brush past her but Kate stood her ground, hands firmly folded across her chest. 'Take one more step and I'll punch ye on the nose, so I will. In future, ye can only come in by invitation. And yer not invited today.'

'You can't do that.'

'I just did.'

'I'm the foreman. I have rights.' She could see his face turning purple with rage and Kate almost laughed out loud at the pleasure it gave her to see him so discomfited.

'So have we got rights, and one of them is that we don't have to suffer you bringing yer mucky ways in here, so push off.'

'You'll be sorry for this, Kate O'Connor.'

'Not as sorry as you,' she shouted after him as he stalked away. Kate ran down the steps, picked up a clod of muck and flung it after him, and now she did let her laughter erupt as she watched him slipping and sliding in the filth in his rush to escape.

Back inside she slammed shut the door, wiping the tears of laughter from her eyes. 'Oh, that was the funniest thing I ever saw. That'll show him, the nasty little shite,' dusting her hands as if wanting to rid herself of something unclean.

But when she looked up at her friend, she saw that Millie's eyes were filled with fear. 'What did ye do that for? Why do you always let yer Irish temper get the better of you? Now we're really done for. He'll give us no work at all now.'

'So we'll find it some place else, or make us own, to be sure,' Kate said on a note of defiance. But as she watched Millie snatch up the leather pieces and begin to stitch with a frantic anxiety, she experienced a nudge of doubt. What had she done? In trying to protect her friend, had she merely made matters worse, risked the family's well-being simply for a moment of personal glory? Kate looked around her at the skinny, snotty-nosed children with not even the energy to play properly, and instantly sobered. She laid a gentle hand on Millie's shoulder.

'I'm sorry, love. I didn't mean to make matters worse but we can't have him doing – what he does do to you. You can't let him bully you like that. Does he do it to all the women?'

Millie didn't once raise her eyes from her work, fingers flying as she stitched with frenetic speed. 'How would I know? Some, I think… all right, quite a few. Not that anyone admits to it but it's easy enough to tell by the look in their eyes after he's come calling. But don't you think you can stop it, because you can't.'

'Why not? If all the women stood together, he'd not be able to take advantage the way he does. Will I ask around, get some evidence?'

'No, keep yer nose out of it. You've done enough for one day. Anyroad, you'd never get them to agree. They'd be too feared of starving to death while they made their protest. We leave all of the arguing to the men, them as is brave enough.' She did stop stitching now, to fix Kate with a fierce glance. 'We women have childer to feed and can't afford to take the risk. So don't you interfere. Don't poke yer snout into our midden, nor into matters you can do nowt to change.'

Kate was stunned by her friend's vehemence. It was the first time they'd ever quarrelled and she felt humbled by the stark fear in her eyes.

'But there must be something I can do.'

'There's nowt. So leave well alone.'

At the end of the week when Millie took in the finished work, she apologised to Swainson for Kate's rudeness, saying she hoped that it wouldn't make any difference, that he'd not withhold work from her as a result. 'Me husband can't seem to get any, d'you see. I depend upon this outwork, to feed me childer.'

In truth, fond as she was of him, Clem was proving to be a bit of a worry to Millie, a big disappointment in fact. It was as if he'd given up on himself, lost all faith and hope in ever being able to provide for his family, and yet didn't seem to understand the price she paid in order to earn a few pennies. He'd help himself to the coins in her purse and go off to the Cock and Dolphin to drink with his mates, saying there was nothing else for him to do.

Swainson gave a sneering laugh, his good eye roving over her with appreciation. 'I'm sure we can think of some way to avoid that prissy little miss sticking her nose in where it's not wanted. If'n we use our imagination.'

Then he went to the door, pulled it open and glanced up and down the street before sliding the bolt across. With a jerk of his head, he ordered Millie to follow him into the back room where he stored the bends of leather waiting to be cut into soles. 'Look sharp about it. It'll have to be a quick one afore someone comes.' Oh, but he'd make her sorry for defying him. He would indeed. She'd certainly think twice in future.

Millie swallowed carefully, gave a nervous smile, and followed him inside.

–

It was a week or two later that Kate finally confessed to Millie that she was pregnant. 'I've fallen again, and this time I've no husband, and I don't even want another child. I want Callum.'

Millie didn't scold or judge her for what she'd done with Eliot. She didn't ask why she'd done it, or what she'd been thinking of to sleep with the master before even his beloved wife had been laid to rest, nor why she had repeated the same error months later. She understood, only too well, how easy it was to make mistakes, and how much in control men were. Didn't Swainson give her a fresh reminder of that fact each and every week. Not being able to come into her home and use her bed had made matters worse, not better. Now he took her wherever he fancied; in his workshop, down by the river, or up against a backyard wall like a common whore. She wondered sometimes if Clem guessed what was going on, but if so, he turned a blind eye, pocketing the money she earned and drowning his sorrows at the pub.

So if Eliot Tyson had shown Kate kindness, of course she'd be ready and willing to comfort him in his grief and loneliness. Now she would simply have to live with the consequences. And if secretly Millie hoped that this new baby, unwanted as it now might be, would help Kate to ease the grieving for her lost child, she did not say as much. Millie had buried two bairns, and knew that however many other children you had, you never stopped loving or grieving for the lost one. Callum couldn't be replaced, but the new little one might help to heal the wound a little, and give her friend a reason for living.

As Kate broke the news, these thoughts flashed through her head, but Millie simply gave a rueful smile and said, 'We'll manage, love. What's one more, with all this lot?'

Chapter Twenty-Two

Lucy sat in the small parlour, looking as if the sky had fallen in on her head. She couldn't believe her own ears. This was the most appalling news. Not at all what she'd expected. 'Would you mind repeating that, Eliot. You say you have given a large sum of money to the *nursemaid*? *Our* money, which we need to save the company.'

Aunt Cissie made a clucking sound with her tongue which sent the two dogs at her feet into a frenzy of excitement. Aunt Vera seemed to have lost the power of speech altogether, sitting bolt upright with her copy of *John Halifax Gentleman*, which she'd been reading when called to this interview, clutched tightly on her lap.

'I believe that it is actually *my* money, but yes, that is what I have done. I thought you'd be pleased to hear that she is to be properly provided for. I believed it appropriate, considering what she has lost. Her son, after all.'

Lucy balled her fists, sat forward in her seat and spat her next words at him. 'You can't do that. You simply cannot do it. We need every penny for ourselves. What *has* she lost? Some pauper brat of no account. No doubt she'll have another baby to fill his place before the year is out. Those sort of people breed like rabbits.'

The muscles in Eliot's face tightened dangerously as he regarded his sister-in-law with frost-filled eyes. 'Might I remind you, this is my son you are speaking of so dismissively, even if he isn't the child of my loins.'

'Oh dear! Deary, deary me,' Aunt Cissie said, sounding flustered, and both maiden ladies shuddered, not wishing to examine matters quite so intimately as these two seemed able to do.

Eliot felt a stirring of pity for them: for their inflexibility, their mulish snobbery, and their very obvious greed in wanting everything he owned to go to them. Perhaps that wasn't quite so true in the case of the aunts, but he was perfectly aware that it was so with Lucy. She'd made no secret from the start that she resented the adoption, that she believed Tyson's Shoe Manufactory should go to her own children. Well, she must simply accustom herself to a bitter disappointment. He'd no intention of ever allowing them to have it.

He manufactured a patient smile. 'As well as the money, I also intend to set her up with decent accommodation. A house somewhere other than Poor House Lane, which is an appalling place to live. Have you ever set foot in there, Lucy? Aunts? I have, and I do assure you that you would not like to. It's a festering sore which should be a source of shame to this town. Those cottages need to be razed to the ground, and will be if I have any say in the matter.'

Completely ignoring the philanthropic aspect of his statement, Lucy stared at him as if he'd run mad. 'A house of her own? A vast overreaction, surely. She gave up the child willingly, used him as a means to gain herself employment. And can you afford to be so generous? Can *we*? Haven't we done enough for the girl already? How much will all of this charity cost, for absolutely no return or benefit?' Lucy paused as if a thought had struck her, and then cast him a sideways glance, pressing her lips into a knowing smile. 'Ah, is it perhaps because you intend to set her up as your mistress, is that the way of it? I've heard the rumours. Dear me, I'm surprised at you, Eliot. And so soon.'

Aunt Vera gave a low hiss deep in her throat and, having found her voice, it came out deep and gruff and condemning. 'I hope not indeed. Poor dear Amelia would turn in her grave.'

Cissie simply sank into yet another litany of 'oh dears', varying them only with, 'What a muddle, what a muddle!' The two pointers whimpered in sympathy and licked her hand.

Eliot turned away, not wishing anyone to see the flicker of guilt that he assumed would be present in his eyes for all to see, addressing his remarks to the view of the river through the parlour window. 'Now you are talking ridiculously. She is a servant girl in need of help, nothing more. And if Amelia is watching, she will entirely agree with my decision. She would consider it entirely proper since she was ever practical and with a generous heart.' He sincerely hoped his much lamented wife could not see how quickly he had replaced her. The shame of his actions were killing him, making him quite unable to concentrate on his work, or do anything properly. He prayed that once he'd set the girl up in safe and decent accommodation, he would finally be able to put her from his mind.

Having got himself back under control, Eliot turned to confront the condemning faces of the women of his family, aware that the more they attempted to boss and organise him, the more he wanted rid of their presence in his home. 'Kate O'Connor might be a thorn in the

310

side of some with her prickly defensiveness and naïve way of viewing the world, but her heart is in the right place and she deserves better than we have given her. And you are wrong, Lucy, about her reason for giving up Callum, which was done with great reluctance on her part, and for the best of reasons.'

'Huh!'

'I rewarded her generosity and trust by neglecting him to such an extent he was stolen before my very eyes.'

'Oh, he was a lovely little chap, it's true.' Aunt Cissie gave a little moaning cry and dabbed at her eyes so that both dogs attempted to climb onto her lap at once, in order to offer her comfort

'Do stop it, Cissie,' Vera scolded, 'and put those dratted animals down. What's done is done and can't be undone. And there really is no need, Eliot, for you to carry this burden of guilt on your shoulders. The girl should have been paying proper attention to her duties. Perhaps it was God's way of telling you that the whole situation was wrong from the start, that you were never intended to father children, of any sort.'

Eliot looked momentarily startled by this bleak assessment of his situation. 'I trust you are wrong in that supposition, dear aunt. I had hoped that perhaps one day I may marry again. Who can say? I may yet have a nursery full of children, God willing.'

Lucy regarded him with fresh horror. What was he implying? Surely he wasn't suggesting that Kate O'Connor might fit into that role? Not for a moment had she imagined such a possibility. A new bride of any sort would be bad enough, before she'd had the opportunity to put the rest of her plan into effect. Lucy held fond hopes of finding him a comfortable, mature wife, one unlikely to give him children. The very idea of the *nursemaid – the girl from Poor House Lane* becoming mistress of this house, inheriting what her own sweet darlings should have, was utterly insupportable. It must not be allowed to happen. In addition to all other considerations, she was far too young, too *fertile*.

'I am sure that when you have had the opportunity to think about my plan a little more, then you will agree it's the right thing to do. We cannot be seen to take advantage of those less fortunate than ourselves. You understand, dear aunts? Lucy?' He lifted one brow by way of cool enquiry. None of them answered.

Eliot strode to the door, glanced back at the three women still bristling with censure and let out a small sigh of resignation. Why did no one ever appreciate that he wanted only to do what was right? Why did people always perceive some ulterior motive, some personal benefit to himself in what he did? His mistress indeed. The very idea. He inwardly shuddered at what they would say if they knew how close he had come to falling into that particular trap. What sort of employer would that make him? Oh, the folly that a man will commit in grief and despair. It was a relief, in a way, that the girl was no longer under his roof. She was far too attractive, too enchanting for words. Dangerously so. But Lucy was right in one respect, he couldn't really afford to be so generous, yet felt he had to do something. How could he ignore her plight after all that had happened?

'Oh, and I intend to continue searching for Callum, so pray keep your eyes and ears alert for news, if you please.'

'You won't find him,' Lucy burst out and then flushed crimson as he frowned down upon her.

'I trust you are wrong in that supposition, Lucy. He is my son after all, and I love him. Good day to you all.' As Eliot quietly closed the parlour door there was a moment of intense silence and then all three ladies began to talk at once. Eliot walked away with a small, troubled smile on his face.

—

Thank God, Lucy thought, as Dennis drove her home later in the carriage, that she'd moved the dratted child far from Kendal. She shuddered to think what might happen if Eliot ever discovered the truth. Lucy was adamant that he wasn't going to be allowed to give away Tyson money to a girl of the lowest class imaginable, who had no rights to it at all. It was an outrage which mustn't be allowed to happen. Yet she felt utterly helpless, trapped in some sort of nightmare. She certainly hadn't gone through all of that trauma to be robbed of what was rightfully hers in the end. She had to do some hard thinking, and fast!

The bills were still mounting, seeming to come in as thick and fast as ever, with no end to them. How she was going to settle a half of them, she really didn't know. And she must still find decent schools for the children. What a coward Charles was, to leave her in this mess. Drat men! Drat everyone! Livid with rage, she knocked everything off Charles's desk with one furious sweep of her hand.

Only when her storm of temper had subsided did she begin to see things more clearly. The answer was obvious. She should take a leaf out of the aunts' book and move into Tyson Lodge, taking her children and maid with her. It seemed to suit them well enough, as they showed not a sign of returning to their own, humbler quarters. In fact, she'd heard Vera saying just the other day that she was thinking of letting out the house they owned in Heversham, since Eliot had so many empty rooms, and the poor man so dreadfully alone now that dear Amelia had passed away.

'If he has so much money to throw around, he might as well throw some in my direction too,' Lucy decided. She was family after all.

Lucy flung open the door and shouted for her maid. The girl came running, as she'd learned to do whenever her mistress called. 'Start packing. We're moving to Tyson Lodge first thing in the morning.'

It was as she turned back into the room that she spotted a folded sheet of paper which had apparently been tucked beneath the blotter. Picking it up, she read the note with care, read it twice in fact, eyes widening with interest, and then a small smile played at the corners of her mouth. So Charles had used the foreman, Swainson, in his plans. Clever Charles. Lucy didn't view what her late husband had done as fraudulent or criminal in any way, only circumspect, a means to protect his family and provide a decent future for them. She slid the note into her skirt pocket and gave it a little pat of triumph. Whatever Charles could do, she could do better.

What with her foolish brother-in-law going soft in the head, not to mention this nasty and persistent rumour of war in Europe; the world, in Lucy's opinion, was running mad. It was indeed fortunate that she, at least, was holding on to her sanity. She would move into Tyson Lodge forthwith, and who knew where that might lead?

It proved to be a wearisome pregnancy, the baby lying heavy, causing Kate to need to use the stinking privy more often than she would care to. She felt listless and tired much of the time, with none of the anticipatory joy which she'd felt when she'd been expecting Callum. Worst of all, she was a burden to Clem and Millie; as if they didn't have enough mouths to feed without her imposing an extra one. She really didn't care to think about what she would do when the baby came, and a part of her didn't care. Yet she mustn't give in. She must get this baby born; then she could resume her search for Callum.

Her time came, still with no sign of a birth being imminent, and somehow it reminded her bleakly of Amelia and her long pregnancy, which hadn't been a pregnancy at all. The poor lady had suffered so much but, in the end, had nothing to show for her labours. Only Kate's bruised ribs as the baby kicked and turned within her, served to remind her that her own situation was entirely different. There would indeed be a baby for her. Unfortunately he, or she, was simply taking a long time to make an appearance.

Millie became increasingly concerned by the delay. 'You're a good two weeks overdue, long past time this bairn made an appearance. Here, take a sip of this, it'll happen do the trick.'

'What is it?'

'Only a nip of gin.'

'I don't want it.'

'Aye you do. Get it down you. We've got to get this baby out somehow, and it'll make for an easier labour.'

Miraculously, the very next day, Kate did indeed go into labour, but it soon became clear that this wasn't going to be the easy birth she'd experienced with Callum, or that Millie had hoped for. Perhaps she didn't quite have the energy she'd had then, her being half-starved and tired all the time, Kate thought, as she sweated and laboured, pushed and heaved when Millie told her to, breathed and coughed and panted at her instruction for hour upon hour with still no baby to show for her efforts.

And the pain was dreadful. She could feel it washing over her, blotting out all thought, all will to survive. One minute Millie would shout: 'I can see the head. It's crowning. Push! Push!' But then it would slip back, and Kate would feel too exhausted to go through all of that again.

'Let me sleep for a little first.'

'No, no, you can't sleep. Come on, sit up. Try again. Childbirth is hard work. Wake up, Kate. Push, drat you!' Millie knotted a sheet to the bed posts for Kate to hold on to, and Clem took the children outside so they wouldn't get in the way. Kate pushed and shouted, cursed and swore, and even at one point, screamed out loud as the pain became unbearable, all to no avail. She couldn't endure another moment, wanting desperately to sleep, to die.

In her mind's eye, she could see Callum grinning up at her, his cherubic face bathed in a golden glow, surrounded by a brilliant light and she wanted to reach out to him, to let some unseen hand pluck her from this bed to which she seemed to be stuck fast, and draw her into that glorious light.

'Callum,' she called, 'I'm coming. Wait for Mammy.'

White-lipped, Millie ran to the door and shouted to Clem. 'Run and fetch Eliot Tyson. We've struggled on us own long enough. It's his child, drat it. Let him do something useful for a change, and make sure he fetches a doctor back with you, an' all.'

It was a girl, finally slithering into the world at two the following morning, yelling the place down as if demanding to know why they'd taken so long about it. The labour had certainly been longer and more painful than Kate could ever have imagined possible and yet survive, requiring the intervention of Doctor Mitchell at his most skilled, to pull the baby from her and stitch Kate up afterwards. She thought she might never walk, or move, again, watching with bleak indifference as the doctor washed and put away his instruments of torture. Then she looked across at the baby, lying serenely in the basket which had held all of Millie's babies, and felt nothing for her either. There were bruises on her head which the doctor said would fade in time and really shouldn't worry her. Kate wasn't in the least bit worried. Why had he told her that? Had she asked? If so, then she couldn't imagine why. The baby somehow had no connection with her at all. But then nothing did. She felt in a daze, numb with pain, with no clear idea of where she was, or how long she had lain on this bed, fighting this endless, pain-filled battle.

There were voices in the room, raised in argument, though she didn't trouble to determine whose, letting the sound drift in and out of her consciousness. And then a face swam into view, one she knew well, and a voice – firm and demanding – a persistent hand shaking her shoulder. 'Kate, Kate wake up. See, you have a beautiful baby daughter.'

She struggled to focus on the face, on the voice, cast a sideways glance up at him. He was smiling, his brown eyes warm on her face, all anger spent.

'I want Callum,' Kate stubbornly repeated, tears flooding her eyes and making his beloved image swim in a blur of colour.

'Of course you do. We all do, and we will find him, I swear it.'

He stroked her hair from the heat of her brow, rubbed away a tear with the back of his hand and she looked up at him in wonder. Did this mean that he cared for her a little, after all? He must have brought the doctor, come to her aid again when she most needed it. Would he carry her off to Tyson Lodge and love her as she so longed to be loved? His next words seemed to confirm this dream. 'We must stop fighting each other over this loss we've both suffered, and what happened between us. It's no good going over and over it. It's done now, but I swear I won't rest till I've found our little man.'

Our little man. How she loved to hear him say that, linking all three of them together. 'It's been months. I tried so hard to find him but...'

'I know, so did I. But perhaps you've been given another chance, to get it right this time. Just tell me, Kate, I need to know, whose child is she? Is she mine?'

Kate was stunned, not quite believing that she heard right. What was he implying? That she lay with anyone?

He was still talking, a feverish glow in his eyes. 'The doctor says she's fine, astonishingly so considering the circumstances, but if she truly is mine, I refuse to allow her to be brought up here. I can't let you stay here either. We've been through too much together, Kate. Amelia would never forgive me if I didn't see that you were both well looked after.'

Been through too much! Was this evidence of yet more guilt? She gazed up into his face, willing him not to have said what she thought he'd said, for him to offer to look after her himself, aching for him to take her in his arms.

'I've found you a pretty little cottage in a yard off Highgate. A clean and decent one, just as you've always dreamed of. A place where you'll be safe and your baby can grow up healthy and strong. But you must tell me. I need to know. Lucy said you would have replaced Callum within the year, and it seems that she is right. So is the baby mine, or not?'

Kate felt a flood of hot anger course through her veins. How dare he even entertain the possibility of her lying with someone else? Could he not understand that she loved only him? Did he see her as some sort of tart who wouldn't know the father of her own child, because she'd shared her bed with too many men? If she could only get off this damned bed she'd scratch his eyes out for insinuating such a terrible thing, so she would. Pushing herself up on her pillows, eyes blazing, Kate told him exactly what she thought of his suggestions.

'What sort of woman do you take me for? Seems to me your mind is filthier than Poor House Lane. And why do you ask? Do you mean to pinch this babby too? While I've strength in me body, won't I fight you every step of the way? I gave you my lovely Callum, and look what happened to him. I'm damned if you're having this one an' all. Get out, damn you. Get out!'

'Now don't lose your temper, Kate. Stay calm. That's not what I meant, and you know it. For once in your life will you stop fighting me. I've no wish to steal her from you. It's just that I don't see how it could have happened so quickly. I mean – Amelia and I – we tried for years, and you and I only twice.'

'I'm not Amelia. Get out, damn you!'

'Kate, listen to me.'

'Get out! *Get out!*'

And this time her screams were such that he took a step backward, startled by her fervour, his face ashen. Millie was at her side in seconds, telling him he'd best go if he didn't want to scare all her milk away.

'Very well. If that's how you want it. So be it,' and turning on his heel, he strode out of the room, tight-lipped with rage.

'Oh, Kate, what have you done? Will you never learn to guard that temper of yours? I think he liked this new little treasure of yours, wanted you to say yes, that she was his. Why didn't you? He'd have helped you look after the wee bairn.'

Clem said, 'He'd've given you more money, lass. He's made of brass, and should be expected to support her, you an' all.'

'I don't want his damn money. He can't buy another child off me. She's mine.'

Millie and Clem exchanged a glance of exasperation. 'All right love, don't get upset. It's not good fer yer milk. Would you like to hold her?'

Kate shook her head and turned away, not wanting to look, or even smell this alien child. Couldn't they see how exhausted she was, that she just needed to sleep?

But Millie didn't seem to have heard because a warm bundle was pushed into her arms. It felt so tiny, so fragile, just as Callum had once felt, except that this baby was as pretty and delicate as a flower, her small, rose-pink mouth already arrogantly pursing with feminine conceit. A pair of blue eyes looked steadily up into hers, proudly proclaiming that she'd arrived at last, and hadn't she done well. 'Just look at the little lamb. Isn't she bonny? And she's all yours. Callum's little half-sister. What are you going to call her?'

Despite herself, Kate found her own lips twitching into a smile and a flood of emotion flushed through her. It was like falling in love at first sight. Instinctively, she drew her close, laid her cheek against the dark fuzz of hair and breathed in the sweet, baby scent of her. 'Flora, she is to be called Flora. My little flower.'

Millie beamed her delight, pleased that mother and baby were bonding so well after what had been a tricky start. 'Right then, now you put her to the breast and get her suckling nicely, while I put t'kettle on.'

Kate did as she was bid, feeling the strength of the child's pull, easing the pain in her that still yearned for Callum. This child was a part of her too, and a part of Eliot whom she had loved more than life itself, though not for the world would she let him know it. She would have done anything for him once but now the world had changed. Instead of supporting each other in their grief, neither could appreciate the other's loss. If there'd ever been the possibility of something growing between them, all hope of that had been lost on the day Callum vanished.

Now, blinded by unshed tears, Kate held her new baby to her breast while her heart ached with joy and despair.

'We'll manage, my precious one, will we not? Whatever the future brings, no one will take you away from me. We'll make sure of that, my precious. And one day, we'll find your big brother, mark my words.'